Surrender Your Dreams

Greetings, Damien, my dear friend. If you've received this message, you are still alive and The Republic is in deep trouble.

If you've received this message, the current exarch has accessed the files known as Fortress Republic. If he is considering this option, then The Republic needs you more than ever.

The Fortress plan calls for an organized collapse of The Republic to a defense zone centered on Prefecture X. It will create an impenetrable barrier between the core of The Republic and the rest of the Inner Sphere. You will soon become aware of the means by which this will be enforced, so I won't waste time here outlining that.

Outside the Fortress walls, The Republic will face unprecedented perils. Our enemies will smell blood and strike; your task will be to help organize the knights and ghost knights to undertake missions necessary for the long-term survival of The Republic. These missions will stretch dangerously thin the loyalty and obedience of the knights; but these missions are vital. The Fortress files contain the operational details of suggested targets and projected mission parameters. Many require your discretion in terms of timing.

There is no one I trust more to do what needs to be done.

D1474745

DARK AGE

SURRENDER
YOUR DREAMS

A BATTLETECH™ NOVEL

Blaine Lee Pardoe

A ROC BOOK

ROC
Published by New American Library, a division of
Penguin Group (USA) Inc., 375 Hudson Street,
New York, New York 10014, USA
Penguin Group (Canada), 90 Eglinton Avenue East, Suite 700, Toronto,
Ontario M4P 2Y3, Canada (a division of Pearson Penguin Canada Inc.)
Penguin Books Ltd., 80 Strand, London WC2R 0RL, England
Penguin Ireland, 25 St. Stephen's Green, Dublin 2,
Ireland (a division of Penguin Books Ltd.)
Penguin Group (Australia), 250 Camberwell Road, Camberwell, Victoria 3124,
Australia (a division of Pearson Australia Group Pty. Ltd.)
Penguin Books India Pvt. Ltd., 11 Community Centre, Panchsheel Park,
New Delhi - 110 017, India
Penguin Group (NZ), cnr Airborne and Rosedale Roads, Albany,
Auckland 1310, New Zealand (a division of Pearson New Zealand Ltd.)
Penguin Books (South Africa) (Pty.) Ltd., 24 Sturdee Avenue,
Rosebank, Johannesburg 2196, South Africa

Penguin Books Ltd., Registered Offices:
80 Strand, London WC2R 0RL, England

First published by Roc, an imprint of New American Library,
a division of Penguin Group (USA) Inc.

First Printing, December 2006
10 9 8 7 6 5 4 3 2 1

Copyright © WizKids, Inc., 2006
All rights reserved

 REGISTERED TRADEMARK—MARCA REGISTRADA

Printed in the United States of America

PUBLISHER'S NOTE
This is a work of fiction. Names, characters, places, and incidents either are
the product of the author's imagination or are used fictitiously, and any resem-
blance to actual persons, living or dead, business establishments, events, or
locales is entirely coincidental.
   The publisher does not have any control over and does not assume any
responsibility for author or third-party Web sites or their content.

This book is dedicated to my family, who have always supported this insane hobby of mine: Cyndi, Alex, Victoria and Sandy (The Wonder Dog).

To my editor, Sharon, who didn't cringe when I asked, "Have you ever seen the movie *Pulp Fiction*?" and who engages me in debates about how many people I'm allowed to kill in a novel. When I told her I wanted to bring *them* back (read this book, you'll figure it out), she didn't even flinch. In fact, she said, "Cool!"

To the other MechWarrior™ writers—Loren, Mike, Randall, Kevin, Ilsa and the rest.

I also want to thank my alma mater, Central Michigan University. Other great places that deserve mention include the Von Luckner Society, the Mariner's Museum in Newport News, Virginia, the U.S. National Archives, the Wings Over the Rockies Museum, and the National Maritime Historical Society.

To Harry Turtledove—my favorite non-MechWarrior writer.

Finally, to the BattleTech™ fans out there who are looking for new twists and turns to the storyline: Gotcha!

BOOK 1

Greetings, Damien, my dear friend. If you've received this message, you are still alive and The Republic is in deep trouble.

If you've received this message, the current exarch has accessed the files known as Fortress Republic. If he is considering this option, then The Republic needs you more than ever.

The Fortress plan calls for an organized collapse of The Republic to a defense zone centered on Prefecture X. It will create an impenetrable barrier between the core of The Republic and the rest of the Inner Sphere. You will soon become aware of the means by which this will be enforced, so I won't waste time here outlining that.

Outside the Fortress walls, The Republic will face unprecedented perils. Our enemies will smell blood and strike; your task will be to help organize the knights and ghost knights to undertake missions necessary for the long-term survival of The Republic. These missions will stretch dangerously thin the loyalty and obedience of the knights, but these missions are vital. The Fortress files contain the operational details of suggested targets and projected mission parameters. Many require your discretion in terms of timing.

There is no one I trust more to do what needs to be done.

You must personally coordinate a number of these missions. One such is Callison: This world is not what it appears and will play a key role in events that unfold in the future. Callison offers us hope in the dark times to come.

A second is on Kwamashu. My greatest advantage as exarch was that, in the rubble of the war, I had access to everyone's secrets. On Kwamashu, the Duchy of Andurien is hiding a secret that they cannot afford anyone to even suspect. There, they are morally weak; there, a fuse must be lit to keep relations strained between House Liao and the Duchy.

Other operations are covert in nature. Some involve assassinations, some require efforts to keep the enemies of The Republic off-balance and at each other's throats. You know some of the secrets I kept, and one of those you now must bring to bear. The Fidelis have been waiting. Use them. Let them fulfill their destiny and help deliver The Republic.

Know this: I trust you as I would a son. I know you will put The Republic first. That is why I have chosen you to carry this message.

Good luck and Godspeed, old friend.

Price of Service 8

Nadir Jump Point
Kwamashu, Duchy of Andurien
Fortress Republic (+886 days)

Hunter Mannheim stared at the newscast being beamed from Kwamashu and fought the emotions that threatened to overwhelm him. A raw mix of fury, frustration, self-doubt and loathing all fought to control him, like a hurricane of emotion with him at the eye. Events were still unfolding down on Kwamashu. The ramifications of their actions became more serious every day.

He had ordered the JumpShip to hold station. No one noticed them in the flurry of ships arriving in-system; they still were painted to look like a Duchy military unit, so no one questioned their presence. The recriminations battering his mind forced Mannheim to stay and watch, to fully grasp the extent of the devastation he had wrought.

He, Sir Hunter Mannheim, Knight of the Sphere, had ordered the detonation of the charges that destroyed the industrial facility in Breezewood. The plan had been to stage a mock disaster for the media to play up that would give the Duchy of Andurien a reason to go to war with the Oriente Protectorate—and keep their minds off trying to poach former Republic worlds. Now the media had a *real* disaster to deal with, a disaster on a planetary scale. Now, the dead and dying provided the reason to go to war.

What he had not known was that the abandoned facility he had rigged with explosive charges for their mock disaster had been used since the end of the Jihad as an illegal storage site for industrial and chemical wastes and by-products. Tens of thousands of barrels of unstable chemicals and biohazard waste that the good people of Kwamashu didn't want to deal with had been dumped there, many buried underground, others stored in the supposedly empty fuel-tank farm nearby. Added to this toxic cocktail were radioactive industrial wastes. The nearby dumping ground explained why so few people lived in Breezewood to begin with, which was a small blessing.

When the Oriente Protectorate had raided the plant under the assumption that it was a new 'Mech assembly plant and therefore posed a threat to the Protectorate, he and his Fidelis troops—disguised as a Duchy unit— had put up a good fight. The plan would have worked if the plant hadn't been a ticking time bomb to begin with—and if the Protectorate hadn't come to Kwamashu in such force as to seize the world. The handful of surviving raiders had managed to make it to their JumpShip and leave the system before anyone thought to intercept them.

He bowed his head, on the verge of crying for the hundredth time in the past week. The explosion at the plant had set off a blast that could be measured on the scale of a tactical nuclear weapon. A firestorm had swept up a significant part of Breezewood, then efficiently devoured the city in an inferno as hot as a blast furnace.

The mushroom cloud from the explosion had risen seven thousand, six hundred and twenty meters into the air and been caught in the jet stream over Kwamashu. Laden with a lethal mix of toxic chemicals and radioactive waste, the cloud spread in two different directions. During the week it took to reach their JumpShip, Hunter had tracked its progress. The "cloud of death," or "death shroud," as it was described by the press, contaminated everything in its path. By the time they had arrived at the nadir jump point, three-quarters of the world had been dosed with a mix of carcinogens, toxic waste and radioactive chemicals, brought down by rain and gravity.

The initial death count from the firestorm had been in the hundreds, but almost immediately people all around the world began to fall sick. The very old and the very young were the first to succumb. Hundreds of thousands of acres of crops had to be destroyed because the soil was contaminated. The government evacuated entire cities, but there was nowhere safe for the refugees to go. Twin killers common to all disasters, cholera and dysentery, took their toll on the millions of refugees. Rioting and looting broke out as panic took over.

Colonel Daum, the planetary garrison commander, had miraculously survived the initial explosion. He sent out a plea for help for Kwamashu to the rest of the Duchy via JumpShips, but it was too late for him. He had been hospitalized almost immediately with lung problems.

Aid was trickling in. JumpShips and DropShips were arriving regularly at the zenith and nadir jump points, sending in transports filled with medical supplies and returning with evacuees. The Duchy military had redirected units to organize disaster relief, but there were millions of people who needed assistance. It was a logistical nightmare. As one commentator put it, it was a catastrophe on the scale of the Tharkad fusion plant meltdown at the outbreak of the Jihad—times a hundred. Another newscaster compared it to the nuking of Outreach. Mannheim found both comparisons heartwrenching.

The cost in human lives was compounded by the damage to the Duchy's economy. Kwamashu was a total loss; not only had the Duchy lost its production capability, but the cost to rescue those who could be saved would be astronomical. Even the most extensive relief efforts would never be enough. The lucky ones would leave the planet. The rest of the population would always wonder about the air they breathed or the ground under their feet, wondering what death it might hold for them—if not immediately, then in years to come.

The Duchy's media machine had turned the disaster into a public relations coup. Public cries of "Remember Kwamashu!" rang on every Duchy planet. All-out war with the Oriente Protectorate seemed inevitable. The war planned by Devlin Stone had found fertile soil on the death fields of Kwamashu. *War. More deaths. More names added to his list of sins.*

The counter on the screen showed the death toll in the thousands. Hunter knew the grim reality. The deaths on Kwamashu were just beginning. There would be thousands more, tens of thousands. He straightened up and shut off the monitor. *All that blood is on my head.* Hunter thought of his wife and children. *What will they think of me?* The shame was almost unbearable. Mannheim already had considered and rejected suicide, afraid to leave even more unanswered questions for his children when the Fortress walls came down.

Thinking of his children prompted him to look for Jeremy Chin, the ghost knight he had worked with on Kwamashu. Jeremy was young enough to be Mannheim's son, and he did not appear to be dealing well with their actions either. Mannheim unfastened the straps holding him to his chair, engaged his magnetic slippers and walked to the corridor, then kicked off from the floor. Chin had lost his impish attitude and confident cockiness. His habit of mumbling to himself that Hunter had noticed developing during the mission had seemed to take on more character. Hunter wondered if the stress had cracked the younger man. *It's hard to know your capacity for guilt until it's too late.*

Jeremy Chin pushed off the wall of the cargo bay with all of his might. Halfway across he tucked his chin and bent at the waist, flipping over in mid-flight to land on his feet. He curled and kicked off again. He had been repeating this motion for two hours, and was wet with sweat from the exertion. He ignored the ache in his legs. In microgravity, you needed the exercise. Jeremy also needed it for another reason.

He looked at the box tucked into the corner. Standing next to it, nearly hidden in the shadows, was a man with his arms crossed. His face was half-hidden by a mask—the kind of mask used to hide deformities. The man wore a mocking, arrogant grin emphasized by the twist in his lip, more damage from the near-fatal blast years before. His hair swept messily off his forehead. Chin wanted to look away from the man's insolent grin, but it took all his effort. The man's voice taunted him.

"All that sweat doesn't change what you did."

Jeremy kicked off again, but this time when he landed he didn't immediately kick off. "Go away!"

Thomas Marik chuckled. "Admit it—you found killing those people all too easy. You're a ghost knight; you've killed before. Taking one life is hard. Much easier to kill an entire population, don't you think? Much like you, I prefer the weapons of mass destruction. If you're going to do the job, use the right tool."

"I didn't kill those people. I was—" His voice broke when he realized the words he wanted to say.

"Just following orders? Oh, please—remember who you're talking to. You could have tossed those orders at any time, but you didn't. I'm particularly glad that you followed your orders, especially your instructions to get me out of that damned hole. But my favorite part still is when you laid waste to the planet. That took me back to the good old days."

His anger swelled. He kicked off again, this time flipping twice in the air before making a hard landing and another stop. "You need to leave."

"I don't think so. Thanks to you, I'm back in the game. I really have missed the carnage so necessary to create a new order. It's gratifying to see The Republic willing to take a lesson from a professional like me."

"Shut up."

"Stone would have been proud of you. Especially the part where everyone will die a slow death. You know, Sir Chin, I could have really used someone like you in the Blake Guard. A person willing to go that extra mile, to take a little pleasure in his work. You would have been a fine member of my order."

He caught movement from the corner of his eye; Jeremy glanced at the doorway to the bay and saw another person step hesitantly into the opening. Hunter. He closed his eyes and kicked off again. He was avoiding Hunter's eyes. Looking into his eyes hurt almost as much as the words Thomas was leveling at him. No—it hurt much worse.

"We should give the order to jump. There's nothing more to be gained by monitoring the situation from here," his fellow knight suggested.

"I agree."

"I've been watching the newscasts from the planet."

He kicked off again. When his boots clicked onto the deck wall, he stayed. "I stopped. Redburn and Levin got what they wanted. They got their war."

The man near the box laughed. "They got more than that, my little knight."

"Shut up," he muttered.

"What?"

"Not you," he replied to Hunter.

"I'm afraid our actions will lead to more than mere war."

The man in the corner offered his opinion. "More than that, Sir Mannheim. Your actions will bring death and destruction to millions." Jeremy ignored him, and hoped that Hunter wouldn't respond to his taunts.

"Yes," he said, his voice strained. "The Duchy will suffer economic issues from the disaster. They want blood. The Protectorate believes they were simply protecting their borders from future incursion. They'll be on the defensive. House Liao will offer aid to the Duchy to gain a political advantage. And every C-bill they spend to prop up the Duchy is one they aren't spending to wage war with The Republic. This war will strain their relationship." He didn't look at Mannheim when he spoke.

Hunter stepped farther into the bay. "That box . . . What's in it? You can tell me now that the mission's over."

Hunter walked closer to the box. Marik moved off to one side, standing nearer to Chin. "Go ahead, tell him. Tell him what you did. Tell him about the best part of your mission."

Jeremy walked down the wall to the deck and over to the box. "Devlin Stone was smart. By the end of the Jihad, he had collected all the dirty secrets of every government. Everyone wondered what happened to the real Thomas Marik after the final battle. He was supposed to have died in an epic last stand, but no body was ever found. I'm sure you've seen the documentaries, heard the speculations that he somehow survived and lived out his final years somewhere secret."

Hunter glanced at the box as if it contained poisonous snakes. "You mean?"

"Meet Thomas Marik. The Butcher of Blake. The Master. The greatest killer of all time."

"Ta-da!" the figure declaimed, swept them an elegant bow, then paused to adjust his mask.

"He did escape the final battle, then?"

Jeremy shrugged slowly. "Stone's notes didn't say. He may have died in the final battle and his remains were smuggled out to the monastery I raided on Kwamashu. It could be he escaped and lived to be an old man like all of the conspiracy theorists say. Maybe the Duchy took him in and hid him—I don't know. He had a lot of secrets that would have been worth extracting, I'm sure. Who can tell what happened? What I do know is this; we have his remains now, and since they were stolen during the battle, it will be assumed that the Oriente Protectorate took them."

Thomas Marik grinned, his teeth gleaming in the darkness. "Everyone wants a part of me."

"My God."

Jeremy nodded once, slowly. "No one knew, other than Stone. If word got out, the Duchy of Andurien would be treated like a criminal state for keeping this secret, and it would make it hard for House Liao to publicly provide them support. More importantly, if they think that the Protectorate has these remains, they will be compelled to try to recover them."

"What will you do with them?"

Chin shook his head and wiped the sweat from his brow. "Redburn didn't give me any direction. Until he does, I have to hold onto them."

"That's right," the shadowed figure said. "Keep me close. We wouldn't want anyone cloning me, would we?"

"So you have his remains, and we have . . ."

"The war. The war I started."

"We," corrected Mannheim.

"Yes, all three of us," the figure added. "Isn't it grand? What shall we do next, my little knight? I was thinking of nuking Genève. Doesn't that sound fun? Jerome Blake would be proud. Let's put some of your newfound experience to work."

"I told you, shut up!" Chin snapped.

Mannheim stared at him. "Are you feeling okay, Chin?"

"I'm fine," he replied curtly. "He just won't shut his freaking mouth."

Mannheim followed the direction of his gaze. "Who?"

"Marik."

"Wonderful! While we're on the subject, you should tell him who knew about the toxic chemicals and biohazards stored in the industrial plant, and how they got wired to blow. Tell him who knew about the radioactive wastes, too. Tell him everything, Jeremy. You've already spilled the beans on me. I'm sure he'd be pleased to know what really happened."

"I won't tell him, damn it!"

Mannheim rested his hand on Chin's shoulder. "Jeremy, you need to relax. You're under a lot of stress. We both have a lot to think about—a lot to atone for."

"Maybe we should kill him," Thomas Marik suggested. "Think it over. Kill him, and you can create your own story for Redburn and the others. We could say *he* destroyed Breezewood. I know you have the skills to pull it off, but do you have the balls to do it?"

"I'm done killing!"

Chin shrugged off the older man's gesture. He didn't want to be comforted. He didn't want to ease his pain. Mannheim didn't know the full truth—and hopefully never would.

"You know you want to tell him," Thomas Marik said encouragingly. "Do it. I want to see the look on his face when you shatter what few dreams he clings to. It will be fun!"

"He's better off not knowing. I did what I had to."

"Son . . ." Mannheim reached out to him again, but Chin stepped back. He had to keep distance between them.

Jeremy closed his eyes to silence them both. A conflict between the Oriente Protectorate and the Duchy of Andurien was good for The Republic. The two of them focused on each other would buy The Republic time and offer hope. Drawing resources from the Capellan Confederation would preserve The Republic. Jeremy clung to those thoughts. They were the only thing that seemed to silence the man in the shadows.

Interpretation of Duty 9

Brandenburg, Callison
Former Prefecture VIII
Fortress Republic (+36 days)

The media ate up the opportunity to film the brave governor of Callison arriving on the front lines to meet the hero who had driven the oppressive Republic forces to ground. Cheryl refused to seek out the cameras, while Governor Stewart waved to them as if she personally was waving to every person watching the event. Cheryl was happy to let it unfold this way. She looked humble and unassuming, which would be useful later. By the time the footage was edited for the evening news, Cheryl was confident it would make a good patriotic documentary.

Of course, they were not actually on the front lines. She had drawn off her *Hellion* and a squad of infantry a good six blocks from the perimeter established around the warehouse district. Light Horse techs swarmed across her 'Mech, slapping on replacement armor patches and welding them into place. She could smell the ozone from their work; the clanging of their tools added to the image of immediacy that the governor wanted. The infantry squad was missing three of its personnel, casualties of the fighting, and two of them were injured, which played well. Their blood-soaked bandages added to the impression that Governor Stewart was right in the fight with them.

Cheryl shook her head.

She stepped forward to meet the governor, and the contrast between them hit her like a slap in the face. She was wearing her piloting shorts and a sweat-soaked T-shirt under her coolant vest. The vest made it look like she was wearing a coiled-up rubber novelty snake on her chest. Her neurohelmet hung in her hand like a dead weight. In contrast, the governor was wearing a dignified dress in a defiant red, as if she were challenging Sir Erbe. The camera crews filmed her every move as she stepped forward and shook Cheryl's hand, flashed the reporters a quick smile and nodded to her personal security. The media was ushered out of view. They had their story, their images, her spin. Now Cheryl and the governor could talk bluntly.

"Governor, forgive my appearance." Not exactly what she wanted to say, but it always helped to be polite.

Stewart waved her hand as if to dismiss the comment. "What is our situation?"

"Sir Erbe surprised me. I expected our push to press him back to the spaceport, but he went for the warehouse instead."

"Pushing him back to the spaceport was our plan, as I recall." She sounded disappointed.

"Ma'am, it is unfortunately true that no plan survives contact with the enemy," Cheryl said, then let it drop. The governor had no military experience, so there was no way to make her understand that adage. "Sir Erbe caught me off guard, but it won't do him much good. He's holed up in the warehouse district and has established a three-block perimeter. I have a variety of Light Horse units formed up around him, concentrated to the south. If he attempts to break out, that's where he'll go."

"What makes you so sure?"

"He's on a planet where the local population does not

support his efforts or even his presence. He needs his DropShips, which are to the south at the spaceport."

"His effort is short-lived, then."

"Not necessarily," Cheryl answered honestly, then immediately regretted it. Governor Stewart was not a military person with a military background. She was a politician. She wanted facts. A battle was an ever-changing thing. As if to emphasize her thought, a rumble of autocannon fire echoed off the buildings several blocks away. "It's possible his force might punch through. The troops under Sir Erbe's command seem very proficient. But even if he does break through and reach his DropShips, we have still handed him a defeat." The last sentence gave Stewart what she wanted to hear.

"Things have changed," Stewart replied. "He is trapped away from his ships. Perhaps we should rethink our strategy."

The original strategy had been to force the knight to negotiate. Cheryl had no doubt that the governor now had something darker in mind. "What do you suggest, ma'am?"

"You have him holed up in the warehouse district. You can tighten that noose. Shell the building he is in. Destroy his defenses. You can destroy this knight and his force entirely."

Cheryl gathered her thoughts. What the governor was suggesting was possible but would be difficult. "In my opinion, it is not necessary to destroy the Republic force. Polls have shown that a significant percentage of the population still has some faith in The Republic, and a move like this might turn those civilians against us. Chasing the knight away with his tail between his legs gives us a sizable victory that does not gain us any enemies." Cheryl focused on the politics involved.

"Forcing a knight errant to flee is a good public relations coup. Destroying him will show everyone that The Republic is really dead. It drives the point home," Governor Stewart insisted.

Cheryl hated to admit it, but the governor was right. She tried again. "What about forcing him to surrender?"

"Surrender is messy. It leaves us with survivors—or worse, hostages that invite rescue missions. If we destroy this Republic force, we alone remain to craft the history of the event. We are left to explain how The Republic acted as an aggressor. No. Surrender isn't desirable, I'm afraid."

Cheryl knew there were no more options. "You want me to destroy Sir Erbe and his entire force."

"Cheryl," the governor said smoothly, "I want you to know that I will fully support your actions, even if the natural course of events results in the destruction of these invaders. I will be the first to hail you as a hero when the smoke clears." The governor had established complete plausible deniability. She would not order the destruction of the Republic force; she would simply take advantage of the results of that event. The blood of her own people would be on the hands of Cheryl Gunson, on the hands of Ceresco Hancock.

"I don't want to be a hero," she said, the plea coming straight from her heart.

"Of course you don't, my dear. Heroes have glory thrust upon them by circumstances. In this case, circumstance has delivered you an easy victory."

I don't want this victory. I want to complete my mission. "The citizens might not understand how this happened."

"This is bigger than Callison, Cheryl. I have been talking to nearby worlds about alliances. If you crush this knight and his force, it will send a clear message about how powerful we are, and how easily The Republic can be defeated. Your victory will be the cement in the foundation of my new leadership. The days of The Republic are gone, and those who resist that message must change their view. Callison will lead the way."

Another distant rumble went off. Missiles this time, and the sound reminded her that the battle was still

being fought. It reminded her of her other obligations.
"I believe I understand, ma'am."

"I believe you do."

As Cheryl turned to walk away, she hoisted her neurohelmet and stared into the blank faceplate. *I do understand. I understand that I have to create my own solution
to my mission.* Inwardly, Cheryl cringed at the realization of what victory might require, even though it was
something she had trained for, something she had come
to take for granted.

They don't call us ghosts for nothing. . . .

The Light Horse Yasha aligned itself over the street
and pivoted the turbojets forward to accelerate. It came
straight at the warehouse complex with its chainguns
blazing. The shells stitched the street and the side of the
building, turning windows into shrapnel and bricks to
dust as the shells impacted. It was the third such pass,
and the stubby fighter was starting to get on Kristoff
Erbe's nerves. The good news was that the VTOL did
only minimal damage and had to take off every few minutes to reload. The bad news was that it remained unmo-
lested except by returning small-arms fire. Its speed and
altitude made it a difficult and highly frustrating target.
Like a damn fly that I can't manage to kill.

The DropShip engines were loaded on the prime
hauler transports, but getting them to the spaceport was
almost impossible at the moment. The Callison Light
Horse had bottled them up pretty efficiently. Every
move he made was quickly countered. He knew that
they might not be able to mass enough firepower to
overwhelm the militia and break out. If he did manage
it, it would be costly.

For now, the warehouse district was safe. He preferred
being trapped there to making a running retreat to the
DropShips. Governor Stewart would have loved that—a
Knight of the Sphere sent into a full rout by a planetary
militia. Nothing would rally dissent on Callison and

other worlds like defeating The Republic in a straight-up battle.

He felt proud that he had messed up her plans by not retreating. He might not have the firepower to break out, but he was confident that the Light Horse lacked enough manpower and machines to break him. *My father would choose the path of least resistance. I can't.*

So now he was under siege. It was messy, it would wear him down, but he would find a way to turn this to his advantage. He had to. Kristoff Erbe saw no other choice than surrender—which was not an option—or death. And he had to believe that no matter how heartless the governor was, she would not seek the total destruction of his force.

Then again, even if she did, who would seek retribution? Would Damien Redburn come to Callison and set matters straight? Was there a Republic out there for Kristoff Erbe to serve? For the first time in his life, he found himself wondering if he was fighting for the right cause. Almost immediately, he suppressed those feelings, pushing them down right next to his true feelings about his father. It was best that such thoughts not reach the light of day.

"Squirrel, Harbinger on secured channel." Adamans' voice interrupted his thoughts.

"Squirrel here," Kristoff replied, switching to the crypto-circuit controls on the comm board and activating his scrambler. "You are in the clear on secure channel one."

"My intelligence team has been reviewing data from our first encounter, profiling the TO&E of the Light Horse and their warriors, detecting patterns of action and tactics based on our battlerom footage. We have some preliminary results, which I am transmitting to you."

Erbe was impressed. The list that scrolled across his secondary display listed every piece of hardware the militia had in the field, and confirmed casualties and per-

cent of damage for the Callison militia. Regular
Republic troops generally achieved this level of detail in
their analysis, but only with a mobile headquarters and
a team of experts crunching the numbers. For him, three
men in the Fidelis dedicated to security as a secondary
duty had performed the task.

"Outstanding, Harbinger. This is incredible data."

"There is more. I am sending you a secured image."

The monitor flickered as the image appeared on the
display. It was the cockpit of a *Hellion* BattleMech. He
studied the digital image captured by the Fidelis camera,
and zoomed in to see the face of the MechWarrior. It
looked like . . . *but that was impossible.* He zoomed in
again. The warrior wearing the neurohelmet in the cockpit of the *Hellion* had stern features, gritted teeth and a
familiar face.

Ceresco Hancock.

Adamans' voice seemed loud in the earpieces of his
neurohelmet. "It is our visitor from the other night.
Based on the patterns of the communications traffic, she
was in command of the enemy forces. She was leading
the attack against us."

"The traitor . . ." he breathed, every muscle in his
body clenched at the realization.

"Say again, Squirrel."

Kristoff Erbe gathered his senses. He closed his eyes
to avoid the image on the display. "Good work, Colonel.
Don't share this image with anyone else. I will handle
this on my own when the time is right."

Altar of Freedom 5

New Dearborn, Ryde
Jade Falcon Occupation Zone
Fortress Republic (−18 days)

Greene walked along the sidewalk toward Veterans Park. He had shed his military jumpsuit in favor of the civilian clothing he had worn underneath. This was more his style anyway, after years of being a ghost knight; being out of uniform offered a great deal of comfort. To most observers he would look like a common laborer—confused by the sound of gunfire and artillery, but still required to get to work. He moved cautiously, but normally enough not to attract the attention of any local law enforcement or Jade Falcon security.

The park was a brilliant burst of color, greens, yellows and light browns shining in the middle of the urban grays and blacks. He found himself smiling when he saw the park. Only a few dozen meters more and he would be to the DropShips. He lifted his wrist as if to check his chronometer as he walked. A low rumble in the distance caught his attention for a moment—artillery fire. *Got to be ours; the Falcons are not big fans of artillery.*

Toggling a button on his watch, he spoke in a low tone that the miniaturized comm system would pick up.

"Mongoose, this is Greene. I'm at the park, heading north to the *Excelsior*. You can begin to fall back."

There was a hiss and the sound of battle from the tiny earpiece he wore. Also miniaturized, the earpiece was camouflaged as an earring. He heard stress in her voice. "Understood. You've implicated our friends?"

"Affirmative."

"See you aboard the ship," she managed, as a cracking sound filled his ear. Whatever was happening a few blocks away, it was intense, that much was for sure. Jayson Greene realized that he was very much on his own.

Lady Synd saw the *Stalking Spider* loom in front of her. Its jump jets had been reduced to twisted metal by her last salvo, but the *Spider* was still in the fight. She wished she could say the same of her *Templar*. The last blast of laser energy from the *Spider* had taken out the remaining armor on her 'Mech's chest. Strands of seared myomer flopped up and hit her windshield, sparking where they had been burned free. Her cockpit was now more like an oven than a control center. The *Templar* moved sluggishly, fighting her commands. She wanted to shift to the right, to try for the *Spider*'s flank, but each step was slow and ponderous, as if she were trying to move through a swamp.

The *Stalking Spider* had taken some damage. Some of her Fidelis troops had peppered its legs with short-range missiles from reconfigured ATVs. Republic troops in a Pegasus hovercraft had made a skirting pass, blasting away at the body of the *Spider*. They had paid a price for their bravery when a laser blast had melted their turret into a permanent position.

The fight wasn't over. The Jade Falcons' push to the park had been stalled by a fierce defense. Her tactical display showed that the Falcons had stopped moving forward and were beginning to entrench into the city, shifting into structures for defense. Not this *Stalking Spider*, though—it was hanging on.

She still had a pair of BlazeFire extended-range medium lasers, which meant she still had a chance of doing some damage. As the *Spider* turned to bring its massive laser to bear, she brought her targeting reticle onto the massive 'Mech and fired a snap shot. One of the lasers missed completely, and she realized that it must have been damaged earlier but had not shown up on her damage display. The other shot, a searing green beam, hit the cocked leg that was closest to her and ran up to the knee actuator.

At that instant, the Jade Falcon fired. The shot grazed her 'Mech's shoulder just enough to jar her. The majority of the energy missed, searing the front of a nearby building. She heard the rumble of the front façade of the building caving in from the savaging it had received, pouring rocks and steel into the street behind her. Her hit must have been enough to throw off the Falcon's shot.

A quick glance at her damage display revealed a harsh truth. One of her remaining two lasers was off-line. The glancing blow must have damaged the power feed in her 'Mech's shoulder. She leaned forward and looked to her left at the shoulder of the *Templar*, which was sizzling hot. The armor was gone there, as it was everywhere.

On the ground she could see Fidelis troops fanning out, assuming defensive positions, firing at the *Spider*. She knew that if she went down before the *Stalking Spider*, it would tear into what was left of her troops. And there had been too much death already. As the *Spider* continued its turn and its laser recharged, she resolved to end the fight then and there.

She urged her *Templar* into a lumbering run—really more of a controlled fall than a full-blown charge. The legs of the 'Mech were slow to respond to her, but she fought the control pedals. Leaning forward, she gritted her teeth and tensed every muscle against the impact. Sweat stung at the corners of her eyes.

The *Templar* hit the front leg of the *Spider* precisely where her lasers had hit it earlier in the battle. Her ears rang, the sound fighting against the metallic grinding of the impact. Her body slammed forward against command couch restraints and she heard her cockpit canopy crack. The abrupt end of forward movement shoved her back into her seat, and her head slammed back hard.

For a moment, she thought nothing had happened. She looked at her tactical display through the mist of the heat that steamed her neurohelmet shield and saw a glare of red. Her fusion reactor and gyro were showing as damaged. Two of her heat sinks had failed. In a daze, she reached forward to the display and felt the *Templar* groan as it moved forward. The leg she had hit was giving way, weakened by the assault and crumpling under the crushing weight of her 'Mech. It collapsed and she fell forward, under the *Stalking Spider*, which dropped down on top of her. The drop to the street below was nothing compared to the impact upon landing. The lights in her cockpit flickered out and were replaced by the emergency lights.

Her *Templar* was dead.

She heard a metallic moan above her, and knew that the *Stalking Spider* was down for the count as well. Lady Synd allowed herself a satisfied half-grin. She disengaged her restraints and grappled her way to the hatch. With any luck it wouldn't be blocked.

Boyne bent over Morella in the rubble of what had been a small corner store only moments before. A searing blast of laser energy had gutted the entire facade of the building, collapsing it onto the first floor. Survivors stirred under the ferrocrete dust and splintered wood of a destroyed piece of furniture. The infantryman should have been dead, judging by the pile of debris he crawled out from under. Instead, he hoisted his weapon to cover Boyne and Morella. Another trooper crawled from the debris as well.

Morella was not so lucky. She looked pale; he could tell she was dying. Boyne ignored the gunfire behind him and leaned over her. Was she already dead? Her eyelids flickered, then half opened. One eye was horribly red

the waist. "You can tell him yourself when we reach the ship." He turned his head and shouted orders. "Fall back by sections. Contact Vasserman and tell him to pull back his vehicles to cover us. Keep up the fire on those Falcons." He activated his wrist comm. "Captain Paulis, I'm at Maple Drive, two blocks north and west of the park. Mongoose is down. Say again, Mongoose is down. I have her and need you here to cover our retreat."

"Crap!" replied Paulis, strain cracking his voice. Somehow it reassured her. It meant he was still alive.

Nausea threatened to overwhelm her, and she tasted bile mixed with the blood in her mouth. "Forget me. Get the troops out of here, Captain," she wheezed. The words seemed to take away what little energy she had remaining.

"You are in no condition to give orders, and I have no intention of taking them now," Boyne replied. "I have ordered a retreat to the ships, and we're taking you with us." He held up his comm unit again. "Stormcloud, this is Iron Will. Drop smoke for cover on my coordinates. No spotting round. Lock onto my signal and fire for effect, full dispersal."

"What about Morella?" she asked. That was not what she meant to say, but the words were what surfaced from her foggy mind.

"She is released," Boyne said, lifting her into the smoke-filled street with the aid of another trooper. The air stung her eyes. "We leave no blood on the field of battle. I simply honored that vow." He pulled his service automatic and pumped off two rounds at a target down the street. She couldn't see his target. She no longer wanted to. *Too many have died. It's time to get out of this place.* Through a haze of pain she saw the smoke rounds hit the street. They hissed and blasted particles in every direction. In a matter of seconds the entire street was thick with smoke. That wouldn't prevent targeting and tracking systems from finding targets, but it made line-of-sight fire impossible. *I warned Redburn this would happen. Damn him. Damn me for being right.*

The image of Morella's body, laying in the rubble, oddly and prematurely decayed, floated in her mind's eye. "What did you do to her?" She stumbled, and Boyne and the other trooper simply dragged her along. Her feet skidded on the ferrocrete pavement.

"Now is not the time."

"Tell me!" she demanded.

"I fulfilled her honor. If it had been me, she would have done the same. It is our way. No blood"—he fired off another round into the smoke that was now behind them—"no DNA. No way for them to know who we really are."

At that moment, Lady Synd lifted her head and saw the yellow-green grass of Veterans Park. Only a hundred meters more . . .

She passed out long before they had traveled that distance.

Overture 1

.

Coos Bay, Oregon, Terra
Prefecture X, Republic of the Sphere
Fortress Republic (–188 days)

Damien Redburn sat in the deep, plush red chair, his feet up on the ottoman. The evening chill had started to set in. He and Sasha had chosen to live in the Pacific Northwest because it reminded him of the planet Northwind, where he had been raised, and offered the prospect of fishing. Before retirement, he had thought he'd enjoy fishing. That seemed like years ago. He had gone fishing six times in the nearly three months since he had stepped down as exarch of the Republic of the Sphere, and now he was willing to admit that he found it boring and cold. Redburn was disappointed that his retirement was not what he'd hoped for. Truth be told, being retired was dull.

He stared intently at the hard-copy book in his hands, as if it could give him solace. Since he had stepped down as exarch, his den looked more like an office; sitting in a comfortable chair and reading late into the night made it feel like a place of rest and relaxation again, rather than a place of work.

Work. It wasn't like in the days when he was leading

the entire Republic. Now work consisted of publicity visits to schools and factory openings, to military bases and factories. Cutting ribbons, shaking hands with schoolchildren, these were the jobs performed by a *former* exarch. There was his book deal; mounds of paper associated with compiling his notes covered his desk. Thinking of it prompted him to look away from his reading and stare at his dark walnut desk. In the falling evening darkness, the mounds of paper, scribbles of notes from meetings long past, seemed to cast odd shadows on the wall near his workstation monitor. *The things I call work now don't make a difference in the universe. There was a time when the decisions I made were important. . . .*

It was the past that truly bothered him. He'd hoped that reading his great-grandfather Thelos Auburn's book, *A Study of Empires: The Third Succession War*, would give him insight, inspiration enough to sit down in front of the pile of papers and begin work on his memoirs. His publisher assured him that people wanted to hear his opinions and views. He frowned, closing the book as carefully as if it were a bible. *No one wants to hear from a washed-up leader. Especially one who made mistakes like I did.*

Damien knew that he was not personally responsible for the current state of The Republic. Knowing that and accepting it, however, were two different things. What Jonah Levin had inherited was a bomb with a burning fuse. Redburn had been duped by Ezekiel Crow, one of his own trusted paladins. Terra had faced invasion by the Steel Wolves. The Jade Falcons had crossed into Republic space and had carved out a chunk for themselves. Then there were the actions of the Capellan Confederation, which saw the peace of Stone's Republic as a weakness to be exploited.

He laid the book on the small table next to his easy chair and felt his face tighten as he thought of the Liao incursion into The Republic. Damien was a veteran of the CapCom war; he had cut his military teeth on the

Capellans in that conflict. *I trusted them all . . . maybe not the Capellans so much, but I trusted the other governments. I assumed, like Stone did, that everyone wanted peace.* Now he saw the governments of the Inner Sphere for what they were, albeit too late. They did not scent sweet peace on the wind, but rather the bitter smell of conquest. That smell sparked their hunger for power, and they rushed forward to consume The Republic like a starving man turned loose at a buffet.

In the past, he had always been able to turn to his stalwart paladins—but even that changed. Victor Steiner-Davion, more icon than man, was dead. Victor offered a unique perspective on Inner Sphere politics that was impossible to replace, and his loss created a void that The Republic leadership would be hard-pressed to adequately fill. Even as he transferred the authority of his office to Jonah—*Exarch* Levin—the Senate had proven itself another disease seeking to feast on The Republic, and its actions started a civil war in Europe.

Damien Redburn had never said the words out loud, but he felt responsible for the events that had unfolded.

A flicker of light from his desk caught his attention. His monitor came to life. He thought that was odd, because he was certain he hadn't left any applications running. Perhaps it was a late-night communication from his publisher, asking for a progress update on his memoirs. As he rose from his chair, he looked at the antique clock on the mantle, saw it was almost midnight and decided that the message was not from his publisher. As he walked to his desk, he wondered if it was a family emergency, if one of the kids had a problem.

He slid into his desk chair, and the leather groaned as he sat. The monitor displayed the logo of The Republic: *Ad Securitas Per Unitas.* He inserted the tiny earpiece in his right ear to listen to the message. *So, not the kids.* The Republic logo was reserved for official communications. His heart beat slightly faster. Perhaps it was Jonah contacting him.

The image on the screen faded and another came into focus. He was looking at a face he hadn't seen in years; he felt like he was seeing a ghost. Fear and excitement widened his eyes. *It's not possible . . . not him!* He opened his mouth to respond to the man on the screen, but the head continued to speak. He stared at the features of the man who had forged The Republic, drinking in his words as if they were life-giving water. After a few moments data being transmitted from Genève flickered on the screen. He leaned in, studying the details as they flowed past.

"My God . . . ," he spoke in a low whisper, meaning it with all his heart. For the first time in months he felt a charge of excitement. "Has it really come to *this*?"

He stepped out onto the terrace, and Sasha looked up at him with understandable surprise. Damien said nothing for a second and just let her look at him. With the reflex action of every military man, he tugged at the uniform coat. It was much snugger than he remembered it; that, or he had put on weight.

"You didn't come to bed last night," she said coyly. "I assumed you had finally started writing your memoirs. Now you show up wearing that uniform. Is there something that you want to tell me?"

He wore the gray dress uniform coat of a paladin. He had not worn it since Devlin Stone had asked him to be The Republic's second exarch, and he had chosen to wear it today for a purpose. *I may no longer be the exarch, but I am always a paladin.* He pulled out the chair next to her and took her right hand in both of his as he sat down. Redburn had held her hands the same way when he proposed to her. He said nothing for a moment. Sasha Redburn broke the silence.

"I know that look," she said, her voice deepening with emotion. "It's the same one you give me every time you are leaving."

He wanted to tell her she was wrong, but couldn't.

Lying to Sasha was not something he had ever done. "I received a message last night. I have to go to Genève to meet with the exarch about it."

"You don't wear that expression for a simple trip to Genève . . . ," she said cautiously. "Not to mention you've dug out your paladin uniform. There is more to this than a trip to Genève."

"Only Genève . . . for today."

"This is not some plant tour or classroom visit. I can tell."

He gave her a small smile. "You're right, my love," he said. "You always are."

"I thought that time was behind us. You've done your bit for king and country, Damien. This was supposed to be our time together."

She knew that with him The Republic always came first. It always had. He thought he was looking forward to spending time with her and the kids. Things had changed more than he expected when he stopped being exarch, and not in a good way. He was no longer the ruler of a star-spanning empire. It was as if he didn't exist.

Until the message last night.

"I was a knight and then a paladin before I was exarch, and that's a lifetime commitment. You knew that when we married. I thought my service was done as well, but apparently it isn't. The message I received last night changed things. I have to go."

"Who called? Was it Jonah? Is it some sort of meeting?"

He squeezed her hands tighter in response. "Not Jonah, dear. I heard from a former exarch. There are duties that I am expected to attend to. I will be back when I have to leave Terra. I won't go without seeing you and the children again." He rose to his feet but kept hold of her hands, drawing her up to stand in front of him. The morning light on the terrace picked out the details of his uniform, and the years seemed to fall away from the former exarch. He took a deep breath and stood tall. *Yes, the uniform is tighter than before, but I feel lighter than I have in years.*

Damien Redburn gathered his wife into his arms for a kiss and a hug. Both lasted a moment or two longer than usual.

Héloïse Montgolfier stood in the large executive office of the exarch, her arms behind her back as if she were at parade rest. She was Jonah Levin's chief of staff, which made her the number-two most powerful person in The Republic when they were in a crisis. The concept of crisis had changed dramatically as of late. The Republic was in a constant state of crisis.

"He says it's imperative that he meet with you."

Levin waved his hand dismissively. "We have too much going at the moment. See if you can schedule something in a week or so."

"He was very insistent, sir. And he told me to mention the word 'fortress.'" She stared solemnly at a point just above her superior's right shoulder.

For Jonah Levin, the man who had assumed the mantle of the exarch from Damien Redburn, that word killed every other noise in the room. His face went hot and cold. "Clear my schedule and show him in."

Redburn entered the room wearing a paladin's uniform. He nodded as Montgolfier left the office, closing the door behind her. Exarch Levin met him in the middle of the crest of The Republic set into the carpeted floor and shook his hand, as if they were posing for a media photo-op. Redburn wanted to laugh, but somehow couldn't muster it.

The current exarch gestured to a guest chair across from his desk and retreated to his own comfortable seat.

"It's good to see you, Damien, but I must admit that I'm quite busy right now—as I'm sure you're aware." It was dramatic understatement on his part. The struggle taking place in Europe between Levin and the rogue senators was being highly publicized.

"I was contacted by Devlin Stone last night."

Exarch Levin stared for a second at his predecessor and then pinched the bridge of his nose as if trying to relieve the pressure of a headache. "Damn it, Damien, that's not funny."

Redburn's expression didn't change. "I wish I were kidding," he said. "Apparently, some of his files outlining his contingency plans for The Republic were flagged with triggers that were set up to send me a prerecorded message—from Stone. The message contained details for operations outside Fortress Republic . . . and a reminder that the rank of paladin stayed with a man for life."

"You're not kidding?"

Redburn shook his head. "I was more surprised than you."

"You know about the Fortress plans, then?"

"Yes." He nodded. "When the HPG went down on my watch, I skimmed those plans along with several other versions. The fact that I received this message indicates that you were not just skimming those files, but actually reviewing them in some detail."

Levin's initial reaction was concern. His people had not spotted any flag on those files. *Who else received a message from Stone last night?* Had the Fortress plans been totally compromised? No. He pushed those thoughts to the dark places of his mind. *Best to focus on what I know rather than what might be.*

While Levin thought, Redburn slid a data cube into the player and played the entire transcript of the message he had received. It did little to alleviate his feeling of dread. *What other little presents have you left out there, Devlin?*

Levin sighed, and Redburn knew the crushing weight of what his successor was contemplating. Levin shook his head slightly as he responded. "If you've read those plans, then you realize the scale of what we're doing. This is a massive strategic withdrawal and entrenching. We pull back to the core worlds of Prefecture X and make it impossible to enter the Fortress while we build our strength for a time when we can emerge and recover The Republic. This is the biggest event in the Inner Sphere since Kerensky's Exodus or the Jihad."

"How can you isolate Prefecture X?"

"You don't want to know. Suffice it to say I have to dust off some technologies whose use is questionable at best, things that Stone had sitting by just for such a contingency. Technologies that our former enemies contemplated using. It's like learning to juggle using weapons of mass destruction."

"Devlin must have understood what you'd be facing. You saw the message. He specifically outlined a number of operations outside of the Fortress that I'm sure you're already trying to figure out how to coordinate. You'll need resources on the outside that can manage the knights and the paladins. Someone to follow through on these operations so that when you do finally emerge, the groundwork is laid for the reestablishment of The Republic."

"Let's not downplay what Stone is recommending," Levin said in a sour tone. "These missions are not like anything we've performed as a government up to this point. We're talking about destabilizing neighboring planets, sabotage, assassinations and even starting wars." As the current exarch spoke, the words obviously weighed heavily on him.

"It makes you wonder," Redburn said.

"About?"

"Maybe Stone was wrong."

After a moment of contemplation, Levin swept the air with his hand, as if to erase Redburn's words. "I can't go there with my thinking. If I start questioning Stone's wisdom now, I might as well step aside and let the Senate run things."

Redburn let that statement stand for a moment. "What's most important is that we both understand the depth of what we are discussing. Our actions will violate principles that both of us have pledged to protect."

"These actions ensure our ultimate survival . . . the survival of The Republic."

"That's what makes it so hard" was all that Redburn replied. He took a deep breath, then let it out slowly. "I can coordinate the exterior missions. They can be my burden to bear."

Levin stared at him. "You're volunteering?"

Redburn nodded slowly, closing his eyes. "If you go by the message I received last night, I have little choice. The fate of The Republic depends on Fortress being successful. Besides, Jonah, you know better than anyone the burden that this office and the title "exarch" imposes. I was in charge when the network crashed. I was the leader that fiddled while Rome burned . . . if you believe the media accounts. This is a way to prove to everyone who I really am. Frankly, it's my last chance, Jonah."

Levin *did* understand. He knew that Damien had struggled to play the cards he had been dealt to best advantage, but that others just saw him as weak and ineffective. Jonah knew differently; he knew Redburn was honorable, that with him The Republic always came first. "I'm tempted to accept your help, Damien. If you've read the plans for Fortress Republic, you know the challenges. You'll be cut off from your family and friends, any hope of military support, even communications with Terra. The people I am sending outside of Fortress are going to face the hardest of times. Even Stone's notes say that."

Redburn smiled. "I know. I wouldn't have come if I didn't know and accept the risks." He ran his hand across the surface of the desk. Jonah wondered if he might be contemplating how long it had been since he had sat on that side of it. "But, my old friend, you have assets available that you are unaware of." Levin thought, irrationally, that there was a twinkle in Redburn's eye as he said this.

"What do you mean?"

"You have heard of the Fidelis warriors?"

"Stone's Shadows? They were a small elite-forces unit during the Jihad. Stone always denied they existed, but there were witnesses to their ferocity. Strange troops. I recall one story where they lost three of their men and they stopped to burn their bodies before moving on against the Blake forces. I assumed they were just one of dozens of disbanded forces or were propaganda, or even myth. So many units were tossed together during that time I never gave them much thought. Are you saying they actually exist?"

"They are real. I know how to contact them. But you cannot. If you, as the standing exarch, were linked to them, it would irrevocably damage the Republic's relationship with multiple governments, including and perhaps especially the Clans. You have a higher calling to answer if you are going to implement Fortress Republic. If I contact them on behalf of The Republic and we're discovered, you are safe to disavow all knowledge of them. In short, old friend, I'll keep your hands clean."

Levin wanted to probe for more information. He had had far too many surprises since he had become exarch. He had to trust Redburn, and so he had to let this go. He skipped to the practicalities. "They'll need hardware, transport and other materiel. Things The Republic happens to be a little short on at the moment."

Damien actually laughed. Jonah couldn't remember the last time he had seen his predecessor even crack a genuine smile. "Actually, they don't. They have their own production capability. In fact, they have a WarShip at their disposal—mothballed since the Jihad, of course."

A covert army? A WarShip? "How big of a force are we talking about?" His mind reeled at the possibilities, and he cursed himself for not forcing Damien to spend more time transitioning the job to him. He wondered just how many other secrets Redburn hadn't revealed, and why.

"They are few in number, by choice. Their skills are more suited for special operations—black ops, really.

Given the path we have set ourselves upon with Fortress Republic, I wonder if Stone didn't set them up for us to use in this capacity."

Jonah leaned back in his chair and carefully placed his fingertips together to form a temple. "I have to tell you, Damien, this is the first thing in a long time that has gone right for us. I'm strapped for troops and equipment. You walk in here and hand me just what I need when I need it. You've sat in this chair. You have to admit, it's a little suspicious."

Redburn leaned back in the guest chair and seemed suddenly weary. " 'Pessimistic' is the word I would have used. It's as if Stone knew all along that peace would fail. If I were in your shoes, I'd hesitate to accept this offer. Trust is hard to come by these days. But I'm the one paladin you haven't used. And Stone must have known that the Fidelis would be needed if an exarch initiated the Fortress plans."

It always comes back to Stone.

Redburn continued. "One never retires from service to The Republic. It seems like I spent my whole life serving The Republic. Since leaving your seat I've been bored—something I've never been before in my life. I feel forgotten, discarded. This opportunity changes all of that. I can do more. I can do this for you, for The Republic." He hesitated, as if he wanted to say more but couldn't. In the yellow light of the office, Levin leaned forward.

"There's more. . . ."

Redburn nodded and breathed out a small but audible sigh. "I feel responsibility for what has happened to The Republic. If I can perform this service, I'll feel as if I've set my soul back on the right path, put to rest some of my own demons. To be blunt, Jonah, I'm the best person for this. The Fidelis warriors are quite . . . *unique.* If their true background was known, it could cause you more problems than they will solve. That's why Stone kept them secret, and why I didn't tell you about them when I could have. My handling them insulates you as

exarch. In short, I give you two words: plausible deniability. What more can be done to *my* reputation?"

Levin was being eaten alive by curiosity to know the
background of the Fidelis, but realized that there was a
potentially high price in knowing the answer. What the
former exarch was offering was to take the fall if something went wrong. That would have to suffice for now.
"You're asking a lot of me, old friend."

"I prefer to think I'm offering you a great deal more.
Coordinating activities outside of Fortress is going to
take someone dedicated, someone who has experience.
You and I both know that I'm suited for just these kinds
of operations."

"What about Sasha? What about your children? You
know that once you're outside the Fortress you can't
return."

Redburn looked somber. "Sasha knows me. She
knows where my priorities lie. She even understands."
His words resonated with Levin. This was a man who
was sacrificing seeing his family, potentially forever.
Stone was smart to choose him.

Levin rose to his feet, pushing himself up with his hands
flat on the desk. For a moment he leaned across the desk
toward his predecessor, scrutinizing his face. *He's aged.
There's a hint of gray in the sideburns, a few wrinkles that
I didn't notice when he came in. Is this what being a former
exarch does to you? I only hope I hold up as well.*

Reaching out he shook the hand of the man across
the desk. "Very well, *Paladin* Redburn. Welcome back
into the game. I'll have Héloïse come in and we can
review some of our thoughts for what will happen outside Fortress Republic, and she'll bring you up to speed
on current events and plans. In the meantime, I will
draft orders for you to assemble a group of knights and
ghost knights for your operations."

Redburn grinned broadly, and once again the years
seemed to fall from his face. "Thank you, Jonah."

"Damien, I think it's me who should be thanking
you."

Interpretation of Duty 3

Brandenburg, Callison
Former Prefecture VIII
Fortress Republic (+12 days)

"**A**re you sure?" the governor asked.

"Positive. I have quarantined the DropShip and crew and have ensured that there has been no outgoing communication traffic. My interview with the executive officers was conclusive. They are carrying a copy of the transmission that Exarch Levin sent out from the so-called Fortress." The moderately sized office of the governor of Callison seemed to get much smaller as Cheryl spoke.

She knew this was what the governor had been waiting for: formal word as to the fate of The Republic. She had used her inside information to plant the seeds suggesting this would happen. Now Governor Allison Stewart would believe Cheryl Gunson possessed a keen sense of perspective.

She handed over the hard copy of the message that Levin had sent out. The paper cut her index finger as the governor pulled it from her. She winced and pulled a tissue from her pocket to catch the blood. She almost laughed. She was a ghost knight, a highly trained special operative, and she was wincing over a paper cut. *It appears that first blood has been drawn, and it's mine.*

Governor Stewart pored over the message as if it were a religious document. "Oh-ho," she muttered to herself. "This is just what I needed."

"Governor?"

"You've read this—you know what the exarch said."

"Yes." She knew that Levin would send a message to the rest of the Inner Sphere, and she had been anxious to see how he would cast the decision he had made. The JumpShip *Star Phoenix* had brought it into the Callison system, and she had ensured that the message was intercepted before it reached the public. In her opinion, it was a good message. Ceresco had met the current exarch when he was still a paladin. As she read the message, she imagined that she could hear him saying the words. *They were good words, too. Pity those words, the truth, be the first victims here on Callison.*

The governor quoted a passage with a mocking tone in her voice. "So formal, so over-the-top. This is what one expects from a paladin nowadays. 'That bright fire . . . shall never be extinguished.' Who is he kidding? Levin is crawling inside the Alamo, hoping that the Combine or the Confederation doesn't finish what they've started."

Cheryl felt compelled to defend him. "His words seemed sincere."

"My dear Cheryl," Stewart replied, for the first time using her first name, and in a surprisingly casual tone. "You lack the subtleties of a political mind, which is one of the reasons I like you. It isn't what he *said*, it is what he *implies*. He is ripping apart the outside of this 'Fortress Republic' to preserve himself and his position of power."

"Do you really believe that?"

"Yes. He has left us to the proverbial wolves. And now we must do our duty to our citizens."

"I will order the media to release Exarch Levin's

statement," Cheryl said, knowing full well that would not happen—not right away, at least.

"No, no, no," the governor protested. "First what is needed is for us to reassure our constituents that they will be taken care of. If The Republic won't do it—well, then we will have to fill that gap."

The image of the governor was broadcast on every holovid screen on Callison, interrupting numerous sporting events, the news, several boring documentaries, and the latest episode of *Immortal Warrior Rebirth*. Cheryl watched the address from her office, leaning back in her chair, studying how Allison Stewart worked.

It was a masterful performance, full of emotion and surprises. The opening was particularly touching. The governor said she had received a message broadcast from "the remains of Stone's Republic." The wording was carefully chosen to indicate that Callison was no longer part of that Republic. She had laid the groundwork, then went on to confide how she had always believed in Stone's vision. Now, unfortunately, it seemed the new order had other ideals, other visions in mind. *She has linked herself to Stone—a safe image for the minds of the public.*

"Exarch Levin has chosen to abandon the majority of The Republic, including our world, your homes—our home" was her next power statement. That would play off the fears people had been feeling since the collapse of the HPG network. Cheryl made a mental note to find out who crafted this speech for the governor. Whoever it was, they were good.

Then, in a motherly tone, she gave the listeners some reassurance. "We may be alone, but we are alone together. My responsibilities have not changed. I am charged with protecting and defending the people of Callison and will do just that." Cheryl's brow wrinkled at those words. She strongly suspected what would follow and didn't want to be proven correct.

"In order to ensure our safety and longevity, I am assuming full control of those parts of the government that traditionally have been managed by the former Republic." The key word was "former." Stewart was telling her people that The Republic was no more.

This announcement was guaranteed to create problems. From what Cheryl knew of the legate, a surly officer named Nehemiah Leif, he would aggressively resist this move. The governor's statement was open to interpretation, but there was no doubt in the mind of the ghost knight what was intended. She was not talking about minor administrative functions in the government: She was going to seize control of the planetary militia.

The governor ended her statement by urging her constituents to maintain peace and order. "The formal statement from Exarch Levin will begin broadcasting as soon as we feel confident that we have adequately answered the questions of the media. Rest assured that I am a loyal citizen of Callison and will do what is right to protect and serve you, its people."

Cheryl shut off the monitor as the question-and-answer portion of the news conference began. Fortress Republic was no longer a concept or a plan; it was reality. She and all others like her were cut off from Terra, possibly for the rest of their lives. It was a reality that she had come to accept over the last few months.

She dragged her thoughts to the governor. Stewart was very good at manipulating the media and the public: Cheryl knew there were things she could learn from such an expert. Her own training in politics and marketing had been thorough, and she had successfully used her talent and experience multiple times in the past; but watching a master at work gave her a chance to fine-tune her skills. Thinking about Governor Stewart's performance led her mind back to her mission . . . it always turned back to her mission.

I have to watch that . . . letting my mind wander. That's what leads to mistakes. My orders are all that I can truly rely on. Orders from a ghost paladin who was no longer available to her. Were those orders still valid? She had studied them back on New Earth, and had reviewed them once or twice since. Cheryl could almost recite them word for word. In the past, if changes to her orders seemed indicated, she could have communicated with Terra to confirm whether a course of action was appropriate. She had rarely taken advantage of that option, but she found comfort in knowing the safety net was there. *Now all I have is my own interpretation of those orders—and perhaps Paladin Redburn, if I could find him.*

She began gathering the paperwork she would take home to review. Around her, the Directorate would be monitoring all channels and information sources for signs of civil unrest; there was some minor concern about the potential for protests, rioting and looting. Cheryl Gunson had responsibilities to tend to.

As she came to her feet, she saw a message from the governor arrive on her priority channel. *Damn.* It was clear she would have little time to rest from this point forward.

With just one additional person in it, the governor's office seemed cramped. Legate Leif of the Callison militia, officially known as the Callison Light Horse, was red in the face when Cheryl entered the room. He was in his early fifties, but as ready for service as ever. He was going bald but not fighting it; he kept what little white hair he still had cropped short. He had a reputation for aggressively defending his troops and his decisions, and Cheryl knew by the fury in his face that she had walked into the middle of a fight.

"Thank you for joining us, Cheryl." The governor gestured to a chair next to the legate. He gave Cheryl a nod which she returned. "The legate and I were just discussing the content of my speech yesterday. He was expressing his, eh, concerns."

Diplomatic to the end. "Indeed."

"As I was telling Governor Stewart, I have not received orders from my chain of command telling me to report to her. That being the case, I have a number of issues with having the Light Horse simply fall under her direct jurisdiction." His voice showed the strain of holding back his frustration.

"I am not sure what I can offer to this discussion," Cheryl replied. "My concern is for the internal affairs of Callison." She watched the governor for some sort of clue about which direction she should go. Stewart's face was unreadable.

"I do value your counsel in such matters," Stewart said smoothly. "Legate Leif, I have shown you the text of Exarch Levin's message. That message does more than imply that he has granted governors a much wider latitude in managing the control and defense of their worlds—a logical position, given the collapse of The Republic. I am simply attempting to comply with the exarch's wishes."

Legate Leif bared his teeth in a menacing smile. " 'Collapse of The Republic,' my ass. I read those orders, and there was nothing in that message about my turning over command of the militia to you. I heard your speech—everyone on the planet did. You painted the exarch as turning his back on Callison. Now you sit there and claim to be implementing his wishes. You made it sound like The Republic betrayed Callison and now you sit here and tell me that you are simply being a good citizen of that same Republic. Governor, you can't have your cake and eat it too."

"I believe you are exaggerating minor points in my speech, Legate," she said without raising her voice. "My loyalty to The Republic has never been in question."

He narrowed his eyes. "Politicians. You play games with words and in the end it's men like me who have to pick up the pieces. The Republic is going through some changes, I admit it. That doesn't mean that I will simply hand you the militia on a silver platter. I serve a higher cause."

"A cause that has abandoned you."

Legate Leif turned and looked directly at Cheryl. "Ms. Gunson, don't tell me that you are buying into this bull?"

I don't want to be dragged into this fight, on either side. "I agree that the message from the exarch offers a broad interpretation. I would think, however, that you and the governor could reach a compromise. Given the current situation and the fact that The Republic is not in a position to offer us clarification, it would seem to be the most effective approach."

Leif waved his hand in the air. "Compromise? On the defense of this world? I don't think so." He rose to his feet.

"Legate Leif, I ask that you take some time to think this over. Consider all of your options. It is the most prudent course of action."

He squinted at her in anger. "Bold words, Governor. You don't have the authority or the force to take the militia from my command. I don't have anything to contemplate." Leif stormed out of the office, slamming the door behind him.

Governor Stewart didn't seem at all fazed. If anything, she looked as if he had done exactly what she wanted him to do. Cheryl shifted in her leather seat and watched her superior.

"He is a very hard-nosed man."

" 'Determined' is the word I would use," Cheryl replied. "He makes a strong case. The message we received from the exarch does not provide specific details for sorting out this kind of situation." She understood how the legate felt. She too felt the pain of being cut off from Terra. Cheryl also understood that this meeting had been carefully staged by Governor Stewart. The governor was laying the foundation for what was to come.

"I am considering going on the airwaves again tonight," Stewart said. "I want to thank the people for their support during this time of transition. I think I owe them a statement about the somewhat rebellious activity of our legate as well. I need to reassure them that I am going to do what is necessary to protect them. What do you think?"

Cheryl said nothing for a moment, thinking hard about the implications. Stewart was shrewd and quite cunning. The people were already frustrated by The Republic. She was giving them a focal point on which to vent their frustrations—the legate and the Light Horse. "If you encourage public scrutiny of the legate and the Light Horse, it may become difficult to maintain order. People have been chafing at The Republic for years, ever since the HPG network went down. Unless your words are chosen carefully, Governor, you might be pushing the public to actions we cannot fully control."

Stewart chuckled and her double chins wobbled slightly. "I always choose my words carefully, Cheryl. I believe the people need to know the truth about the legate and his position against Callison."

The truth as you want them to see it. "I understand."

"Do you, Cheryl? You see, I think that if the public does protest the legate's position, we will find it necessary to take some action. As you said, things can get out of hand. And in the end, my dear, something will need to be done about the legate and the Light Horse."

Cheryl had no doubt about what the governor was implying. Mobs were violent, uncontrollable beasts when unleashed. Accidents happened. Violence occurred. In the midst of such fighting, people can be hurt—or worse. What Stewart was asking her to do now crossed a line that she had been able to avoid up until this point. She was capable of doing what the governor was asking, but it was the part of being a ghost knight that she hated. There were times when certain actions had to be taken in the best interests of The Republic. *That doesn't mean I have to like this . . . not at all.*

"Indeed, Governor, something will need to be done."

Price of Service 9

The plain office was furnished with old furniture that had been retrieved from storage. The former military base was in the early phases of being recommissioned. Knights and other personnel worked tirelessly, repairing the buildings, reclaiming the grounds, repairing 'Mechs in the massive bays, training new troops. Some parts of this building were still in ruins, but this office recently had been patched and repainted. The abandoned fort was slowly returning to duty.

Hunter Mannheim and Jeremy Chin had followed a carefully planned, long and circuitous route from the Duchy of Andurien to Callison, one of few refuges available to knights and paladins left outside Fortress Republic.

"Reporting as ordered, sir." Mannheim stood at rigid attention.

"Drop the formality," Damien Redburn said, looking up at the knight from his seat behind the battered metal desk. He tossed the handwritten letter across the desktop, but Mannheim didn't look down. He knew what it was; he had written it. "Your resignation is not accepted, Hunter."

Anger flickered across the knight's face. "You cannot deny me—"

"I can and do," Redburn cut him off. "Right now we need men like you, and I'm not going to accept your resignation because you are feeling guilty for what happened on Kwamashu."

"Sir. With all due respect, it's not guilt. I committed a war crime, an atrocity. You can't allow me to continue to serve as a Knight of the Sphere—my action taints the rest of the order. Tens of thousands, perhaps millions will die because of me."

Redburn tilted his chair back carefully, not sure where the stopping point on the old chair was or if it was working at all. "Sit down, Hunter. I want to tell you some things you don't know." The knight took the guest chair and sat at attention. Redburn tapped his fingers against his chin as he searched for the words to express what he had to say. He knew Hunter was an honorable man, and he knew the pressure honorable men put on themselves. The time had come to take away some of that pressure and bear the burden himself.

Damien Redburn did not find this easy. None of this had been easy.

"Sir Chin never revealed his orders to you?"

Hunter shook his head. "All he told me about was that box and its contents. The boy is not coping with this very well, by the way. He talks to himself—and seems to answer himself, too."

"I know," Redburn replied. He took a deep breath. "Hunter, this isn't easy for me to say. You are not responsible for what happened on Kwamashu. I am."

"You, sir?"

"I am, as is the ghost paladin."

"I don't understand."

"Before we sent you on this mission, we knew we would have to hit Kwamashu in order to get the remains of Thomas Marik. That act alone would spark tensions on the border. At the same time, we developed a list of probable target cities for staging what you were told would be a mock disaster. Breezewood was one of three potential target cities. It made that list because it was a dump for toxic and biological waste. That was why the other cities were on the list as well."

"Sir?"

Redburn sighed. "We knew a mock disaster might not be enough to start a war, and the theft of Marik's remains might also not be enough. So we targeted three cities that would create a real disaster."

Hunter's face reddened with anger. "Why wasn't I told?"

"Because it would have forced you to make a moral decision. The final choice of targets was left to your ghost knight."

"What?"

"Chin selected Breezewood. He made sure that when you detonated your charges, it set off a much broader cataclysm. He was under orders not to share that information with you. While I'm pleased that he adhered to those orders, I'm afraid that's what is making him ill. He has taken on the burden of this, all of the guilt."

Redburn could actually see Hunter processing his words. "My God—sir. Don't you realize what you've done? Not just to me, not just to the Duchy, but to that boy."

"I do," Redburn assured him. He closed his eyes for a moment, wishing he could pray. The former exarch wanted to pray, but was worried that God might answer those prayers. *There are many things in life I will have to atone for. This is only one.* "I need you to maintain your mantle as a knight. I've brought some of the Fidelis with me to help rebuild your force and that of Lady Synd. I know you feel what I did was wrong. I can only say that it was necessary for the long-term survival and welfare of The Republic. But that doesn't make it an easier burden to bear."

Hunter was still angry. "I gave up my wife and my

children so that I could be known as the Despoiler of Kwamashu.''

"No one knows other than the ghost paladin and Sir Chin. None of us will ever speak of this again."

"That will have to be enough," Hunter replied coolly.

Redburn seemed relieved that Mannheim had mentioned his family. Reaching into his uniform shirt pocket, he pulled out a data cube and laid it gently in front of the knight. "I had a feeling you'd take it this way, and you have every right to feel as you do. But the exarch wanted you to know that your guilt is mislaid. He authorized me to speak to your wife and children before Fortress Republic went active. I told them that you would be facing the greatest challenge given to a knight. I told them you would be asked to do things that were against your nature. I explained to them that they would not see you again for several years. I gave them two days. They understood, Sir Mannheim—in ways that will impress you. They recorded these messages for you. Hours' worth. What you think taints you in their eyes only makes you a better man. They would not want you to quit your service to The Republic. But don't take my word for it, listen to them."

Hunter picked up the cube as if it were a delicate flower. He looked at Redburn.

"I know," Redburn said.

Chin prowled about his small quarters like a trapped animal. Like most of Fort Defiance, the room had been reconditioned. The air stank of the chemicals used to purge the last of the must and mold from the old ductwork. Despite its disinfected smell, his room was a mess. His cot was disheveled as badly as his appearance. The furniture was not aligned to the walls but placed almost randomly. Neatly aligned to the foot of his bed, however, was the wooden box he had kept constantly in sight even after his arrival on Callison.

Long months in the DropShip had taken a toll on the

young ghost knight. His hair was short now, but that only highlighted the gray starting to show at his temples. He was surprised every time he saw it in the mirror.

The ghost knight monitored the news of Kwamashu and cringed at how the media had distorted the catastrophe. He had been there. No, more than that, he had caused it. Jeremy knew exactly how big the disaster was. There was just a hint of pride associated with that— pride in a job done right. A pride tainted by the enormity of the crime.

And it was a crime. A war crime made worse by the taunting words of the man who followed him everywhere. Jeremy had tried to silence his voice but couldn't. It was like trying to drive away a shadow.

He saw Redburn and Mannheim enter his room. He ignored them—maybe they would get bored and leave. It hadn't worked with the psychologists who had come to visit him, but he felt it was still worth the effort to try it.

"How are you feeling, Jeremy?"

"Tired," he said, a hint of anger in his voice. "I enjoy my time with Doctor Trever best. Nice lady. Painful needles. She didn't tell me that I'm crazy, but from that look on your faces, I'm sure she told you that I am. What did she say? Psychotic? Schizophrenic? Or am I simply a garden-variety mass murderer?"

Redburn lifted his hand as if to stop the words. Jeremy saw his gaze fall on the small wooden box. It sat silent but ominous. "Jeremy, I have told Hunter everything about your mission. I thought you should know. God knows he had the right to hear it."

Chin looked at Mannheim then back at Redburn. "Great. Thanks a lot. Now he can hate me, too." He stared at his fellow knight. "You have to hate me. I set you up from the start. I didn't just betray you, I turned my back on everything I believe in. I turned my back on being a knight."

"I don't hate you, Jeremy," Mannheim said solemnly.

"You have to. I killed those people. And a lot will die over the next few years because of me. You have to hate me."

"No, Jeremy," Hunter said gently. "I can't hate you any more than I hate myself. I was there, too."

Redburn stepped forward. "Jeremy, Hunter and I have talked. I think the two of you should spend some time together. Maybe you can find ways to cope with all of this."

Chin stood still, then shook his head at something only he heard. He closed his eyes and said nothing.

"Sir Chin?" Redburn prompted.

"They gave me medication. It makes *him* less . . . tempting, quieter. You have to tune him out or he keeps you up all night with his raving. He wants me to kill you. He says you deserve it for what has happened to The Republic. He says that this is all your fault, Paladin Redburn—not mine."

He: *Thomas Marik.*

Hunter stepped forward. "Tell that son of a bitch he has to go through me first," he said confidently.

Chin smiled grimly—the first time in months. "Yes. I think I will."

"We need to get you well again."

Jeremy looked thoughtful. "There's only one place I can hope to find peace." Only one place in the universe. The journey back was going to be longer than the flight away from that world. Much longer.

"Then that is where we will go."

Altar of Freedom 1

Training Facility Lion
Northern Mopelia Island, New Earth
Prefecture X, Republic of the Sphere
Fortress Republic (–45 days)

Lady Crystal Livingston Synd was happy to admit that the Fidelis troops had performed exceptionally well in the training exercises with her troops. Given the recent challenges faced by The Republic, they seemed like a godsend, which automatically made her suspicious of them. False hopes had appeared in the past and quickly faded to bad memories. Adding to her apprehension was their refusal to speak of their origins. She had met with their senior officer, a commander named Boyne, who was quite professional and competent, but he simply ignored any personal questions and any questions about his troops, their past or the Fidelis' goals, no matter how strongly she pressed. Exarch—no—*Paladin* Redburn had warned her that she would have no luck penetrating the veil of Fidelis secrecy. That didn't mean she wouldn't try.

The training facilities on Mopelia had proven to be excellent as well. From her perch on a ledge overlooking the grass-covered valley, she could see the exercises unfolding. Captain James Paulis was leading a mixed combat team attempting to shake out the Fidelis troops from several knolls they had reinforced. Paulis was a Republic soldier to the core. His tactics and approach to battle were right out of the academy curriculum: He sent his forces along the flanks, and once they were in position, he pressed the center.

She stood at the top of the hill in her 85-ton *Templar* and gazed down. She was an observer on this exercise, piloting her *Templar* under the call sign Mongoose only to gain a position from which to view the mock battle.

Incorporating the Fidelis warriors into her unit had proven somewhat stressful, but not exactly in the way she had expected. Her own troops were combat veterans of the Tenth Principes Guards. It had taken some flexibility on her part to merge the units together, though the Fidelis had adopted the Republic rank structure quickly and without complaint, and even more work to integrate their fighting styles and tactics. The truth was that the Fidelis troops had proven themselves superior to standard Republic forces. In an occupation where rivalry and competition were important, this added tension.

This exercise was proof of the disparity in the troops' skills and tactics. The rolling green grass in the valley below her was dotted with the occasional jut of pink granite rock or dark-emerald clump of brush. The Fidelis defense points were on top of the knolls, foxholes and bags of dirt hastily filled in and positioned to resist the assault.

The Republic forces entered the valley from the far side. Fast-moving Rangers and Maxim and Saxon APCs swept along the flanks, while infantry poured down the center. Two BattleMech lances anchored the right and left flanks. Their mission objectives were simple: to take the tops of the three knolls. The Republic troops outnumbered and outgunned the defenders in the exercise.

Lady Synd watched as the attack force reached the valley floor, a long, narrow, flat area interrupted only by the knolls. By adjusting her cockpit sensor feeds, she was able to magnify the image of the battle unfolding below. The defending force opened up first on the troops advancing down the center, aiming for the fast-moving ATV force that led the charge. A squad of hoverbikes and the ATVs caught the initial bursts of small arms and mortar fire. They were using dummy rounds, but even these kicked up enough smoke to mark their kills and create a realistic fog of war. Those two squads ground to a halt, but the rest of the force reached the bottom of the first knoll and began to charge up. On the flanks, the 'Mech forces split up and moved around the first knoll, driving fast for the other two reinforced positions. The 'Mechs unleashed low-power laser bursts up the hillside to little effect: The hilltops represented perfect hull-down positions.

Synd studied the troops under her command. The Republic troops were executing a textbook assault, yet something told her that the Fidelis troops were going to persevere. She could feel it in the pit of her stomach.

The attack force in the center trudged up the hill under sporadic fire. She could see the blanks firing from the hilltop, muzzle flashes, the smoke of battle. Could they hold?

The Republic forces reached the hilltop and suddenly there was a massive white cloud of smoke blasting out from the hilltop in multiple directions. The attack force, five squads, had been plastered white with the mock-damage smoke. A perfect trap. They had been lured in and taken out. The simulation computer recorded the deaths of the assault squads.

Her attack force froze, stunned by the sudden blast and the massive cloud of white smoke that rose from their attack on the center. Working from the vantage point of observation, Lady Synd hadn't been tricked. She knew a trap and a diversion when she saw one. The other two hilltops were not hunkering down. One did nothing. The other had infantry troops running down the hillside closest to her, right on top of a Kinnol tank and a 'Mech there that had twisted around to see the source of the first blast.

The Fidelis troops were like gorillas. The vehicle fired just once before they were on it. They swarmed onto the top of the vehicle and opened the hatch before it could be buttoned down. White puffs of smoke emerged as dummy grenades were tossed in. Three of the troops dropped inside, not waiting for the "dead" crew to be evacuated.

Another two squads hit the *Blade* as it turned to respond. They didn't bother to fire on it, they just climbed up it. Like ants assaulting a milkshake, the power-armored infantry scaled the exterior of the 'Mech before it could bring its guns to bear. They reached the cockpit in three heartbeats. Two more and they registered a kill on the simulation computer, taking out the MechWarrior. Within a few minutes the 'Mech was running again, as was the *Blade*, now under control of the Fidelis. *How had they bypassed the security protocols so quickly?*

The assault on the third hilltop was slow and ponderous. The Republic 'Mech and infantry forces were in no mood to duplicate the events on the first hilltop and had no idea what had occurred on the other side of the battlefield—until the *Blade* and an armless *Targe* fired at the rear of the attacking force, devastating blasts at essentially point-blank range. The simulation computer logged the data and fed the results to the attackers.

At the same moment, the top of the hill erupted. The assault force turned to meet the captured *Blade* and *Targe*, not aware that at this precise moment the Fidelis forces on the hilltop had emerged and charged down. A *Stinger* was caught off guard by the infantry and blown up. A chaotic fight erupted as the forces mixed up in a jumble at the foot of the hill.

She watched and nodded. *They are very good.* But were they going to be good enough? Her mission might require more than what even the Fidelis could muster.

Redburn had been right; they would give her an edge, but nagging doubt still tugged at her thoughts. Skill alone might not tip the scales.

The bunker was part of the training facility used by the Fidelis on New Earth. The decor was one step up from Spartan: simple block construction covered with a dull coat of gray industrial paint, and white fluorescent lighting that only added to the dinginess. The holographic situation table, however, shone like a jewel in its surroundings. It offered resolution that Lady Synd had seen only on models used by the knights and paladins in their exercises.

Captain Paulis stood at the table. The debrief on the exercise had been completed two hours ago, but anger still showed red on his face, highlighting the remaining white dots of damage powder from the simulated battle. His forces had been beaten by the Fidelis' unorthodox tactics, even though both forces had deployed mixed Fidelis and Republic troops. His failure simply pointed out to Paulis that his opponent had executed a superior plan—and that bothered her Republic officer.

Boyne's face offered nothing. His expression showed interest in the briefing, concentration when she spoke, but there was none of the lighthearted gloating she had expected, none of the camaraderie between Boyne and Paulis that was common among military leaders. Also missing was a sense of rivalry: Boyne simply did what he was told to the best of his abilities, period. His ego had been checked at the door.

Also in the room was her ghost knight, Jayson Greene. At least, that was the name she had been given. Ghost knights tended to live in a universe where they changed their names and identities as often as their clothes. Greene was short, and looked older than anyone else in the room due to the gray in his sideburns and his hair. There was no air of mystery about him; he appeared to be a soldier just like any other. Of the three ghost knights that Redburn had brought to their meeting, Lady Synd considered she had drawn the best of the lot.

She punched a control on the table's edge and the system came on, showing a city that filled the three-by-three-meter table. The holographic buildings flickered into existence, the green of the parks came into view. It was a moderate-sized city that could have been anywhere in the Inner Sphere, home to over a hundred thousand souls. This was their target.

Her voice was crisp. "It is time we discussed our objective. So far, all I've told you is that we are going against the Jade Falcons to perform an extraction of friendly personnel. Now it is time for you to hear the details. You've met Major Greene already. I have asked him to provide the operational details. Major Greene?" She turned to him.

He cleared his throat. "Our mission is to go to the world of Ryde, to the city of New Dearborn, and raid a Jade Falcon–held research facility. Our intention is to mislead the Falcons into thinking that we are a Lyran Commonwealth attack force. Our objective is to extract five scientists who work at that facility, and their research data. Our implication of the Lyrans has to be subtle, but sufficiently clear for the Falcon's Watch to piece together. We will then depart the system with the scientists."

Boyne said nothing, but crossed his arms as he thought. Captain Paulis jumped in, speaking directly to Synd. "Sir, are we going to have the forces to pull this off? The Jade Falcons are not going to simply let us land and take what we want without putting up a fight. They're bound to come right at us with whatever they have—and we have the challenge of fighting this battle in an urban combat zone."

She understood his concerns: She had voiced them herself to Paladin Redburn and had gotten nowhere. "The Republic is stretched very thin at the moment. We go in with the resources we have."

"Are we going to attempt a diversion of some sort, something to lure them away from our target?" the captain pressed.

Boyne surprised her by answering that question. "It would not work. The Jade Falcons are not fools. A diversion would have to be significant in size and present a significant risk for them to pay any attention to it. To offer such a risk, we would have to draw too much from our primary force, which would severely diminish our chances of success. I believe a diversion is not the answer." Synd was more surprised by the fact that Boyne was offering an opinion than by his accurate analysis. *Now that we are working on the details, he has something to say.*

"Captain Boyne is correct. I have reviewed this operation many times, and a diversion is simply not going to work given the size of our force. Major Greene, please display possible landing zones, our objective and projected Jade Falcon response."

Greene activated the controls on the table and the lighting changed on the holographic city. The park area and the spaceport at the edge of the city in the far corner of the map pulsed a brighter shade of green. One building turned a dull yellow that made it easy to see in the middle of the city. Synd had the same thought every time she saw the map: There was far too much distance between the LZs and the objective. At the far east and west edges of the map pulsed two red circles of light.

Greene used a laser pointer as he spoke. "The city limits what we can do. The Jade Falcon garrisons are in the suburbs on the far east and west. We could land outside of the city, but as you can see, that would stretch us out like a snake. The Falcons would be able to cut us off from our DropShip once we reached the central city. That leaves us with either the city park, or the spaceport to the south."

"The spaceport is too far away; it creates the same problem as landing in the farmlands in the outskirts of New Dearborn," Captain Paulis noted.

"My thought as well," Greene said. "That means using the city's centrally located park as our LZ." He pointed to it. "It gives us two wide boulevards to work with, and puts us only eight blocks from the target. If we work in two columns, we should be able to reach the facility in just a few minutes.

Boyne added, "Hopefully before the Falcons can respond."

"That would be nice," Paulis said, drawing a grin from everyone but Boyne.

As if on cue, the red dots in the suburb turned into glowing red lines racing into the city on every major highway and road. Like a vice clamping on the park and the research facility, they wound tighter and tighter until the simulation stopped—with the red lines forming two bubbles around the research facility and the park. The simulation underscored the threat Lady Synd had recognized the moment she had looked at the plan.

Greene plowed on with his analysis. "Our current intelligence indicates the Jade Falcons have two Trinaries in their garrison, as well as two companies of local militia and elements of a Provisional Garrison Cluster. The heavy hitters are veterans of Alpha Galaxy rotating to Ryde for rest and refit. Our sources on Ryde say that the local forces are heavy in 'Mechs and vehicles. I would rate these troops as veteran. Their garrisons are placed with easy access to roadways that can get them on us quickly."

There was a pause as they each surveyed the map. Synd watched them staring at it, searching for something that would give them even a momentary advantage. Boyne broke the silence. "That river running north and south just to the west of the park. What can you tell me about it?"

Greene smiled. "The River Rouge. We've been thinking the same thing, Captain. There are a lot of bridges there. The river is plenty deep and the shore is built-up: Hovercraft and 'Mechs can cross, but there's no way for them to climb the other bank. There are a dozen bridges over the river, and it would drain our limited resources too much to blow them all."

Boyne's brow wrinkled in thought for a second or two. "Lady Synd. My people are trained in combat engineering. You have seen that they operate well in small groups. We do not have to take out all of the bridges—only key points that will bottleneck the Falcons and buy us time. I can send out three-man teams using power armor equipped with jump jets during our initial approach. They can take out a bridge or two each. It will not prevent the Falcons from coming, but it will slow them down."

She thought for a moment. It was a good option. "Interesting, Captain Boyne. I think we need to look at the details. A combat jump into a city is tricky, but this just might work."

Captain Paulis pointed to the map. "The garrison force off to the east will have the advantage of this major highway. If we can clog that up, we can force them onto secondary streets. As Captain Boyne pointed out, we just have to slow them down."

"I have considered that avenue as well," Synd said. "But blocking the highway is somewhat trickier. There are no bridges or underpasses. It is a straight pipeline into the heart of New Dearborn. I do not see a way for us to tie up that road enough to make a difference."

Boyne walked around the holographic table to the side where Greene stood. His eyes never left the table. Synd watched him. *He's already fighting the battle in his mind.* There was something about Boyne, about the Fidelis, that made them grittier fighters. They were always mentally in a battle. *Clansmen are quick to the fight. These Fidelis tend to take their time, to think things through.*

Boyne pointed to the map. "Major Greene, tell me about those buildings." His finger loomed into space near the highway. Greene handed him the laser pointer, and Boyne highlighted two tall skyscrapers, one on each side of the main road into the city. Greene picked up his noteputer and stabbed away at it, pausing twice to confirm the coordinate in the city.

"One is the New Dearborn University Hospital. Thirty-two stories tall, it is the main hospital for the city. Over eight hundred beds. The other building is a commercial property. Office building, twenty-eight stories tall, no unique features."

Boyne turned to Synd, and his dark eyes made contact with her own, as if he were staring into her soul. "These two buildings are unremarkable except for where they are positioned. I propose we send two squads to that location, plant shaped charges along the base of those structures and collapse them across the highway. The debris field will be enough to block the road entirely and force the Jade Falcons onto secondary streets. If we time it right, we can even drop the buildings on them as they pass."

"Are you crazy?" cut in Captain Paulis. "Greene just told you, one of those buildings is a hospital. You'll be killing hundreds of innocent people."

Synd jumped in. "Captain, it is Major Greene. Captain Boyne"—she weighed her words carefully—"while your proposal is creative, I hope to find another option."

Boyne did not waver. "I understand your concerns, Lady Synd. The loss of life is not a small matter. However, my suggestion is motivated by the desire and necessity for this mission to succeed. After all, my life is on the line, as are all of yours. We are going to suffer significant losses to the Jade Falcons even if this plan is successful. Unless there is an alternative, I ask that my proposal be considered."

She felt her jaw tighten. *Damn.* She knew that he was right. At the same time, she was sworn to protect the citizens of The Republic. Even though the people of Ryde were under Jade Falcon occupation, they were still her people to protect. As a soldier, she understood that the mission came first . . . but at this cost? The plan he was suggesting repulsed her. It was the kind of thinking that kept her up at night.

"I appreciate your candor," she replied. "Your suggestion will be taken under advisement. In the meantime, I want all of you to come up with alternative plans of attack. We will reconvene here tomorrow at 0800 to review options." The two captains saluted and left the room. Greene lingered behind.

"Sir Greene, what do you make of these Fidelis troops?"

He cocked his eyebrow. "They're the most aggressive— no, most fanatical troops I've seen in awhile. You watched the exercise earlier today. They didn't just dig in, they launched an assault against a superior force and won. They go at fighting like Capellan Death Commandos. Maybe that's where Stone found them—their training is top-notch; to the man they have more expertise than our standard Republic forces. They seem dedicated and highly motivated. They've fully integrated with our regular forces with no issues other than our men running pools as to where they really came from."

The men aren't the only ones curious about their origins. "I agree with your assessment, but I'm also worried. This suggestion that Boyne has made, to take out the buildings—it's as if he has no regard for the casualties."

"I think he is putting the mission first." He paused, opening his mouth as if to continue speaking, then closing his mouth without uttering a sound.

"What aren't you saying, Sir Greene?"

"M'lady, you and I have gone over this data together so many times it hurts my head. While Boyne may come across as a little indifferent, let's face it: His plan might buy us the time we need to bring off this mission."

She frowned. He was right, and that was what hurt the most. "When I became a knight, I thought of myself as more than a soldier. This assignment has reminded me that even a knight must follow orders."

If this is what we have to do to preserve The Republic, is the price too high?

Price of Service 7

Breezewood, Kwamashu
Duchy of Andurien
Fortress Republic (+860 days)

"**P**ickaxe, this is Rook. What is your position?" Sir Mannheim demanded as a Streak missile blast snaked in on his 'Mech's left leg. The armor there was gone long and deadly minutes ago, and he was grateful that the Streaks were only a twin pack. Cumulative damage was making his *Shockwave* sluggish, and it now required every ounce of his skill to balance and pilot.

"We've hit their flank to the north of your precious damn factory, Rook," returned the agitated voice of Colonel Daum. "We've got a full company of them tied down here in the city. I sure as hell hope this is worth it."

Hunter watched Jeremy Chin's Fox hovercraft dash at full speed across his field of vision, turning on the fly and letting go a barrage at a Protectorate squad of Purifier battle armor attempting to reach the perimeter of the plant. The tall antennae of the Fox whipped in the wind. Tied to its tip was a real fox's tail that lashed around as the vehicle roared down the street at full throttle.

Mannheim was distracted enough by the sight to chuckle.

"Roger that, Pickaxe. We have forces knocking on our front door and may have to abandon this facility."

"My people have fought and died to save that place!"

Hunter fired his missile rack again, this time at the Po tank making its third run into the open. The missiles popped across the top and turret of the tank, forcing it once again to seek cover. He noted that he had only two reloads left. After that the missile rack would be dead weight on his BattleMech.

"Stand by, Pickaxe," he replied. Changing the channel, he tied into Chin's Fox, which had gone up two blocks, turned around and was roaring back to take another glancing shot at the Purifier troops. He waited until Jeremy fired, then opened the channel.

"Foil, this is Rook. It is time to cook the chicken," he said as the Purifiers strafed the Fox, giving as good as they got on this pass. Hunter wanted to help, but all he had left was his large laser and he was saving that for the Po when it reemerged.

"Do we have a fix on Colonel Daum?" Chin's voice sounded ragged, rushed, wired on adrenaline.

"He's to the north, bogged down in the city. One of the Protectorate companies has him fully engaged."

"Damn it!" shouted the ghost knight. "You have to tell him to disengage and get out of the city, Hunter."

"I will try, but he's as stubborn as they come." *I wish he were fighting on our side.*

"More blood . . ." Chin's voice sounded lost.

"Say again?"

"Nothing. Damn. We need to go west, head to the DropShips. Before you key the blast, get our people out and signal Daum to evac as well." His words sounded urgent, almost panicked. Mannheim watched as the Fox dove into the complex and ran west, moving as quickly as it could.

Fifteen minutes seemed like an hour as The Republic's mock-Duchy force disengaged from the industrial complex and moved away to the low ridge to the west.

The force was dramatically smaller than the company that had landed on Kwamashu. The vehicles and 'Mechs that had survived were in dire need of repair. Jeremy Chin watched anxiously as the Fidelis squads set the pace. The Fidelis troops had suffered losses but they seemed surprisingly low. His impatient check of the Fox's chronometer made him wonder if it was working.

"Foil to Rook. Are Daum and his people out of there?"

"I got word to him. He should be clear by now."

Jeremy's palms were slick with sweat. "Should be" wasn't the same as "yes, he is." He should take time to check. Each passing moment meant that more of the Oriente Protectorate raiders were pushing into the complex. More blood. He glanced back at the small wooden box he had recovered from the monastery. It had slid around in the back of the Fox's cramped piloting compartment, but was still there, wrapped in the embroidered cloth it had been sitting on. He could feel the contents of the tiny coffin taunting him, as if he had awakened a ghost that still wanted to bring chaos to the universe. *This bastard knew about shedding blood.* Now he was a witness to more carnage—even if it was from inside the box.

"Knowing you, you'd enjoy this," he said to the box as the Fox rose over the ridge.

He wanted to signal Colonel Daum once more, but time was working against him. "Rook, this is Foil. Request your concurrence to detonate."

"Foil, this is Rook. You're green."

Jeremy keyed in the code to detonate the explosives. Not just the ones Sir Mannheim's team had planted, but all of them. He hesitated on the last sequence of the code. Time stretched, then snapped back.

The blast erupted, and Ghost Knight Jeremy Chin bowed his head.

It looked like everything was going as planned. Sir Mannheim watched the string of explosions, orange fireballs that rippled into the sky on massive boiling clouds of black smoke. Then a shock wave rippled out from the plant, a circular blast pattern of incredible proportions. The ground shook. Scrub trees between his force and the plant disintegrated. His 'Mech lost its footing, sagged to one knee, then dropped to the ground, slamming him around the cockpit. He tasted blood from the corner of his mouth; his voice-activated mic stud had cut his cheek. *Salty flavor.* Then—*The blast shouldn't have been that big. . . .*

As he struggled to his feet, he saw the Fidelis troops laying on the ground. *No, he hadn't imagined it.* As his *Shockwave* fought to regain its footing, an image burned itself into his brain.

The entire industrial plant and at least five blocks in every direction was engulfed in a roaring column of fire that soared thousands of meters into the sky and was still rising. The conflagration was yellow, orange and red, mixed with black churning smoke, still racing upward. Suddenly, he felt a wind behind his *Shockwave,* blowing toward the industrial complex. Dust, dirt and the debris from the shantytowns flew through the air as if a tornado had touched down.

He could not comprehend the existence of the inferno. Forced to find a frame of reference for comparison, his mind leaped to holos he had seen of nuclear weapon attacks made during the Jihad. For one wild moment, he wondered if they had somehow made such a horrible mistake. The fire was so intense that it was sucking in the surrounding air for fuel. Another rippling wave shot out from the plant, less intense this time, but still strong enough to knock men down. Of the infantry, only a few of the Fidelis managed to stay on their feet.

The column of fire and smoke seemed to become larger, wider, until the flames filled his vision. The sound was like a roar of summer thunder that never seemed to reach its crescendo but strained to release more and more energy. There was a low rumbling roar like a distant freight train that seemed to compete with the thunder. The entire city of Breezewood was being devoured by the firestorm. Yet another blast rattled his *Shockwave*, a grim reminder that the disaster was not over, that it was growing, not subsiding.

And what about the people? Breezewood was a rundown shadow of a city, but hundreds, perhaps thousands would now die. And—oh, God—Colonel Daum. "Pickaxe, this is Rook. Do you read me?" All he got back was a low hissing and an occasional crackle. *All those men and women . . . we've got to help them.*

The wind that had tried to suck his force into the fire seemed to hold for a moment then rush back out. Now, however, the air was superheated. The infantry hugged the ground, scuttling in retreat until they could stand and fall back in earnest. He didn't have to give the order. Mannheim's force retreated at speed from the ridgeline as debris and a haze of searing smoke poured toward them. The column of flames had stopped its climb and was starting to collapse. Mannheim checked his chronometer and was stunned to realize that ten minutes had passed since the initial blast. In his heart, he had hoped it was mere seconds.

He heard a beep from his 'Mech and recognized it as an environmental warning. He checked the instruments and saw a slight radiation level warning for outside his cockpit. Impossible—unless . . . for a moment he convinced himself that the Oriente Protectorate must have used a tactical nuclear weapon. He found himself balling his fists in anger. *How dare they?*

Then logic took over. There had been no flash. A nuclear blast would have triggered radiation warnings far sooner than this, since they were a mere two kilometers outside the city. No, something had been released into the air by the blast. "Foil, this is Rook. I'm getting a low-level external radiation warning. It could be that my equipment is damaged."

Ghost Knight Chin replied, sounding weary. "No, Rook. I've got the same thing here. We need to fall back immediately."

"I can't figure out what happened."

"*I* happened."

"What the hell does that mean?"

"Nothing—everything. Look, we need to get our troops out of all this. That firestorm is only going to spread."

Chin was right. Mannheim gave the order to retreat to the DropShips.

As he gave the order, Hunter shook his head. All the dead. All the blood. It's all on our hands. For the first time since he became a Knight of the Sphere, he found himself questioning the man who had formed The Republic.

Interpretation of Duty 6

Munich Spaceport
Brandenburg, Callison
Former Prefecture VIII
Fortress Republic (+35 days)

Approaching the DropShip unseen didn't require even a fraction of her skill in nighttime operations. The crowd worried her more than the forces under command of the knight: Military personnel had rules of engagement; they showed some degree of control in their operations. Even with her own operatives planted in the crowd, there was a chance that someone in the mob might see her and shoot, thinking her to be part of The Republic force.

Moving in the black shadows between two of the hangar buildings, she slithered among stacks of old crates and barrels. The *Aurora*-class DropShip sat some eighty meters from the buildings she stood between. The nearby transport was much larger and more imposing, but for her the *Aurora* was the threat. Its bristling turrets represented death. It was a military vessel on a military mission, and she knew that Sir Erbe would be aboard her. The *Aurora* was her objective.

She could hear an occasional shot from the far end of

the tarmac and the ping of the round hitting the ship. She knew the gunfire was a minimal threat, and she was sure Sir Erbe's troops did too. Her agents in the crowd occasionally provoked gunshots to add to the tension and keep the infantry on the ground under cover.

Holding her night-vision binocs to her eyes, she swept the area. She saw glimpses of infantry near the rear landing struts, but that was it. There could be others who were concealed or wearing infrared-suppression clothing or armor, but the ground under the DropShip appeared clear. She switched to motion-sensor mode and held her gaze on the ship; she saw only a few figures moving inside the DropShip's cockpit, right by the armored windows.

Getting aboard the ship was going to be easier than she had thought. Tucking the night-vision gear in her pouch, she moved quietly around the barrel she had been using for cover and crouched low. The reflective lights of the spaceport cast long, pale shadows in the night. Adjusting her thermal-suppression face mask, she moved into the shadow created by a large, rectangular garbage can and used it to get closer to the DropShip. As the shadow stretched, she crouched even lower.

She paused and checked under the DropShip again. Still no sign of activity. Good. She waited for five long seconds, then dashed across the final distance. No sound, no alarms, no activity. Her target was the forward access hatch. From there she could easily get inside the ship. The chin turret mounted under the bridge would be manned but was turned toward the perimeter fence and the protesters. She went right under it, reaching up and touching it as she paused under the belly of the DropShip. The hatch was a mere twenty meters farther. Reaching it would test her dexterity and gymnastic skills, but she knew she was up to the task.

She stepped forward, and suddenly a blanket of force hit her from above. Kicking out, she tried to get free. *Damn it!* The ferrocrete seemed to reach up and slap

her down. She felt weight and knew someone had
dropped on top of her. Someone had been hiding on the
bottom of the DropShip.

Someone was damned good.

She kicked again and heard a grunt. Her opponent
chopped at her leg near the knee, hitting a reflex point
that stung agonizingly. She suppressed her cry of pain
and pushed back to try and get her footing. The leg that
had been hit was numb and hung like a dead weight, as
if it were asleep. She whirled on her good leg and
dropped low, leveling a hard punch.

Her opponent saw it coming before she had thrown it
because he arched his back and the punch went past him.
He brought both hands down on her shoulder, but she
saw that coming and her body dropped, absorbing most
of the impact. She rolled and came to her feet; feeling was
already tingling back into her leg. "You want to dance, big
boy? Let's rock," she said just under her breath.

The figure adopted a low fighting stance. With the
hand on his extended arm, he motioned her to bring the
fight to him.

She knew he was waiting for a charge, mentally preparing his counter. She didn't play to that; instead, she
darted off toward the starboard landing strut. She preferred to make the enemy react to her rather than sacrifice the initiative. The strut would offer cover and give
her something to use against her larger foe. Jumping and
rolling in the air, she went between the pistonlike struts,
rolling to her feet and ready to continue the fight. She
waited, but her opponent wasn't following her move.
Where is he?

There was a flash, brilliant like the sunrise. Flash gre-
nade. Instinctively she shielded her eyes, but it was too
late. She was blinded. She mentally shifted to blind-
fighting mode, but her assailant had regained the initiative. She felt a dull thud on the back of her neck. Her
ears rang as she punched, hitting something covered by
light body armor—a chest? An armored fist hit her jaw,
and as she turned to absorb the impact, she felt a kick

to her side. Her head felt like it was going to explode as she dropped to her knees. The hit to the neck had been harder than she thought. Shaking her head, she held up her right hand as her eyes struggled to adjust.

Many hands grabbed her, and she felt restraint straps dig into her wrists. She smiled thinly. It had taken a lot of them to bring her down.

The shooting was sporadic and annoying—a psychological rather than a physical threat. The bullets from civilian-owned rifles ricocheted off the hull of the *Onondaga*, forcing the infantry patrols to stay close to the ship for cover. The shooters were mixed in with the protestors who had started to camp at the edge of the spaceport. Firing back meant risking hitting innocent protestors, so his orders still stood.

His mission had gone sour before he had landed on Callison; he had come to grips with that. Other knights might have made a stand by now, but Kristoff was determined to control the situation. He had learned long ago that control was important to him. The things in his life he couldn't control, he didn't try to—like his father's actions during the Jihad. The things he could control, he held onto with an iron fist.

He had been called to the tactical operations room; someone had been caught attempting to board the DropShip. He was glad for the interruption to his thoughts. Erbe walked quickly through the ship to the lower deck. When he walked into tac-ops, he immediately noticed two things: The intruder was a woman, and she was wearing a sophisticated infiltration suit, capable of stopping a bullet or a knife. She was wearing a hood and had her hands bound behind her. Apparently Adamans made the capture; he was standing next to her with his hand on her shoulder, and Erbe could see sweat glistening on the parts of his face visible through the night mask. Adamans smiled broadly, proud of his prize.

Erbe didn't wait to hear the report. He pulled off the hood and stared for a moment in silence.

"Sir Erbe, good of you to make it to Callison on schedule," said Ghost Knight Ceresco Hancock.

"Ceresco."

"If you will have this gentleman remove my restraints, we can get down to business," she said. Her lip was swollen, but her voice rang with confidence.

He nodded, and Adamans pulled out a massive knife. With practiced precision he reached behind her and flicked his wrist, cutting the strap. The Fidelis looked to Sir Erbe, who motioned for him to sit, then took a chair across from their visitor. "You could have contacted me through channels. There was no need to sneak up on us."

She shrugged. "I like to keep my skills in practice, and I felt the risk was minimal. Besides, all transmissions are being monitored, and while I have some control over that process, I couldn't risk blowing my cover. I must admit I hadn't planned on someone strapping themselves to the belly of the DropShip behind that turret. My compliments to your troops." She cast a glance at Adamans, who nodded to acknowledge her praise.

"You'll find that the Fidelis are not your run-of-the-mill Republic soldiers. They are as cunning as they are deadly," Erbe replied.

She rubbed her jaw. "I am forced to agree."

Kristoff addressed the Fidelis warrior. "I have some things to discuss with Ms. Hancock. Adamans, will you give us a few minutes alone?"

He rose. "Ceresco Hancock, it was my pleasure to meet you." Kristoff was amused that she was caught off-guard by Adamans' attitude. He left the room before she could respond.

As soon as the door clanged shut, Kristoff launched into a litany of recriminations. "You took off from New Earth without bothering to confirm our plans; we've been on the ground for two days and the only thing I hear from you is an attempt to break into my DropShip; I have landed on a world of The Republic that is apparently on the edge of open rebellion; I have well-organized protestors taking shots at my troops and my ship. I'd appreciate an explanation for any or all of this." He felt he'd managed to keep his anger in check.

Her smile was almost gentle. "Sir Erbe, I had to leave as quickly as possible so that I could begin my mission here. Yes, this world is currently hostile to The Republic— Governor Stewart has seen to that. I have attained the position of head of the Directorate of Internal Affairs, and hopefully have gained her confidence in the process. Outside this ship, my name is Cheryl Gunson. Believe me, things have been challenging for both of us."

"If you tell me what your mission objectives are, we can work together."

She shook her head. "I wish I could, but I can't. You of all people know how important keeping a secret can be."

He flinched. *Was this about his father, about the Jihad? Why would she bring that up?* Kristoff knew that other knights knew about what had happened back on Towne, but that was his father's mistake, not his. His face tightened. "What do you mean by that?"

"You've dealt with ghost knights before. You know that a large part of our success is the secrets we keep."

He took a deep breath and cursed himself for over-reacting. "You're right, of course." He thought for a moment. "My biggest problem seems to be that Stewart has taken control of the militia and whipped up public sentiment against our presence."

"She all but ordered the legate killed," Ceresco said flatly. "Her lust for power is just starting to roll. Left unchecked, she will pose a threat not just to The Republic but to any system within jumping distance."

"My mission doesn't deal with her," he replied. "I have to secure those DropShip engines and the military hardware from the militia. I assume she's your problem."

She nodded once. "The first part of your mission has become trickier. Those engines have been moved from their original warehouses to a position about a kilometer into the city proper, in the old section of town. I will give you the coordinates of the warehouse, but getting to them is not going to be easy."

"Will the governor fight?"

"Count on it. A battle against a Knight of the Sphere, innocent people being killed by aggression on the part of The Republic—it all plays perfectly into her hands. The people could be united against The Republic for years.

"The Light Horse is already on alert. She doesn't know why you are here, but she's actively looking for a way to draw you out. She wants a little war—and she wants it on her terms."

Kristoff relaxed for a moment and smiled. "We have at least two things on our side. I don't have to hunt for those engines, because you can tell me right where they are. And though the militia may outnumber us, I have the Fidelis warriors."

"I'm impressed with them so far," she said, rubbing her jaw as if remembering Adamans' skill.

"You don't know the half of it. The Fidelis are beyond special forces. I trained with them extensively on New Earth, and they put even our elite Republic troops to shame."

"Interesting," she replied. "Why didn't Redburn use them when he was exarch, I wonder?"

"There's not a lot of them, for one. We stripped away half their numbers just for the missions assigned by Sir Redburn. Also, the leading theory among the Republic troops is that they've been held in reserve because they're tainted somehow."

"Tainted?"

"I'm sure you heard the stories told about Stone's actions during the Jihad, how he did whatever it took to achieve victory. Well, the Fidelis are easily the equal of the Word of Blake's elite strike forces. It's possible that Stone struck a deal with some of the Wobbies during the Jihad and got them to turn traitor in return for full pardons. At least that's the idea of the moment."

"This is a new one to me. I've only ever heard the

popular version of Stone's fight—how he was an honorable man and soldier."

"Trust me," Kristoff said sadly. "There was a dark side to him as well. All that mattered was victory."

"Well, if they can help tip the scales in a fight, that's all that matters to me. There are a lot of ways to get to the warehouse where those engines are stored, but only a few roads that you can use to get them back to the DropShip."

"So we run the risk of getting bottled in."

She narrowed her gaze. "I can help you. I have access to full schematics of the city, right down to the sewer pipe diameters if we need them. You'll have to go fast in order to pull this off. Because I head up Internal Affairs, if I know when you plan to move and exactly where you are going to be, I should be able to manipulate things so that the Light Horse is in the wrong place at the wrong time."

"So you'll need to know our plan."

"That's right."

Kristoff rubbed his hands together. "I'll get Colonel Adamans in here to lay out the operation."

She checked her chronometer. "Let's do it. I can't risk being seen here—with the enemy." She grinned, and her swollen lip twisted her smile.

Altar of Freedom 3

New Dearborn, Ryde
Jade Falcon Occupation Zone
Fortress Republic (−18 days)

Ryde was never described by visitors as a beautiful world. Its three continents hung in a shroud of cold, sulfurous atmosphere. The atmosphere was so thin that the crew had been weaned to it by changing the air mix on the DropShips and slowly training their bodies to deal with the difference. All three continents sported agrodomes and were dotted with heavy industry and mining operations. Dull brown mountains jutted into the thin, wispy clouds that swirled in the upper atmosphere. From her perspective on the cramped command deck of the DropShip *Excelsior,* the landing seemed to be going smoothly. With Captain Galloway's permission, Lady Crystal Synd was strapped into an out-of-the-way jump seat, listening to their progress on a headset plugged into the bulkhead.

There had been six hundred and eighty million inhabitants on Ryde before the Jade Falcons landed. Malvina Hazen, the media-proclaimed "Terror of Ryde," had faced only light resistance when her forces had attacked the world. Despite that, the Falcons wanted to make sure that the locals understood the price of resistance. In a sports stadium in the capital city of Heaven's Gate, they had rounded up sixty-eight thousand civilians. One out of every ten of that number was separated from the group and slaughtered. The image was broadcast around the world, and the Falcons allowed holovids of the event to be smuggled off-world. The message was clear—tangle with the Jade Falcons, and you pay a price in blood and carnage. It was a lesson that Lady Synd had no desire to repeat.

The twin DropShip of the *Excelsior*, the *Pontchartrain*, came into view for a second off the starboard bow. The ships were approaching the world in close proximity to each other, as they had traveled on the entire journey in from the nadir jump point. The Falcons would know they were coming, but there was a slight chance that their sensors might tag one of the ships as an echo. It was a narrow hope at best, but at this point Lady Synd was willing to take any edge offered.

Based on the distribution of the Falcons' aerospace assets, they expected any attack force bold enough to come to Ryde to hit Heaven's Gate. If she was making a direct assault to retake the world, that was the place Lady Synd would land. Conversely, the Republic ships pitched out of orbit in unison on a high-speed burn. Their trajectory was just within the safety limits but designed to catch the Falcon aerospace elements hovering over the wrong site.

The city loomed in the distance as the ships dropped low to the ground. They were flying fast and close toward the city over yellow-green grassy plains. Now they would break off, each going after their initial objectives. They would rendezvous at the landing zone in Veterans Park for the deployment of the main attack force. She leaned forward and activated a secure communications subsystem to the other ship.

"Major Greene, the time has come. Good luck to you and Captain Boyne. See you on the LZ," she said.

"We are running our communication program right

now, m'lady. The Jade Falcons will think that we're something other than Republic forces," he replied. "See you on the ground." Suddenly the *Pontchartrain* listed away from the *Excelsior,* off to its objective—the John Cabin Parkway. The *Excelsior* slowed slightly and lurched off on a different vector, this one taking it above the bridges over the River Rouge.

She felt the ship quake slightly and vibrate as the rear starboard pod opened. The ship banked gently and popping static filled her earpiece, followed by the voice of Captain Paulis. "Rat Squad has deployed," he reported.

"Excellent," she said out loud. "Captain Galloway, take us in. I've got to get to my 'Mech."

Captain Boyne charged across Woodward Avenue to the ground floor of the New Dearborn University hospital, his squad only a few meters behind him. The building seemed much larger in real life than it had on the holographic table. John Cabin Parkway, the main artery for half the city to navigate in from the suburbs, sprawled just beyond the building and intersected the avenue on which he and his team had landed. Boyne turned the head of his modified Gnome battle armor and surveyed the area. The drop had gone without a hitch. If anyone noticed his troops on the ground, they had fled for cover . . . just the way he liked it.

"Braddock, double-time your team across the parkway and begin work on Bravo target. I'll handle Alpha. Stick to the operational protocol."

"Fire alarms first, explosions second. Got it, sir," replied Braddock. He was not a Fidelis warrior, but Boyne felt he had proven himself to be competent. Boyne activated the mission timer on his Gnome's right forearm. The running clock was reflected on the armor's faceplate.

"Assume overwatch pattern Epsilon. Begin the evac of that building now," he barked to his own team. Even with the fire alarm giving warning, this was going to cost lives. "Teuber, you are our eyes. Take your position on the roof of the next building and monitor comm traffic. I must know the moment you detect the Falcons."

"Service!" replied Teuber. "My blood will not fail you."

Boyne stared upward at the skyscraper. In a few minutes it would cease to exist. He did not approve of the evacuation orders that Lady Synd had attached to his mission. Better to simply collapse the buildings across the Parkway and not worry about the civilians; she had added a factor that reduced the chance of success for the mission. What he would not admit to his team was that he respected the knight for making that call. It took courage to do what was morally right, and Boyne respected that.

Sir Greene was unaccustomed to operating in the open. He was a ghost knight, an intelligence officer. He was trained for military operations—hell, he had spent years in the military before being recruited for service as a ghost. That had been last decade. Since then, he had lived in the shadows, using dark alleys and smoke-filled bars to protect The Republic. Commanding troops in battle was something he knew, and an area of expertise that he had not tapped in years.

The truth was he missed it.

He angled his Maxim armored personnel carrier forward onto the green grass of Veterans Park. The *Aurora*-class *Pontchartrain* loomed over him as he turned the APC around to get his bearings. He was to lead the drive south into the heart of New Dearborn. Once there, he would locate the scientists and extract them. Damien Redburn had provided him with a secondary objective: to copy, and then corrupt, the records of the research that the scientists were working on. In his written orders this was explicit: "This research material presents a direct threat to the future of The Republic." *No pressure there.* That would also give him the window of opportunity to leave the Falcon after-action investigators a little more evidence that this strike had indeed come from the Lyran Commonwealth.

Greene would have preferred to have been the pilot of a BattleMech in the battle, but he had to agree when Lady Synd pointed out to him that it simply wasn't practical. There was no way to take the 'Mech into the facility once they arrived. He felt far more exposed in the APC than he ever would have in a BattleMech.

He was taking a lance of troops with him while Lady Synd established a defensive perimeter and secured a corridor between his strike team and the DropShips. It would not do any good to secure the researchers, steal their research material and then be trapped by the Falcons. The Fidelis troops in his lance gave him a boost of confidence. Weeks of watching them train made it clear that they were a force to be reckoned with. He wanted to pity the Jade Falcons when they engaged the Fidelis, but then he thought of the massacre of citizens on Ryde and felt that the Clan warriors would be getting just what they deserved.

"Strike Team Dagger form up on me," Greene signaled. Captain Paulis was with him, piloting a *Griffin.* "We do this just like the exercise. Let's put the pedal to the metal." Before any of the Fidelis warriors could ask him what he meant by his last comment (he had come to expect them to question the use of colorful commands), Sir Greene throttled the hovercraft APC on an angle that took him into the center of the city.

Crystal trotted her *Templar* to the south, where the edge of the lush green and yellow grasses of the park reached the city streets. Each step made the ferrocrete roadway grind and groan under the stress. The buildings facing her effectively functioned like a blank wall, the only gaps the streets and dangerously narrow alleys that sliced into them. She saw hotels, stores, other businesses. According to the sensors on her tactical display, she had lost the magnetic anomaly reading on Captain Paulis'

Griffin, but knew that their units were about four blocks apart.

"Deploy the artillery ASAP," she ordered. The Sniper had been designated for a gentle hill in the park. That position would allow it to provide covering fire to the force to the south. The other piece, a smaller Padilla, had been positioned near the DropShips to protect the LZ and hopefully hammer any Jade Falcons that might punch through. Her force was a mobile strike team. They would secure the corridor between the research facility and the LZ and delay any Jade Falcon attempts to get into the heart of the city. On paper it sounded a lot easier than it was in real life.

There was a low rumble, almost like an echo of distant thunder. She instinctively checked her sensors but saw nothing. Twisting the torso of her *Templar*, she saw threads of smoke rising over the rooftops of the nearest buildings. It could just be a fire in the city, but she knew differently. Those fires came from the bridges over the Rouge River.

"Rat Squad, this is Mongoose," she said as her fingers worked the tactical display controls, fine-tuning them for resolution. "Sit rep."

The sound of gunfire blasted into the earpiece of her neurohelmet and she quickly turned down the volume. Rat Squad was nothing more than six troopers equipped as combat engineers. They were half the city away from the LZ, and could not be supported if they needed help. The background noise told her that they were under attack from an autocannon. That meant tanks or 'Mechs. Something was already going wrong.

Damn.

"Rat One achieved the objective and is heading this way," came a voice through the muffled blasts. "Rat Two has taken out one bridge but has encountered opposition on number two target. Falcons are moving forward jump-capable units and have secured a bridgehead on our side of the river."

She paused. There was nothing she could do from

where she was; they both knew it. "I will detach a relief force and send it your way, Rat Two."

There was a swirling hiss of static in response and the muffled, breathy voice of Rat Two coming back online. "Negative, Mongoose. We will complete our objectives. Let Captain Boyne know—" There was a pause. In her mind she could see the battle, see the tiny three-man squad running for cover. "—Let him know that we honored our oath—to the man." The comm channel cut off.

Those men were going to die. She could hear that in Rat Two's voice. It was relaxed, calm, resolved. She didn't know the oath of which the soldier was speaking, but she knew the sound of men preparing to sacrifice themselves. "Alpha Lance," she said smoothly, pulling up the tactical diagram of the bridges and roadways Rat Squad was covering. "Rat Squad reports enemy contact on our side of the river. Fan out to the coordinates I am sending you and prepare to fight a delaying action."

Greene's Maxim rocked from the blast that hit just in front of the APC. The hovercraft swung wildly toward the sidewalk and took out a newsstand, or maybe a phone booth—Greene wasn't sure and didn't care. Their attacker was a Jade Falcon *Loki* that now stood right in front of the three-story research facility.

Captain Paulis moved forward in his *Griffin* and opened fire. The wave of autocannon slugs from the modified *Griffin* hit the right side of the *Loki*, furrowing nasty gashes in the armor-plating on the torso and arm. The *Loki* twisted at the torso as if it had been punched. It lurched from the impact, and a laser barrage from its primary weapon missed Paulis. Instead, the coherent light hit the building just past Paulis, showering the area with a hard rain of jagged glass and chunks of brick.

"Gunner, armor-piercing!" Greene barked. The APC was not designed for close-in fighting, but it still had teeth. A green light flickered on the board—the rounds were loaded and locked. "Target that *Loki* and fire for effect."

The hover APC recoiled as the turret let loose a blast of ammunition. The *Loki*'s right arm took the brunt of the stream of shells. The battered arm suddenly seemed to lose power, dropping down and becoming limp. It swung lifelessly at the side of the 'Mech. The Jade Falcon MechWarrior seemed unfazed by the damage. Instead of moving out of the line of fire, which would have been a sane reaction, he broke into a run and charged forward.

For a fraction of a second, Greene was taken aback by this tactic. Then he reminded himself that these *were*, after all, Clan warriors. *No, strike that. These were Jade Falcons—arguably the toughest of the Clans.* He toyed with deploying the squad in the back of the APC to provide cover, but he knew he would need them when they penetrated the research facility. Instead, he juked hard to the left, turning the APC down a side street to get out of the line of fire. *I'll just swing around and hit its flank as it passes.*

He heard Paulis fire as he banked around. Then the *Loki* lumbered into view, and he was stunned by what he saw. Two squads of Fidelis and Republic troops assigned to his team charged straight at the *Loki*. Some of the men held their positions and fired their assault weapons at the three-story-tall 'Mech. The other power-armored troops fired their jump jets and headed straight into the *Loki*'s path.

The Jade Falcon pilot, confined by the narrow corridor of the streets, slowed to assess his situation. That pause was a mistake. Sir Greene saw sparks of small-arms fire from the ground troops flickering across the *Loki*'s cockpit glass. The Fidelis troops, in their jump-jet-equipped Kage armor, didn't waste time firing, but instead latched onto the Jade Falcon 'Mech with their mechanical claws and swarmed up the battered war machine.

The *Loki* pilot slammed his 'Mech into the side of a building, crushing one of the armored troops. A sickening red smear ran down the side of the 'Mech as he torso-twisted in an attempt to shake the other Fidelis free. They held firm. Greene wanted to fire but couldn't without risking hitting his own troops. The Fidelis troopers scurried up the BattleMech to the head. He saw a flash and knew it was the blast of a satchel charge. The cockpit of the *Loki* seemed to flare orange inside. Black smoke billowed out. The *Loki* suddenly stopped moving.

The troopers jetted away from the 'Mech as it fell forward. It plowed into the ferrocrete roadway, tearing up huge chunks of the road and radiating cracks in every direction. A water main shattered and a hydrant broke off; it was like a rainstorm had settled over the intersection.

Greene's squads landed next to the downed Battle-Mech. One of the Fidelis surveyed the side torso where the bloody smear of a fallen comrade remained, a red-brown blur that had once been a man. He ignited his flamer, hosing down the stained area. The move caught Sir Greene off guard. *What the hell is that all about?*

Even before he had finished his thought, he saw two of the troopers pull out the limp body of the Jade Falcon MechWarrior, who was either dead or so near death that it was a moot point. As he watched, a Fidelis warrior pulled out a huge knife and cut off the head of the MechWarrior. The head, complete with the neurohelmet, rolled a full eight meters before rocking to a slow stop.

"Did you see that, sir?" The voice of Captain Paulis sounded in his headset.

"Yes, I did."

"What are you going to do about it, Major?"

He licked his lips and stared ahead. Switching to a broad channel for all his team to hear, he spoke in his best command voice. "Move out and secure the perimeter of the objective." He toggled to a command frequency. "Mongoose, this is Strike Team Dagger. We ran into some opposition, but are at the objective."

"Roger that, Dagger One," Lady Synd's voice replied. "We are being pressed from the west. No word yet from our friends to the east. Will keep you posted."

No word from Boyne? Greene wasn't concerned. Boyne had proven himself in training to be fully capable of dealing with difficult situations.

Teuber called in from his perch with pure military precision. "Captain Boyne, we have a Jade Falcon attack force moving down the John Cabin toward us. You have three minutes before they are on us. Multiple targets— BattleMechs and support vehicles. I am feeding tactical data to all units." Boyne adjusted his comm unit to clear up the background static from the arm-mounted control unit.

"Affirmative, Teuber. Stay in place until we blow, give us a damage assessment, then link up."

"I will not fail."

Boyne knew he would not. From where he stood in the lobby, Boyne surveyed the chaos roiling around the base of the hospital. Hundreds of people were milling around, looking up for smoke. The fire department and police had arrived, and he had ordered them to evacuate the patients. They were dumbfounded by his request. They were not military . . . not Fidelis; they simply didn't understand the need to follow orders.

A nurse came up to him and patted his shoulder armor. "You're The Republic. Have you come to take out the Falcons?"

"You must leave, now," he answered through the external speakers on his battle armor.

"You *have* come to save us?" the nurse demanded, stunned as he pushed her through the lobby doors to the outside.

"This is just a raid. You are in danger. You must leave," he urged, pushing her hard. A fireman grabbed the nurse and pulled her away as she leaned back toward him, back toward the hospital.

"You can't do this. They'll kill us for this. That's what they do. They'll make *us* pay." He could see the terror in her eyes. He knew she was right, but did not respond. His faceplate hid the expression on his face.

Using a series of eye-blink combinations, he checked his HUD display. His troops were clear of the building. He had a green light from Braddock on the other side of the John Cabin Parkway—the signal that he was ready to go.

Activating his external speakers, he barked out a command. "This building is going to collapse. Run away! Get clear!" He waved his massive arms in the air.

Panic set in.

Good.

He jogged across the street and checked again. His people were clear. Boyne transmitted to his entire team at once. "We are clear. Stand by for blast." *Clear as we can hope to be.*

Teuber called in from his perch. "Sir, Jade Falcons are closing fast. Contact in thirty seconds."

He toggled the detonation code into the comm unit on his arm. There was a rumble, a roar, and a massive blast of concrete dust filled the air.

Price of Service 1

Training Center Opal
Bernardo
Former Prefecture VI
Fortress Republic (+739 days)

Damien Redburn stepped in front of the holotable, deliberately using the backdrop of planets hovering in midair for dramatic effect. "Gentlemen, we are ready."

There was a pause, then Ghost Knight Jeremy Chin spoke up. "About time," he said sarcastically. "Sir." Frustration rang in his voice. Redburn had sent the two knights only a handful of messages over the past two years, and they were always the same: "Stand by for further orders." They knew the basic concept of their mission, but none of the details. Now, two years since their meeting on New Earth, Redburn had shown up at the training facility where they had been isolated with their troops. Chin had seemed on edge since they had received word of the former exarch's arrival in-system.

Hunter "Hunt" Mannheim winced at the younger knight's words. In all his years of service to The Republic, he had never met a peer knight who demonstrated the arrogance and consistently childish behavior of Jeremy Chin. At first, he assumed it was just how the younger man dealt with pressure, a release from the long months of training they had endured. Then the practical jokes had started.

His bed had been short-sheeted, which he found slightly funny the first time. When it began happening once a week, it became annoying. There was no question that Chin was the culprit; the regular Republic troops respected Sir Mannheim too much to consistently prank him, and the Fidelis simply lacked interest in spending their time and energy on such frivolous activities. By far the worst incident had taken place during a training debriefing. Chin had programmed the holotable display to show a fake three-dimensional image of Jessica Marik—naked. It went beyond embarrassing, but even the normally reserved Fidelis officers had laughed.

Hunter jumped in before Paladin Redburn was forced to respond to Chin's rudeness.

"I believe what Sir Chin is trying to say is that we are looking forward to beginning our assignment."

Redburn nodded. "I understand," he said, and gave the ghost knight a faint grin. "We had to wait for the right circumstances to come together. I believe we have arrived at the optimal conditions, and so the time has come for us to strike."

"Sir," Sir Chin pressed. "When we met two years ago I thought it was pretty clear that Devlin Stone had picked our target himself. So why all of this sitting and waiting?"

Redburn sat. "The problem is that a lot of the orders Stone left for us regarding the Fortress plan were pretty cryptic, written to address vague circumstances or conditions that he predicted but we just didn't see coming. There are many precise instructions, but many more passages that Exarch Levin and I had to interpret."

"Ah, a Nostradamus for the modern age."

Hunter glared at the ghost knight. "You should watch what you say about Devlin Stone, Sir Chin," he said, emphasizing the knight's title in a low, dangerous voice. Chin kept his next comment to himself, obviously used to this particular tone in Mannheim's voice and how to respond to it. The tension of the past two years was clear in the relationship of the two knights.

Redburn ignored the exchange and continued. "Recent events have created conditions we consider the right ones to activate your mission. As you know, the Oriente Protectorate has been flexing its muscles throughout the old Free Worlds League. They had hoped to leverage the Capellan Confederation to apply pressure on the Duchy of Andurien. The Capellans apparently had plans of their own. The net effect is that the balance of power along the border of the Confederation and the old Free Worlds League seems to be shifting. Stone's notes on your target indicate that in such circumstances, we would need to destabilize it."

Hunter sat up straight in his chair. "Sir, we have trained for nearly every conceivable mission type while waiting here on Bernardo. We're ready—more than ready."

Redburn nodded once. "I believe you are. I am now able to tell you that your target planet is Kwamashu." He turned to the holographic display and manipulated the controls. The map showed the Duchy of Andurien, a blinking golden dot indicating the world of Kwamashu. The display zoomed in.

Kwamashu was a green and blue world with a few dull tan areas of desert. The planet had three large continents and two smaller ones, one of which was a desert. Most of the cities, only a few of them sizable, clustered on the large continents. Millions of people called Kwamashu home. The Duchy of Andurien considered it a relatively self-sufficient world. Not exactly a gem in the crown, but a world whose vast and varied industry helped keep the Duchy a viable entity. Especially now that much of that industry was converting to the production of military goods.

Hunter wet his lips. *Action at last.*

"Your mission specifics," Redburn continued, "are outlined in this briefing. JumpShips await your departure orders." He handed a datacube to each of the knights. "You both have unique orders associated with this mission. These orders will not be easy to fulfill, but I trust that you won't let down The Republic."

Sir Mannheim said nothing for a moment, focused on the cube in his hands. The Republic. The meaning of those words had changed since he had met with Redburn and the other knights on New Earth. A coordinated effort was unfolding outside of Fortress Republic to ensure the continued existence of The Republic, and it was finally his turn to contribute. He had heard many unsettling rumors of assassinations, coups and even revolutions supposedly perpetrated by Knights of the Sphere. *The definition of being a knight may have changed for some, but not for me.*

"We won't let you down—or The Republic."

"Don't promise so quickly," Redburn warned. "The exarch and I have sorted through the options and are left with no choice but to ask you to start a war.

"Of all the missions we have initiated since Fortress Republic was established, I have been looking forward to this one least of all. Sir Mannheim, Sir Chin will help you analyze the data, choose the appropriate target and devise a plan of action. His training as a ghost knight allows us to trust his discretion in this operation, and you must honor his orders as well as your own."

Hunter glanced over at Chin. His usual cheerful, boyish expression seemed to have faded in the last minute of conversation. He suddenly looked deadly serious and years older.

Mannheim said slowly, "I, too, have been dreading that this would be our mission."

"I know you won't fail me. I trust you to do what is right." With those words, Redburn rose to his feet. "The time has come to put all your training to the test."

Hunter nodded and rose to his feet to salute the paladin. *So this is what The Republic has become.*

"You're the intelligence expert. What do you suggest?" Chin rubbed the datacube he had carried with him since meeting with Damien Redburn two years earlier. Mannheim had noticed in the many months they'd been together that the cube was always in the younger knight's pocket or in his hand. He treated it like a talisman; his regard for it bordered on obsessive. His sudden silence now was uncharacteristic, but Mannheim had long ago chosen not to try to figure him out. The ghost knight touched the holotable controls and a small dot on the west coast of one continent pulsed red. He launched abruptly into his plan. "The best way to start a war is to give one side or another a good reason to fight. The best place to make this happen on Kwamashu is the city of Breezewood." He pointed to the pulsing light. "We'll stage a disaster in an old part of town dominated by an industrial complex abandoned after the Jihad. We will lure in the Oriente Protectorate with false information that the facility is a military threat. When they come, we'll blow up the entire complex. With proper media manipulation, we can convince the citizens of Kwamashu and the government of the Protectorate that the Duchy is arming itself for a military incursion. We'll feed the Duchy false reports of casualties from the Protectorate strike that leveled their complex, and they'll want revenge. Both sides will come at each other never suspecting third-party intervention—us."

Hunter ran his hand over his brush-cut hair. "I assume you've considered that we can't just show up on this world as ourselves."

"Really? You think that's important?" His voice was filled with fake surprise. "Geez, Hunt, this is my line of work. I'll go in early and pose as a Duchy liaison telling them that a secret team is coming in to set up a 'Mech assembly facility in the old complex. Your force will have to disguise itself as a Duchy of Andurien unit being sent in to provide additional security. That will buy us the freedom to wire the entire complex for a spectacular mock disaster once the fighting breaks out."

"How will you lure the Oriente Protectorate to Kwamashu?"

The ghost knight chuckled. "This is the old Free Worlds League, remember? First off, there are SAFE spies everywhere—and because the region is so fractured politically, even if the Protectorate doesn't learn about it from its own agents, someone will sell them the information. There are also potential contacts in Breezewood that I can pass the word to. We're setting up a 'Mech production facility right on their border. This is something they can't afford to ignore. They'll have to send a strike team in to take it out." As usual, Mannheim found Chin to be annoyingly confident in his opinion.

He expressed his biggest concern. "There will be no civilian casualties, right? This is a fake disaster."

The ghost knight paused and rubbed the datacube in his hand. His eyes drifted from Mannheim to the cube. "There shouldn't be," he said quietly. "If we do this right, there will be minimal risk to the people of Breezewood."

Mannheim stared at the image of Kwamashu that hung in the air in front of him. Starting a war was not as simple as staging a fake raid, he knew that much. This plan had a lot of moving parts, any one of which might go wrong. "How can you guarantee the timing of the Protectorate raid?"

"If we leak the date that the assembly plant will be ready for production, chances are pretty good they'll hit on that day or just before. They'll want to take it out when the money has already been spent to rebuild it but before it has a parking lot full of BattleMechs ready for combat."

Hunt paced around the glowing image of Kwamashu, keeping his eyes on the ghost knight at the controls of the holotable. "When we met two years ago, Paladin Redburn indicated that you, as a ghost knight, might receive additional mission objectives that supercede my orders. Do you have any such orders, and if you do, will you share them with me?" There, he'd said it out loud. If Chin was honorable, he would be honest with him.

The question seemed to embarrass the young man.

His face turned red. He seemed to be suddenly aware that he was rubbing the datacube and stuffed it in his pocket as he spoke. "I have several orders that augment this mission. One is a secondary target that I must achieve when the Protectorate makes its move. I can't share that with you right now. The other orders I have are"—he paused, searching for the right word—"inconsequential to the success of this mission."

"I'd like to be the judge of that."

"I understand. But I'm still not telling you my orders."

"Why?"

Chin smiled. "Because they don't impact anything we've just discussed."

Those words did not put Hunter Mannheim's mind at rest. If anything, they made matters worse.

Damien Redburn stood at the window, looking out over the spaceport. *He's aged a lot since he stepped down as exarch,* Mannheim thought to himself. He had requested a meeting with the paladin in hopes of learning about Chin's orders. It might be a wasted effort, but it was worth a try. Redburn was scheduled to depart soon; it was now or never.

"Hunt," Redburn greeted him, reaching out and shaking his hand. "I trust the planning goes well now that you finally know where you are going and why."

He nodded. "It does, sir. It feels good to move forward." He hesitated, then continued with a deliberate understatement. "I have to say, this ghost knight you've teamed me with has proven to be quite different from any other I have met."

Redburn grinned. "Jeremy is a good young man—'young' being the operative word. He's headstrong and self-centered, and though he may seem a little cocksure, I've been assured that he's very capable. His record shows him to be a little hard to control, but highly effective."

"I'm going to cut to the chase, sir," Mannheim replied. "In my experience, you have the best chance for success in an operation of this type when you have all of the data up front. Chin has separate orders from you. I believe I need to know those orders if we are to have the best chance of succeeding."

Redburn's grin faded. "I knew you'd feel that way, Hunt. Hell, if I was in your shoes, I would feel that way too. Unfortunately, it doesn't change anything. Chin's got two sets of orders that he cannot share with you."

"Sir—"

"I wish there was another way. His secondary target is so sensitive in nature that we simply can't risk even your knowing what it is. And I specifically requested that he not reveal his other mission parameters to you."

"May I ask why?"

Redburn looked out the window again. "These Fidelis troopers I assigned to you, Hunt, they're quite remarkable, aren't they?"

"Sir? Uh, yes." The deliberate change of subject caught him off guard.

"Effective and mysterious at the same time. You don't know this, but Devlin Stone himself told me about the Fidelis. It wasn't until just before the Fortress walls went up that I had the opportunity to tell Exarch Levin about this hidden resource. I carried that secret for years—and there are parts of that secret, such as their origins, that I still haven't revealed to a soul. You know why?"

"No," Mannheim said, looking out the window himself as the workers far below unloaded a transport ship.

"Revealing some secrets can do more damage than good. What I've asked Jeremy to do is something I don't want him to share with you right now. What I've asked him to do would only burden you and might place the mission at risk. This burden he alone must bear for now."

Hunter said nothing, but looked his former leader straight in the eyes. *If Redburn says it's risky for me to know what the orders are, I'm going to have to trust that.* "I understand, sir."

The former exarch turned his gaze once again to the dock. "Tricky business . . . starting a war."

Hunter almost laughed at the understatement. "I have had two years to reflect on the possibility of this mission, and it still keeps me up at night." It was as close to a complaint as he allowed himself.

"We are living in strange, stressful times. I've had to ask many knights to shoulder heavy burdens that stretch our code of honor to the breaking point." Redburn put his hand on the window. Hunter did the same and felt the glass leach heat from his skin. "This may be hard for you to accept, but I feel for you. I know I'm asking a lot from you. I have been asking men and women to make heroic sacrifices for two years now, and it never gets any easier. But the need for such efforts doesn't seem to diminish."

Hunter bowed his head. Putting the Oriente Protectorate and the Duchy of Andurien at each other's throats was good for The Republic: If they focused on each other, they would not spend their resources attempting to carve up those worlds outside the Fortress' protection. At the same time, there was a weight associated with these orders. Because of his actions, thousands, hundreds of thousands, would suffer and die. This knowledge woke him several times each night.

"I find myself thinking of my family, the kids—my wife. I'm not sure what they'd think of me given what I have to do in this operation."

"It would change nothing," Redburn assured him. "You're still the man they love. You're simply being asked to do something that is extremely difficult, and extremely worthwhile." He reached into his pocket as if to reassure himself that something precious was still there.

Hunter shook his head. "There's a price for this service, sir, and that price is a piece of my soul."

Redburn rested his hands on Mannheim's shoulders. "Rest assured that your soul is not the only one being paid as part of the cost." His meaning was clear: Redburn himself was putting his life and soul on the line as well.

Mannheim wanted to plead with him to reconsider the mission. Redburn understood how difficult this was—he had just said so. With that thought, however, came a sudden understanding that the mission *couldn't* be changed. The realization left him stunned for a moment: If Redburn accepted that the sacrifice was truly necessary, then it must be so. He straightened his spine. "Thank you for your time, sir."

"Thank you for your service," Redburn replied, firmly squeezing his shoulders. The gesture triggered a memory of Lady Crystal Synd, who had parted from him the same way two years ago. He wondered if his fellow knights were dealing any better with their orders than he was.

Interpretation of Duty 8

Brandenburg, Callison
Former Prefecture VIII
Fortress Republic (+36 days)

"**H**arbinger, this is Squirrel." Sir Erbe was speaking from the cockpit of his *Hellstar* as he angled slowly and carefully along the edge of the intersection. The area of Brandenburg in which the target warehouse was located was run-down. Older buildings lined the streets, most no more than four stories tall, many abandoned years ago. Kristoff was not concerned about the buildings. What bothered him was the lack of people. Since they had pushed off at 0430 hours he hadn't expected a lot of people on the streets, but there should have been someone. So far, not a hovercar and not a soul.

This mission should be quick and simple. But nothing on Callison yet had demonstrated either of those attributes. Someone, probably some low-level clerk, had moved the DropShip engines his unit had come to recover. They had been moved before he had even landed on Callison (otherwise he would have suspected the governor's hand in the situation), relocated nearly a kilometer away from their original warehouse near the spaceport. Facing an angry mob at the spaceport perimeter fence, a governor who was leveraging events to increase her own power, and partnered with a ghost knight with her own agenda, Sir Erbe felt that he had been dealt a bad hand. But he was determined to play the game with the cards he had been dealt. That translated into a stealthy raid into the city to recover the engines.

"Squirrel, this is Harbinger. I read you five by five," Adamans replied from his *Goshawk* two blocks away. At least, the warbook on Erbe's battlecomputer said it was a *Goshawk*. The Fidelis had a habit of modifying hardware to fit the skills of the MechWarrior piloting or driving the tank or 'Mech. In this case, the result was that Adamans' *Goshawk* lacked the shoulder armor plates common to the design, and instead carried antipersonnel pods near the knee actuators and some additional armor plating on its torso.

The Fidelis had modified his *Hellstar*, removing the four Ripper Series A1 particle projection cannons and replacing them with two extended-range large lasers and a pair of large pulse lasers, along with an improved targeting and tracking system. He'd liked the new configuration when he had trained in it on New Earth.

"Any word from Infiltrator One?" Infiltrator One was the designation of a special squad of troops that Adamans had created. Equipped with Oni battle armor, these troops were scouting for the advance force.

"Stand by," he replied, pausing to change channels. "Infiltrator One reports no sign of any hostiles between us and the objective. Target is clear: no civilians, no militia."

Damn strange. He was moving through the streets with a reinforced company of infantry, BattleMechs, tanks and other gear. They had moved out several blocks from the spaceport, and so far no one had even bothered to call the police. It didn't make sense. "Hold up, all units hold position." Sir Erbe looked at his tactical display. The grid of streets and buildings didn't offer him a clue. Infiltrator One was eight blocks to the north and two to the east. The original plan had called for a direct penetration to avoid attracting attention. His mind shied away from the thought that kept coming at him. *This smelled like a trap.* But how was that possible?

"We should be running into something, local law enforcement at the least."

"Affirmative, sir," replied Adamans. "I suggest we shift to our right flank, deploy three blocks to the east. If someone is moving to cut us off, we can find them by changing our plan."

"I concur. All units, redeploy due east onto Woodward Avenue. From there we will proceed north."

The comm channel came to life a moment later as he angled his 'Mech to the east. "This is Grinder Two. I have a roadblock at the Woodward intersection." Erbe checked his tactical display. Three blocks north.

"Wiper Three on discreet. I have obstructions here as well as some protestors stepping out onto the street. Wait—small arms fire. Taking evasive." Wiper Three was a Shamash recon vehicle, a lightly armed hovercraft built for speed. Others began to call in. The shift to the east was not going to work except for the 'Mechs. He saw a roadblock of hovercars, four deep, blocking the street ahead of him. Rock-throwing protestors emerged from around the corners, and he heard the pinging of small-arms fire. Kristoff could punch through easily; stepping on a hovercar with his 'Mech would leave a small fire behind but cause him no damage. But if they busted through, people—citizens of The Republic— would die. That was not why he came to Callison. In fact, killing civilians would play right into Governor Stewart's hands. Time to turn that knowledge to his advantage. *Alright, Chubby. Do you expect me to retreat? Sorry, this boy doesn't do what his father did. I don't give up so easily.*

Time to change plans. He had no doubt that they would encounter the same situation to the west. He could move forward to the warehouse, or back to the spaceport. A typical commander who recognized that his plan had been compromised would fall back. They would count on his making that decision, which was a darned good reason to not do it. "All units, fall back to the original plan. Move north and secure the warehouse." *I refuse to cut and run.*

He turned his *Hellstar* and heard the *thunk* of a bullet hitting his cockpit windshield. The impact didn't even mar the ferroglass, but it did remind him that the dangers outside were real.

"Flash, flash, flash," called a new voice over the comm channel. "This is Angelfire One. I have multiple contacts closing the rear door. Repeat, rear door is being engaged. Relaying sensor data now." This trooper was part of a unit assigned to keeping the route to the spaceport open. This contact was not protestors. Angelfire One was painting vehicles and a *Mangonel* BattleMech closing in. The Light Horse was on the field.

Their plan had been compromised. He would be willing to lay even money that it wasn't any of the troops aboard the *Onondaga*; betraying their operation would have put their own lives at risk. But there was someone else who could have done it: Ceresco Hancock. He discarded that thought almost immediately. She might be a ghost knight, but she still was a Knight of the Sphere. She wouldn't deliberately send Republic forces to their deaths. *It couldn't be possible.*

The instinct of any military commander would be to fall back to the spaceport. Erbe knew that's what the Light Horse would expect. *But I'm not playing their game.* "All units form up on my position. We will take the warehouse and set up a defensive perimeter. All units, double time!" Kristoff Erbe barely resisted the urge to break out his 'Mech into a full run, knowing it was too dangerous on the city streets.

Cheryl angled her *Hellion* around the block as if she piloted a BattleMech every day. In reality, it'd been a long time since she'd been in a cockpit. When Governor Stewart announced that Cheryl would lead the operation to ensnare The Republic forces, everyone assumed she would pilot Legate Leif's assault 'Mech. She chose to assign that 'Mech to Captain Natel and take over his much smaller *Hellion*. She joked that it was so small it might not attract attention—not that any three-story humanoid war machine bristling with weapons wouldn't draw a stare or two as it charged down the street. . . .

Her line hit the flank of the Republic forces. She'd laid a good trap. She made sure the roads to the warehouse were open. She'd even managed to relocate the civilian population away from the battlefield without protest the previous day by faking a natural-gas leak. She intended to pinch Sir Erbe's forces on the main road. Using protestors as one arm of the trap played to his sense of honor as a knight—a cheap shot on her part, but she didn't care. With even a minor threat of his rear route being cut off, he'd be forced to withdraw to the spaceport. A Republic retreat away from the local militia would open the door to negotiating a settlement and would give Governor Stewart her much-desired moral victory. She could force Erbe to the bargaining table and complete her mission.

Her *Hellion* turned the corner into the battle zone. In the darkness of the early morning hours, smoke curled up and obscured the white shimmer of the streetlights. She saw a couple of fires, buildings set ablaze by missile or autocannon rounds that had gone astray. She saw the mangled remains of the Light Horse's lone Saxon APC falling back toward her. Its armor was crumbled, buckled and burned. It looked like an aluminum can that had been played with by angry children; she was shocked that it was still moving.

The *Hellion* reeled from a hit. Gauss round. She could tell by the kinetic force; it was like a punch. She staggered back a step or two to maintain balance and felt the *Hellion* struggle. Her damage display showed that the round was stuck in her right torso, immediately under the missile rack. She scanned the area, locating the towed artillery piece that had done the damage half-hidden around a corner three blocks away. The Fidelis had taken the shot at maximum range and hit; a testament to their skill.

She locked her long-range missiles onto the towed gauss rifle and listened as the Holly system churned a salvo into place and primed the warheads. The moment she heard the audible click, she fired. The ten missiles whirled around one another mid-flight then slammed into the target area. The building erupted in flames, smoke and debris, momentarily obscured. Now she could see that her Po tank also had suffered a few hits from the gauss. She concentrated her scans forward on the rifle, but could not find it. It had either been buried in the attack or moved at the last moment.

Her tactical display told her that Sir Erbe was redeploying—but not where she had expected. His rear guard, where she had applied only light pressure, seemed to be collapsing. She hadn't sent much against them, wanting to allow the knight a graceful exit back to the spaceport. But he seemed to be pulling back those forces, intent on moving forward to the north.

A rumble erupted to her right, in the vicinity of the Saxon. A barrage rained down on what was left of the armored personnel carrier and finished the job that had been started moments earlier. The vehicle stopped moving and the hatches flew open. The crew didn't make it out before the APC became an inferno as secondary explosions lit off. She lost sight of it in the black smoke.

Movement caught her eye and she saw a Centaur battle armor crew, armored infantry with light artillery mounted on their backs, scramble across the rooftop a block away then drop out of sight. They had fired their portable artillery onto the street from the rooftop—a three-dimensional calculation ordinary troops would not risk. She had underestimated the Fidelis.

It wouldn't happen again.

If Sir Erbe wanted to cut off his line of retreat, then so be it. "This is Midnight Angel to Sweep Lance. New orders. Advance to the main road and shift north. Street-by-street sweeps. All units, vector north by northeast and turn their flanks." *If he wants to reach the warehouse and dig in there, I'll let him.*

A Light Horse VTOL, a batlike Yasha roaring on stubby turbo jets, swung to the north of the warehouse. The Fidelis troops on the roof—a squad of Kage battle-armored infantry—rose on their jump jets and traded a few rounds with the circling VTOL. The exchange was inconclusive. In the dim morning twilight, Erbe could only see the plumes of the jets and the sparks off the armor of the Yasha as it took hits.

The decision to pull away from the spaceport was risky, but it gave his troops the advantage of initiative. He knew that the militia's battle plan would be to push them around and force them back to the spaceport. His choice to forge ahead ruined that plan. Besides, he had come for the DropShip engines, and he planned to get them. Fidelis scouts had reported that the warehouse holding the engines was large and reinforced, big enough to hold BattleMechs and support vehicles. The buildings around it were shorter, giving an entrenched force an advantage in the field. It would have to do as a refuge.

A wave of long-range missiles dropped on his *Hellstar*. Half of them hit, ripping into his metallic hide. The box-like assemblies on the 'Mech's shoulders held his extended-range large lasers and the one on the left bore the brunt of the assault. The damage display showed that the cooling coil on that unit had taken a hit. The laser would fire, but he would have trouble using it in a prolonged fight.

He turned and saw the militia squad, a hoverbike unit, turning on a dime now that they had his attention. *Time to test out that laser.* He pivoted the box down and twisted the torso of the *Hellstar* so that the small cluster of hovercraft were lined up. He fired. The weapon made an unexpected crackling sound, but discharged. A beam of emerald light lanced out just in front of the fleeing infantry squad. He angled it back, burning a trench in the ferrocrete and dragging the beam into the lead pair of hoverbikes. The first one dipped down hard and exploded in a ball of bright orange light that lit up the entire block. The other one caught a glancing blow and crashed into the nearby building. The driver bailed out and limped off, backlit by the burning wreck of his vehicle. The other hoverbikes split up and broke away to regroup elsewhere.

Kristoff hated this. Even though he had turned the tide of battle so that he was calling the shots, he was fighting a defensive operation. He preferred fighting out in the open, not in urban environments. He excelled at mobile battles; siege combat was costly for everyone involved. He couldn't afford costly.

Fires several blocks away were casting weird lights and shadows against the sides of nearby buildings. The damage proved that his troops were putting up a good fight for a withdrawal. Past where he had fired at the hoverbikes, the hulking *Mangonel* finally lumbered into view. Its presence here meant one thing: The path to the spaceport was closed.

The *Mangonel*'s girth filled the entire street. Locking his quad pack of pulse lasers onto the behemoth, he waited for the tone. Erbe heard it as the militia pilot twisted his 'Mech's torso to align his massive autocannon.

Erbe fired first: It was no contest. The pulse lasers sprayed a burst of crimson light onto the Light Horse 'Mech. The bulk of the assault 'Mech made it an easy target. The closely grouped shots burrowed deep, churning into the thick armored hide of his foe. The *Mangonel* rattled under the laser barrage as Kristoff felt his cockpit temperature surge. His lasers whined loudly as the capacitors started their recharge cycle, and he felt the fusion reactor under his feet step up output. The *Mangonel* was a dangerous foe, so he immediately juked to the left, shifting so that the warehouse was to his rear and a two-story office building gave him some cover from the counterassault.

The Light Horse 'Mech had taken the damage near its autocannon, and the holes glowed red from the heat. The assault 'Mech fired. A stream of shells arced out. Two found their mark, hitting his left arm below the elbow actuator and pushing the limb away from the torso. The rest of the shells hit the building he was using for shelter, digging into the roof and walls. The entire building seemed to crumble as flames burst out with a roar.

On the rooftop of another building he saw a squad move in the shadows. They emerged for a moment from behind a group of chimneys and took cover behind a decorative row of bricks. He knew them. Infiltrator Two. They were the elite of the Fidelis infantry and they had the *Mangonel* in their sights—at cockpit level. From their perch in the shadows they leveled their rifles and fired. Their modified shells peppered the cockpit ferroglass. Kristoff used his viewscreen controls to zoom in. Unlike standard small arms, the modified weapons and rounds used by the Fidelis were damaging the ferroglass. Circular pockmarks formed where the rounds hit. An inferno round hit as well, lighting up like a Molotov cocktail but burning much hotter. Half of the cockpit windshield was on the verge of being penetrated and was burning brilliant yellow.

The Light Horse MechWarrior knew he was pushing his luck. Walking backward nearly half a block, he retreated behind a building.

"Good work, Infiltrator Two," Erbe signaled. He could swear that he saw one of the men give him a thumbs-up. "All units, shepherd those prime haulers into the warehouse. We need to get those DropShip engines loaded and ready to roll. Colonel Adamans, form a defensive perimeter around this structure and the surrounding buildings. Send out a squad to secure water and food in case we're here awhile. Deploy our mobile artillery infantry and come up with a plan for dealing with that Yasha when it comes back."

"Affirmative, sir." His tactical display showed Ada-mans' *Goshawk* already on the far side of the ware-house, covering the north.

The sun was just beginning to come up over the hori-zon. A bloodred streak filled the sky horizontally as the rising sun lit up the purplish clouds. It looked like it was going to be a beautiful day on Callison. *I only wish I could say the same about my corner of the world.* Sir Kristoff Erbe took a moment to admire the sunrise.

He watched as the early morning light illuminated the smoke from the battle all the way back to the spaceport, and finally examined the question he had deliberately ignored in order to concentrate on reaching the ware-house. *How did the militia know where we were going to be and when?* He knew the answer; had known it from the moment the militia showed up. Ceresco had set him up. *What would cause a fellow Knight of the Sphere to turn against her own people?* He couldn't make her actions make sense.

Now it was also his mission to make sure that she was apprehended and brought to justice. The Republic may have retreated into its Fortress, but that didn't mean the law had retreated with it.

Overture 2

New Earth
Prefecture X, Republic of the Sphere
Fortress Republic (–92 days)

The operations meeting room was secured in so many ways that the occupants assumed it was overkill for a reason. Not only was there physical security in the form of armored troops in the hallway guarding the door, there were also obvious jamming devices in the corners of the room. Patrol dogs sniffed the corridors and perimeter of the complex where the meeting was held.

Eight chairs were arranged in a single horseshoe-shaped row around the central podium, which stood vacant. The video workboards that lined the walls were shut down and locked out. There were multiple data-analysis terminals in the room; they all had the same screen saver that announced they were secured. Security for this meeting far surpassed the normally tight security of ordinary military operations.

The people in the room milled about in essentially three groups. The first was obviously the Knights and Knights Errant of the Sphere. Their uniforms announced their status. The second group was dressed in discreet gray uniforms bearing no rank insignia or other identification, and their hairstyles were far too casual for standard military personnel. One of them desperately needed a shave. The last group consisted of two officers wearing the uniforms of the Republic of the Sphere. Both wore the insignia of the Principes Guards on their arms; both wore an expression that betrayed their combat experience.

There was no mingling between the groups.

Redburn entered the room and in unison, the armored guards on the hallway side closed the doors. When he reached the podium, he stopped for a moment to survey the assembled soldiers. All conversation ended in the time it takes a heart to beat twice. Most of the people in the room looked genuinely surprised to see him, which he understood—Damien Redburn was old news.

"Please be seated," he said, by way of checking the sound levels. His voice sounded loud for the size of the room.

He launched immediately into his message. "I am here under the direct orders and auspices of the exarch," he stated, making eye contact with each person in the room. "What I'm about to tell you is important enough for the exarch to allow me to handle it personally. Obviously, this is highly classified, and nothing conveyed here can leave this room. Understood?"

A low "yes sir" rumbled back to him. Redburn noticed that he was warm and adjusted the temperature in the room down a few degrees from the controls in the podium.

"In a short time, the exarch will be executing a plan called Fortress Republic. This plan was devised by Devlin Stone himself and left to the exarchs who followed him. The scope of this plan can be compared to Kerensky's exodus from the Inner Sphere. Quite literally, The Republic will collapse in on itself, executing a strategic withdrawal inside the borders of an area roughly mapped by Prefecture X. An iron curtain will be put in place that will prohibit ·entry into Fortress Republic space. Anyone attempting to enter the Fortress will have little chance of surviving, let alone succeeding in penetrating these defenses." He paused for a moment. Stunned looks swept the faces of those gathered before him.

"Sir, how can you possibly secure an entire region of space?" asked one of the knights. "It would seem there are too many ways in and out, not to mention HPG traffic."

Redburn allowed his voice to become deeper. "You will have to trust me on this, Sir Mannheim: There are ways to enforce such a barrier. It is best that no one in this room know the details of that enforcement."

Damien took a sip of the water that had been provided for him and continued. "For an undetermined period of time, The Republic will remain in the Fortress preparing for the appropriate moment to return and reestablish itself within the Inner Sphere. In the meantime, the knights will protect the long-term strategic interests of The Republic by executing operations outside the Fortress.

"These missions are atypical for knights and those they command, but these missions are necessary for the survival of The Republic. We—*I* will be asking a great deal from each of you. Exarch Levin recognizes the utmost importance of these missions, which is why he has sent a paladin to lead you.

"While Fortress Republic is being implemented, there is a risk that outside interests could cripple our plans. The missions that you will undertake are aimed at preventing the Houses and other factions from seizing the initiative during the existence of the Fortress. Many different operations will unfold over the next few years— many of your brothers and sisters who are not here today are also undertaking missions. The scope of these operations is massive; some will take years to fulfill." He paused, letting his words sink in. Jaws hung open; faces were drained of color. *They're soldiers first and foremost. They'll do what's right.*

"Each knight here will be paired with a ghost knight."

He gestured to the three men whose uniforms lacked insignia. "You also will have some unique military assets at your disposal: I am tapping a secret resource that Devlin Stone set up for just such an eventuality. They call themselves the Fidelis, but chances are you will know them by the name used in the history books: Stone's Shadows. They are highly trained and well-equipped commandos. Their numbers are limited, but their contributions will be invaluable, given the nature of the missions." He reached under the podium, pulled out a small file box and walked to one end of the row of chairs.

To each of the people in the room, save the two military officers, he handed a set of orders in a sealed envelope marked MOST SECRET, and a black datacube. Each envelope was torn open, the orders reviewed. He watched the faces of the noble men and women pledged to serve The Republic. More than one face regained its color. Some tightened. Some turned red. He saw anger and frustration. No one spoke.

Redburn returned to the podium. "Some of you will deploy immediately. The rest of you are on standby until your missions are given the green light. Please note that it may be months or even years before you are asked to execute your orders." Again there was silence.

"Ghost knights, your paladins have provided you with orders that supplement the support you are giving the more public efforts of the knights. These orders are "eyes only," though you may share that data with your coordinating knight at your own discretion. The orders of the ghost knights in these missions supercede those of the knights in all cases." He saw two of the knights look at each other, understandably puzzled by his statement. The time he had spent with the ghost paladin planning these missions had convinced him that this dual structure was necessary for the success of the operations. The ghosts normally didn't coordinate efforts directly with other knights, and forcing them to work under the knights errant would hinder the full use of their skills and abilities.

"You were all chosen specifically for your talents,

your psychological profile and your skills. I worked with the ghost paladin and, in at least one case, the exarch himself to match you to the mission you've been handed. I suggest that you access the secured terminals here, review the data on the cubes I've handed you and pair up with your opposite assets in the room. I am going now to a secured room just down the hall. I'm sure some of you will have a question or two, and I want to make sure you have a chance to ask them." He managed to get one step from the podium before the knight who had spoken up earlier, a tall, lanky warrior named Hunter "Hunt" Mannheim, raised his hand to get Redburn's attention.

"Sir Mannheim?"

"Sir . . ." Mannheim paused, not sure what title to associate with Redburn, but then pressed on. "It's the Fortress Republic plans and timing. Will we have a chance to see our loved ones before we depart?"

Damien Redburn looked down for a moment. He had been dreading this question because of the answer he would have to give. "For security reasons, we cannot allow that. You will all be departing from New Earth before the Fortress walls go up. All of us, including me, will be separated from our families for the duration of this crisis. I'm sorry." He paused for a moment to make eye contact with the knight. "This impacts me as well. There is a price for the freedoms we defend. Until now, only a few understood the full measure of our commitment to preserve The Republic. You, all of you"—he waved his hand to encompass the entire room—"are going to show the Inner Sphere the extent to which The Republic will go to preserve itself." With those words, Redburn left the room.

"They're not what I expected," Knight Kristoff Erbe said in a low tone to the older knight standing next to him. They had spent several minutes reviewing their mission orders, and then the knights clustered quickly to compare notes and opinions.

"Who, the ghosts?" Hunter Mannheim replied. "You've never worked with them before, I take it?"

"No," Erbe said, giving the group of them reviewing their datacubes another glance.

"I have once before," Sir Mannheim replied. "They're—well . . . different."

"I have never worked with a ghost, but I've heard stories," a tall female knight added. "A good friend of mine has spent months working with one. They are on an undercover mission together right now."

"Anyone I would know, Crystal?" Hunter asked.

"Alexi Holt," she replied with a confident grin.

"Oh, I've heard of her," Erbe replied. "If she's on a mission that means that we . . ."

"Yes," Lady Synd interrupted. "She and Jones have finally found a way to penetrate ComStar security. Both are deep undercover."

"Too bad," Mannheim commented.

"What do you mean?" she asked.

"If they had gotten into ComStar sooner, they might have made none of this necessary." He waved his hand at the room, but the other two knights knew that he was speaking about their missions.

"I don't think so," Erbe replied. "Even if the network was back up, the enemies of The Republic would keep coming. The blackout was simply an excuse. I think that this plan, as crazy and difficult as it is, is probably the best strategy the exarch could think of."

Mannheim frowned. "Not the exarch. Not even the former exarch. No, this came from Stone himself. That is our best hope."

Sir Erbe paused for a moment. "I wonder just how many meetings like this are taking place."

"I know some knights are being recalled to Terra. Others are being transferred to worlds in other Prefectures. I assumed it was simple reassignments. Now . . ."

". . . now it seems that there is more going on than meets the eye," finished Mannheim. "Much more."

*   *   *

"Which one of you is Erbe?" the ghost knight asked the tight cluster of knights. She was short, almost tiny in stature, with stunning blue eyes and high cheekbones that made her seem stern. Her tone and the conviction in her voice made her seem much taller, more imposing. Kristoff Erbe, former knight of Towne, studied her for a moment before reaching out to shake her hand. "I'm Kristoff Erbe." Her grip was as firm as his own, almost but not quite a challenge. *So, this is a ghost knight . . . not at all what I expected.*

"We'll be working together. I'm Ceresco Hancock—at least that's what you can call me until I go undercover."

He forced a smile. "I'm looking forward to working with you."

She shook her head. "That's doubtful . . . but I appreciate the sentiment. I assume you've reviewed your orders?"

He glanced down at the paper in his hand. "Yes, I have. It seems straightforward enough. My orders didn't mention your role, however."

"I know," she said, declaiming the words for best dramatic effect. "There's a reason for that. From what my orders state, the primary thing we need to coordinate is the timing for your end of the operation." She said much without saying anything at all.

"My operation seems pretty straightforward," he repeated. "I assumed you'd be there to gather intel for me."

She smiled, and he did not find it reassuring. It was the sinister grin of someone who knows something you don't. "That's part of my role. I have to go in well in advance of your mission. Knowing when you're going to show up is critical to my part of the operation."

"Any chance of your sharing with me what your end of this mission is?" Sir Erbe pressed.

"None," she replied. "Suffice it to say, we have different objectives." With those words she waved her hand to the terminal where she had been working . . . an invitation for him to sit with her.

* * *

Damien Redburn watched Lady Crystal Synd step into the room. She was tall and had a narrow frame. She was not a poster child for the knights errant: Her face was drawn and sallow and her nose was, well, big—Roman and sloping. She moved like a specter, as if she floated. That was deceptive; he had read her battle record. She was a master tactician and a deadly fighter. That record was one of the reasons he'd chosen her.

"Lady Synd." He gestured to the chair opposite the ordinary desk in his makeshift office. She slid into the seat without a word. "I take it you want to discuss your mission."

"That is an understatement, sir," she replied. "I have looked over the mission and the resources you plan to assign me. They are insufficient for a mission of this scope."

Redburn had expected this reaction, and it had nothing to do with Crystal Synd herself. Any knight would have questioned her assignment, given what he was sending her in with. "I understand your concerns, but you must accept that there are no other resources I can assign you. You hit Ryde with the forces I'm giving you. You extract the scientists as required. Hopefully you can get them inside The Republic before the wall goes up. If not, the key is that they are out of the hands of the Jade Falcons."

"Sir." Her voice sounded strained. *Probably not sure just what to call me or how far she can push it.* "You have me dropping on Ryde with a reinforced company. There are not enough forces for a diversion. We have to hit this research facility with everything if we hope to pull this off. The Jade Falcons will respond in kind. They will come at us with the full force of a planetary garrison, a garrison of experienced combat troops."

"That is correct." *What else can I say to her?*

"The odds are stacked against us achieving the mission parameters," she stated flatly. She avoided saying that victory was impossible. That was promising. Redburn licked his lips. "I know I'm asking a lot of you. That is why I'm sending the Fidelis troops with you. They are expert fighters, a deadly force."

She hesitated. "Perhaps I'm not the person to lead this, sir. I just don't see a way to pull this off, not without extreme losses."

Redburn nodded twice in understanding. Losses. Knights were soldiers, they followed orders. Officers of The Republic, on the other hand, were not used to suffering the casualties she was anticipating. "You are *exactly* the person to lead this mission, Lady Synd. I chose you myself, and with good reason. Yes, you are going to take losses, but you are a fluid tactician in a fight. You are a skilled warrior who knows that the mission comes first. You understand that losses are necessary in war and will do what you can to minimize those losses. I wouldn't want anyone else on Ryde representing me or The Republic.

"I am going to repeat myself: Your mission is critical to the long-term success of the Fortress Republic strategy. I can't tell you why, but these scientists can't remain working for the Jade Falcons. It is impossible for me to replace you as the leader of this mission; furthermore, I can't imagine doing it. You are the best resource for making this work."

She stared at him with her hazel eyes, saying nothing, staring not just at him but into him. Redburn let her break the silence. "I understand, sir. I will not fail you."

"I know you won't." He rose and saluted her. She cocked her head slightly, confused by the gesture, and returned the salute.

He sauntered into the office Redburn was using as if he were a drifter rather than a sworn protector of The Republic. Ghost knights were like that. He had brown hair and a coy grin on his face. As Redburn rose to his feet, he slumped into the guest chair at an odd angle, almost as if he were watching a holovid rather than meeting with the former exarch of The Republic.

Cocky, arrogant, self-assured, immature . . . yes, his profile seemed correct. "Sir Chin. Have a seat," he said after the fact, as he resumed his own seat. Jeremy Chin smiled at the use of his formal title. It was something that most ghost knights never heard used.

"You know why I'm here?" he asked.

"I think so."

"Let's see then, you tell me," Chin replied. His tone was overconfident, a sign of his age.

"You have a concern about your portion of the mission. You're worried about the moral implications of what I'm asking you to do."

Chin nodded. "You're dead on, sir. You have me doing something here that is, well, *dirty*. I've done some borderline stuff as a ghost. As you know, it's sometimes part of the job. This is something that goes way beyond that."

Redburn had been prepared for this discussion. "You're right, Jeremy. This is very dirty work." He sighed, and leaned back in his seat as if he were prepared to bare his soul. "Hell, it's worse than that. What I'm asking you to do is downright wrong, morally, legally and ethically. And it's going to be worse because you are not kicking off the mission right away. I need you on standby for months, maybe much longer."

The ghost knight was surprised at Redburn's confessional tone. "Sir?"

"Listen," Redburn said, leaning forward across the table. "This is one of the plans that Devlin Stone himself suggested. I'm not fond of it. Like you, though, I am here to serve The Republic. Like you, I follow orders. You aren't going to like this, not at all. Hunter Mannheim would hate it even more, if he knew the full truth. No one likes blood on their hands. You'll do it, though. Your record tells me that. At night, you'll curse me and my children and their children. You'll hate me; and you're right to do that. In twenty years' time, though, you're going to look back and see how important your assignment was." Redburn felt that the best way to deal with Chin was to be up front. He only hoped he hadn't gone too far with his blunt answer.

"Twenty years, eh?" Chin said, clearly stunned by the openness of the former exarch. "You're asking me to do something pretty radical . . . sir. All on the promise that someday it'll be worth it. I'm not looking forward to sitting and waiting until you give us the go signal and the target world. Sitting and waiting, thinking about this. It's going to drive me nuts."

"That's the mission you've drawn, son," he replied. "And telling you this—that's the mission I've drawn."

"The second set of orders I have; the monastery and the, er . . ."

"The *artifact*?" Redburn ventured.

"Sure. I was going to say the box, but artifact will do. I have to be honest, that part of the mission seems a little strange. Not to mention you've given me no orders as to what to do with it once I recover it." It was a side mission that he was going on—a side mission that Stone himself had described.

"You're right." Redburn smiled thinly. "I haven't."

Lady Synd saw him brooding and walked over to him. Older than the other knights in the room, Hunter Mannheim looked angry and agitated. "Sir Mannheim, are you alright?" she asked.

"Hunt. Call me Hunt," he countered. "And no, I'm not alright. Thanks for asking, though. That counts."

"It's your family, isn't it?" she probed.

He looked at her, his expression almost confused. She realized he hadn't been thinking of them at all. "Rita knew what she signed up for by marrying me. The kids are used to my not being around. This is longer than I ever thought I'd be gone, but Judith and Ron are good kids. We raised them to appreciate what they have living on Terra, living in The Republic. No, that's something I can work with. It'll be hard, but they'll be fine." He said the words as if he wanted to believe them more than he did.

"Something else, then?"

Hunter looked at her and she could see the furrows on his forehead, as if he were struggling with what he had been handed. "I'm working in the dark. My orders are to prepare for a mission that, on the surface, seems a bit nefarious."

"None of these missions is very typical."

"At least you get to ship out soon. I have to go and sit on my hands indefinitely."

"Maybe you won't have to go at all."

He shook his head. "I doubt that. Redburn wouldn't have brought me here if this wasn't destined to be a reality. I just find myself wondering about this mission. If we have to do these things to save The Republic, is it really worth it?"

"You are questioning that—*really*?"

He bit his lower lip. "Yes . . . no. No, I'm not. I know that Stone had a hand in determining these operations and that I should trust his judgment, but this mission is not right. These are not the actions one should ask of a Knight of the Sphere."

"I can understand that," she replied.

"I always held knighthood up to a higher standard. Frankly, it scares me to think that in the end we're just officers following orders."

She put her hand on his shoulder and squeezed. "We're more than that, Hunt. We are Knights of the Sphere. No matter what you have to do, you must always hold on to that truth. I realize it's not much, but it's all I can offer you. I hope it helps."

Altar of Freedom 4

Ghost Knight Jayson Greene ran down the hallway of the research facility to where the infantryman stood with a group of men and women wearing knee-length white jackets. The infantryman wore the insignia of the Principes Guards; Greene assumed the people with him were the scientists. Greene was painfully aware that they had no time for delays. The situation was too fluid—fighting already had erupted outside the research center. The image of the downed *Loki* and of the decapitated Falcon MechWarrior still burned in his memory.

"Sergeant, what's the damned issue here?"

The infantryman looked downright *relieved* to see him. "Sir Greene, these are the scientists we were sent to rescue. They won't get into the APC."

He glared at them. "You must leave now. Do what the sergeant orders. We have to get you out of here." He put every ounce of command he could muster into his voice.

"Now see here," an older man said. "Are you in charge of this fiasco? I'm Dr. Andrew Brunner. My people and I have no intention of just up and leaving our work."

"Dr. Brunner," Greene began anew, curbing his frustration. "I have been sent by the exarch himself to extract you from your current situation. The Jade Falcons are closing in around us. We don't have time for debate. You and your team have to leave, and leave now."

Another scientist spoke up, a female by her voice, though a test would have been warranted to confirm that she was indeed a woman, based on her appearance. "We won't leave without our families." Several of the others muttered and nodded in agreement.

Sir Greene quickly reviewed his options. He could have them dragged into the APC, but that would be messy and take time that he didn't want to spend. He cursed himself for not seriously considering that these men and women might not want to be rescued. It really limited his options for dealing with this.

He grasped Dr. Brunner's shoulder, looked him full in the face and lied. "Sir, we have already sent out teams to recover your families. We'll rendezvous with them when we reach the JumpShip. Right now, you need to move and move fast."

Brunner studied his face, as if trying to decide if he was telling the truth. The older researcher finally nodded. "Very well," he muttered, and started down the hall. The other scientists followed in line. The sergeant stopped in front of Greene.

"Tell Captain Paulis to get these people out of here. Fall back with all units. I have a few things to wrap up."

"All units, sir?"

"The mission comes first, Sergeant," was all he offered as an explanation.

"Sir, I'm not sure about leaving you here alone."

Greene flashed a smile. "I do my best work alone."

The Jade Falcon *Dasher II* rushed into the Veterans Park like a sprinting athlete. Its target was the Padilla, and it would close before the artillery piece could bring its massive firepower to bear. Lady Synd caught the movement from the corner of her eye and turned her *Templar* to face the threat. The *Dasher II* was going to be hard to hit, but the Fidelis had modified her *Templar* with an improved targeting system. Time to put it to a real-world test.

She used her joystick to center the targeting reticle on the *Dasher* and waited for the lock tone. Her pair of Defiance PPCs sounded a high-pitched whine as they fired, unleashing two streams of charged-particle energy downrange. The heat in her cockpit rose slightly from the discharge as the manmade lightning bolts both found their mark on the pumping legs of the *Dasher*. A rain of armor plating, smoke and a flicker of fire was the result. The *Dasher* missed a step, then another, then fell, sending a burst of laser fire into the Padilla as it dropped. It plowed a long furrow in the soft sod of Veterans Park, stopping just short of the Padilla. The artillery piece mounted a pair of Harpoon short-range missile racks and pumped both of them into the *Dasher* to make sure that it was down permanently. Gray smoke rose from holes in the thin back armor of the facedown BattleMech.

Synd let a smile rise to her face, but then she was hit by a shot from a *Black Hawk*. A withering sputter of crimson laser pulses stitched their way up her *Templar*'s left side. Operating on pure instinct, she reversed her 'Mech, jogging backward far enough to allow her to get a good angle on the Falcon attacker.

They don't call me Mongoose for nothing . . .

The green-gray Falcon *Black Hawk* had come from the direction of the Rouge River; the fact that it had jump jets meant it simply had flown over the river, ignoring the missing bridges. It moved fast along the edge of the park, followed closely by two squads of Falcon elemental troops. The Falcons were living up to their fearsome reputation, and she wasn't sure just how long they would be able to hold off the defenders.

The elementals ran straight at her while the *Black*

Hawk slowed to a walk and attempted to obtain a target lock on her *Templar*. She stopped and jerked her own targeting system to lock onto the *Hawk*.

She fired simultaneously with hearing the target lock tone, using the pair of charged-particle cannons and both of her extended-range medium lasers. The heat in the cockpit spiked, and she felt like she was in a sauna. Her PPCs found their mark, but one of her lasers' emerald beams missed, slashing a long scar into the office building behind the *Black Hawk*. Flames lapped from one of the burned-out windows.

The hits rocked the *Black Hawk* backward, and it reeled as if it were going to fall. But the Falcon Mech-Warrior was made of stern stuff: He fought the impact that had seared and blackened the front of his 'Mech and rose back to a fighting stance. Then he fired.

The attack was the worst fear of any MechWarrior: an alpha strike. The *Black Hawk* fired everything it had, all six of its lasers at once. She lost sight of the enemy behind a barrage of death. The attack didn't just hit her *Templar*, it overwhelmed it like a tidal surge. Her damage display flickered yellow in multiple areas, indicating the hits.

She staggered a step, fighting the damage and the heat. The elementals would be on her in a minute. Once the Jade Falcon pilot recovered from the devastating heat generated by an alpha strike, her problems would only get worse.

Suddenly she saw Fidelis jump jet troopers land on the overheated *Black Hawk*. It had to be Boyne. They seemed to engulf the 'Mech as it stood idle for a critical few seconds, steaming in the cool air, venting as much heat as possible in order to rejoin the fight.

Explosions from planted munitions went off at the knees, hips and head of the *Black Hawk*. Vulnerable as she was at the moment, some portion of her mind was impressed by the precision and speed at which the infantry moved. The Falcon MechWarrior activated his ejection seat; the canopy blew clear and he rose into the air, blasting away from the 'Mech. One of the Fidelis infantry rose on his or her jump jets in pursuit, firing as they went. A laser beam stabbed skyward at the ejection seat as it reached its apex. The parachute never opened. The chair dropped like a dead weight to the ground. As her infantry landed on the ground near the ejection seat, the Falcon elementals suddenly turned to face the threat to their rear. Lady Synd managed a few feeble steps in pursuit, but her *Templar* was still struggling against her control.

"Captain Boyne" was all she could say.

"We see them," he replied curtly.

The squads intermixed in mid-jump, the elemental troops of the Jade Falcons slamming into the jump-jet troops of the Fidelis. It was the most vicious battle that she had ever seen. Lasers and a flamer erupted in the air. It was impossible to tell who was who in the swarm as both sides dropped to the ground to continue the melee. Synd jabbed at her foot pedals and pushed the throttle forward. Her *Templar* slowly came back under her control. Each step was agonizingly slow. *I have to save those men.*

Even as she closed with the infantry battle, the fighting began to diminish. She saw one of her Fidelis troopers fall, cut nearly in half by an elemental. That elemental found himself under fire from three other troopers and was reduced to a mangled and half-melted slab of meat and metal. One of the Fidelis warriors pulled his sidearm from his hip and stabbed the barrel into the joint between another elemental warrior's helmet and suit. He fired. There was no chance of a miss. The head of the elemental was half torn, half peeled backward.

Then it was over . . . at least for a moment. The Jade Falcons were not just dead, they were disemboweled. A Fidelis trooper moved to each of his fallen comrades and seemed to press them hard in the upper shoulder. She didn't understand the gesture, but made a mental note to ask about it later. Smoke drifted over the small patch of grass where they had savaged one another.

Synd had been a Knight of the Sphere for years. She had fought in many battles, and prided herself on maintaining a level of honor on the field. That was her duty as a knight. This battle, this mission—this was not honorable. This was war at its bloodiest. When he gave her the Fidelis, Redburn had given her a killing machine, and she had turned them loose. "Boyne."

"We were successful, m'lady," Boyne replied. "We destroyed a handful of Falcons when the buildings fell. They have been forced onto secondary routes in order to approach the park."

"The evacuation?"

There was a pause. "Many lives were saved. Per your orders."

Another voice came over the comm channel. "Lady Synd, this is Dagger Two." That would be Captain Paulis. Her tactical display showed that the *Griffin* he piloted was entering Veterans Park to the south of her position.

"Go ahead, Dagger Two."

"I've brought back the scientists, and they are secure," his winded voice replied. "Major Greene stayed behind to complete his objectives. He said you'd understand."

He was going to copy the research data from the computer network there. "Did he stay alone?"

"Yes, sir. I put a squad at the edge of the LZ to assist in his recovery if he runs into problems, per our plans."

"And the scientists?"

"They are boarding the *Excelsior*. The Falcons seem to have pulled back for now."

Boyne cut in. "They have stopped coming at us piecemeal for a moment. This would suggest that they are concentrating their forces for a cohesive strike."

Synd checked her sensors. There was no sign of Jade Falcon activity on short-range sensors. Long-range showed movement and possible fusion reactors just at the edge of her scanning range—which was about six blocks in the built-up city. From what she saw, Boyne was right. The initial attacks had been probing efforts with the forces they had in the vicinity. Now they were preparing for a real assault. Sensors indicated it would come from north of the park.

"We will form up to the north, moving in to secure the first two blocks or so of the city on that side of the park. We need to hold them off long enough for Major Greene to rejoin us."

There was a pause, then Paulis replied. "Lady Synd, we have recovered the scientists, which was our primary objective. . . ."

She cut him off. "You have your orders, Captain." Giving orders and making them happen, however, were two distinct things.

The Jade Falcons came down on Veterans Park only twenty minutes after Lady Synd's force moved out of the park to seize the city blocks and buildings in the Falcons' path. The urban area was going to invite the worst kind of fighting; point-blank range, building to building. Making matters worse, the Falcons had arrived with enough firepower to ensure victory.

Synd's *Templar* moved into the middle of a street— which one, she didn't know. Shots from a *Gyrfalcon*'s autocannons rattled her 'Mech as she stepped forward. It was obvious that the *Gyrfalcon* MechWarrior was unimpressed by the firepower coming down the boulevard at it. Artillery rounds from her Padilla landed everywhere around it and even on it, but the *Gyrfalcon* did not even flinch. It methodically moved closer as she stepped behind a building for cover.

This new round of fighting had been raging for only a few minutes and already it had been costly. She looked down the street perpendicular to the approaching Falcon force and saw one of her Saxon APCs tipped on its side and belching clouds of black smoke. The roadway around it was torn up with gouges from missed gauss rifle rounds, leaving nasty furrows in the street. Dead bodies, her troops, lay nearby. Some had gotten away, far fewer than those who had died.

"Lady Synd," Captain Paulis' voice sounded like he was screaming for a medic. "I have to fall back. My force has taken heavy losses."

"Hold the line, Captain."

"My 'Mech is coming apart at the seams, sir." He panted the words, at the edge of pleading with her.

Boyne's voice cut in. "I have three squads here along with Lieutenant Argosy's *Thunderbolt*. Argosy can hold here and I'll bring my men to your position."

"Infantry won't stand a chance. We have three Falcon 'Mechs and a tank coming down Maple Drive to the park. Anything entering that corridor is toast."

"We will be there in five. Prepare to give us suppression fire." Boyne's voice was confident.

"You'll be slaughtered, Captain."

"We will do our duty."

"Cut the chatter," Synd said, leaning out just enough to fire a blast from her PPCs down the street and into the *Gyrfalcon*. The azure blasts were aimed low, hitting the legs of the Falcon 'Mech and momentarily stopping its movement. "Boyne, no heroics. Do what you can. Paulis, give him covering fire when he needs it. We have to buy time for Major Greene."

The building she was hiding behind rumbled and rocked, and she stepped away from it and back into the street. This Falcon MechWarrior was no fool. He was blasting her cover. "Remove the building and you remove the cover." Urban Warfare 101. *I took that class as well, my friend. . . .*

She cut over to the next block and moved north. She would find an alley or street that cut back to the right and hit either his flank or rear. *We have to buy Sir Greene time to complete his mission—that was her focus.*

But at what cost?

Interpretation of Duty 1

Training Facility Serpent
Northern Mopelia Island, New Earth
Prefecture X, Republic of the Sphere
Fortress Republic (–83 days)

"She's left?" barked Kristoff Erbe, Knight Errant of The Republic. "We never coordinated my end of the operation—she focused entirely on determining when I should arrive on Callison. She didn't brief me on her mission or operational objectives. We didn't even share communications protocol."

"I understand that you find the situation frustrating," Damien Redburn replied. "Lady Hancock was allowed to use her own discretion regarding what she shared with you. I, however, am prepared to answer any of your questions that I can at this time." He leaned on the desk in a spare office that he had appropriated, tucked away in the Fidelis training facility.

"Why all the cloak-and-dagger?" Erbe asked, his anger receding slightly. He wasn't really angry that Ghost Knight Hancock had left without letting him know; all her communication with him so far had been professional and to the point, and good-byes were for friends. What made him angry was that he was operating entirely in the dark, and he did blame her for that.

"In the initial briefing I gave your group, I stated that the missions of the ghost knights would take priority over any other objective. Regrettably, revealing her orders to you would compromise the integrity of both missions. I can tell you that Lady Hancock spoke to me regarding her concerns about this mission at length and with great passion." Redburn's understatement almost made Erbe smile; even in his minimal interactions with the diminutive Hancock, it had been clear that she was feisty, and a tiger of a debater.

Redburn continued. "The operation on Callison is important to our long-term future. I was recalled to duty by a message from Devlin Stone. In the accompanying documents, he indicated that Callison is more than it seems, and needed to remain loyal to The Republic throughout the Fortress period. Per his instructions, I worked with the ghost paladin to develop orders for Lady Hancock that will challenge her abilities, and test you as well. According to Stone, Callison offers us hope, Sir Erbe; remember that in the weeks to come."

And hope is in small supply right now. "I feel that I'd be better prepared to be tested if I knew what I was up against."

"I realize that, but your request is moot." Redburn walked around the desk and sat down. "Now then, if you want to discuss the parameters of your orders or any other aspect of your mission, I'd be happy to assist you."

It was obvious that he wasn't going to get anything more from the former exarch—no, paladin. Erbe hated secrets, especially secrets that involved him. Fine. Best to play this out for what he could. "So why do you think that Callison is so important?"

He was surprised at the half-shrug that Redburn gave him. "Callison is mostly unremarkable, except that it has managed so far to avoid being drawn into the recent turmoil. It has strong industry and a good garrison force that has succeeded in maintaining order.

"I have pored over records looking for some sort of secret on the planet. There is no reference to a hidden stockpile of military hardware, but on Callison that is almost a moot point. It has a large industrial base that has already started converting to military armament production. There were two military bases that were decommissioned after the Jihad, but there was nothing remarkable about them, either."

Redburn put his elbows on the desk and leaned forward as he continued. "Callison is a single jump from both the Lyran Commonwealth and the Marik-Stewart Commonwealth. That puts it in position to launch a rapid response if either side starts something that places the border in jeopardy."

"That doesn't fully explain why Callison. My mission is to go there and recover a pair of completed DropShip engines and strip materiel from their militia. Your explanation also doesn't tell me whether my going there will reveal any of the planet's secrets."

"You're right, it doesn't. For some parts of your mission, you simply have to remain in the dark."

"So I'm asking again; why Callison?"

Redburn grinned. "The true answer is simple. Callison is important because Devlin Stone said it was."

"A holographic message recorded years ago tells you to go to a world, and you send in troops?"

"A fair question, my good knight. To find your way on this mission, you'll have to embrace the concept of faith. I knew Devlin Stone." A broad grin erupted on his face as if he were embracing a fond memory. "If he says that Callison is of value, then it must be."

"You place that much weight on faith?"

"You of all people should understand faith. Faith is what we must rely on once Fortress Republic is put in place. When you look at that planet on the surface it seems ordinary. But a world is more than its resources. Look at the people; look at their leaders."

Erbe bristled at the seemingly innocent comment. *Was Redburn going to say it out loud? Was he going to bring his father, his family, into this?* "What are you saying, Sir Redburn?" His voice sounded harsh, even to himself.

The former exarch knew he had struck a nerve, and now he pressed on it. "One of the reasons I chose you for this assignment was your background and the history you've struggled with. For many years you have faced unspoken, invisible challenges and met them successfully."

He had said it. The gauntlet had been tossed. Kristoff Erbe had faced this issue his whole life. His response rarely varied. "Don't judge me by what my father did or didn't do. I'm my own person. The sins of the father end with him."

Redburn smiled in an attempt to ease the tension between them. "You were chosen for this mission because of *your* past, not your father's. You've struggled your whole life against an enemy you can't fight. I was merely pointing out that you have vast experience dealing with faith. Whether you know it or not, faith is what has helped you through those challenges. Given what is going to happen with Fortress Republic, that same faith will get you through these challenges as well."

"Faith," he repeated thoughtfully. He had never thought of it that way. He believed his father had made some poor choices; his father's decision to deal with the Word of Blake during the Jihad had been controversial, to put it mildly. Kristoff Erbe had been fighting the ghost of his father's choices his whole life, and that fight had given him an inner strength. He never apologized for his father's actions, but he recognized that the taint touched him. Becoming a knight was one way he had found to begin purging that past. "As you obviously suspect, this is a difficult subject for me. Prejudices are hard to fight. People's perceptions are complicated when you ask them to recognize change. I am my own person. If you think it's faith that has driven me to separate myself from my family history, well—that's as good an explanation as any. I am not my father; I'm choosing my own path in life. Don't try to judge me by the actions or inactions he chose decades ago."

Redburn simply nodded and moved on with the discussion. "Which leads me to discussing Governor Stewart." He paused.

"I've read her intelligence file," Kristoff said, happy that the subject had changed. "Interesting woman," he said, indulging in a little understatement of his own.

" 'Interesting' can be a virtue, Sir Erbe, but she's more than that. You've read the reports, so you know that she has begun to work with several crime families that operate on Callison and neighboring worlds. It appears that our good governor is hedging her bets on the future of The Republic. These families can provide Stewart with a significant power base."

"The report on her indicates that she's ambitious, but there were no details of her plans."

"A weakness of having our HPG network down—intelligence reports now are often fragmented and incomplete, so we aren't sure just what she's up to. But she demands careful watching when you land. She's obviously the kind of person who could take advantage of Fortress Republic to advance her own goals." Erbe had suspected the governor was a risk; Redburn was giving him the warning in plain language. "Perhaps it's a mistake for me to show up in force. I certainly shouldn't need much military force to recover two engines and remove some militia hardware, and landing with significant troops might tip our hand. Maybe I could go down alone and simply negotiate with her for what we need?"

Redburn shook his head firmly. "Your orders stand. We can't afford for you to be taken hostage if the situation is too volatile or if the governor chooses to take advantage of Fortress. Besides, despite what people may think by the time you get there, The Republic still stands. Your showing up with a Republic force will help soothe any concerns of the local population."

"These troops you've given me . . ." Kristoff seized

the opportunity to discuss another concern. "The Fidelis appear to be very skilled at what they do and they're equipped with some of the best gear I've ever seen. But none of them have experienced real combat, and that could be a serious liability to the mission."

Redburn smiled knowingly. "You should get to know them. The officer assigned you, Adamans, commands a battle group. He is one of the best of a superior force. Go somewhere neutral, spend some time with him. You will find that their lack of experience is offset by what they bring to the table."

Erbe leaned back in his seat. Redburn was making a valid point. He didn't know the Fidelis, and he definitely didn't understand them. He had tried to crack their stoic exterior, but to no avail. He straightened his spine. "I will not fail you. I will make this work."

"I believe you will," Redburn replied. "Callison is important; important enough for us all to try."

Sir Erbe nodded. *Callison is important because Devlin Stone said so.*

They entered the building together, but Kristoff Erbe had his doubts. On the outside, the building didn't look like his idea of a bar. In fact, the island of Northern Mopelia had offered very little in the way of entertainment. But as he stepped into the dark room, he saw that it was a bar, of sorts. A bar as interpreted by the Fidelis.

First of all, the air was clean. The Fidelis apparently didn't smoke, which Erbe actually appreciated. Second, the men and women inside were not typical bar patrons. To a man, they wore pristine military casuals, clean and pressed. He saw no half-drunken gazes as his eyes adjusted to the dark. Each patron acknowledged him with a respectful nod, and he returned the gesture.

Adamans wore the rank of colonel on his epaulets; many of the Fidelis in the bar hoisted their drinks as if toasting him, as if acknowledging their pride in his affiliation with The Republic. Adamans and Erbe slid into the chairs at a corner table. The bartender, obviously a veteran from his muscular stature and cropped hair, limped over to the table carrying two bottles. One leg seemed oddly large, and Erbe realized he had seen this condition before. The bartender had a budded limb, regrown after the loss of the original limb. When the procedure was done poorly, as was clearly the case with the bartender, it left the patient deformed.

The bottles were dark and cold, and he assumed they contained beer. He lifted his bottle and took a drink. It was beer alright, dark as night and so thick that it almost had a texture. When he swallowed, he immediately felt the alcohol hit his system. Like everything else about the Fidelis, these beers were not ordinary. He looked at the label; it was black with yellow letters spelling BEER.

"I'm glad you accepted my offer of a drink," he said to Adamans.

The Fidelis officer took a swig of his own drink and nodded. He ran his hand through his short black hair and appeared to relax—as much as any of the Fidelis ever relaxed. "I appreciate the company. With all of the planning and training scheduled for the next few months, such an opportunity is rare and enjoyable."

Erbe looked around the bar. There were no advertising posters. The place was clean, almost too clean. Other than being dark, it simply didn't feel at all like a bar. "I must admit, Adamans, I wasn't sure the Fidelis actually had bars and drank."

The man chuckled—also a new experience for Erbe. "I assure you, Sir Erbe, we drink. Personally, I strive for moderation, as I have been known to be a nasty drunk. The Fidelis drink, we fornicate, we have children, we grow old. We are just like you—only different."

Philosophy worthy of a Capellan seer. "You must admit that compared to regular troops of The Republic, the Fidelis seem out of the ordinary."

"Not to us," he said, taking another swig of his beer. The knight did the same. "We are simply the products of our past."

"That can be said of nearly everyone."

Adamans shook his head. "Not so. What is your lineage?"

Erbe was surprised to arrive at a serious topic so quickly. "Well, my ancestors were from the Federated Suns. I was raised on Towne, and did not leave there until after the fall of the HPG." Thinking of his family conjured memories of the chaos of the Jihad and the pain of the challenges he faced then.

"How does your past guide your life?"

"Let's just say that my past is not what makes me who I am." *My father's past is what forged me. I refuse to make his mistakes.* For the second time in the same day, he acknowledged that he had become a knight in an attempt to purge the wrongs of his father's past. It never seemed to be enough.

Adamans took another drink of his beer and licked his lips. Kristoff didn't match him this time; the alcohol content of this beer was much higher than the drinks he was accustomed to, and though the Fidelis officer did not show that he was feeling the effects of the drink, he decided it might be hard to tell. "From the day I was born, I was raised and trained to be a Fidelis warrior. I learned every role of our society, every assignment in the military. This role was mine because it was my father's, and his mother's before him. He had the right to set me on this path. From birth I knew my role and duty." He took another small sip.

Erbe studied him silently, then ventured, "It sounds like a caste society."

Adamans frowned. "We do not believe in castes. They limit freedom. We know because of the Great Betrayal that freedom and choice are important. We still sing the stories of that time, and of our bonds with The Republic."

"The Great Betrayal?"

Adamans pondered the question. "I must choose my words carefully, Sir Erbe. The Fidelis keep our history to ourselves. This is more than tradition; it is law to us, our creed. The Great Betrayal was a pivotal moment for our people. We had been betrayed and left for dead by those who were of our blood. They forgot us, but we refused to die. The custos ensured our survival. He led us down the road to our home.

"The betrayers came and claimed to be our friends. The custos knew better. He trusted them only as much as necessary. When we learned of their betrayal, he changed us forever. He taught us that freedom, with rules and guidelines, was the key to our survival. We shed the old ways that held us back. We found The Republic and tied our future to the Great Father—Stone."

The mention of Stone prompted Erbe to raise his beer in a toast. "To the memory of Devlin Stone."

Everyone in the bar, even those he felt sure could not have heard him, stood and raised their drinks. "To Devlin Stone!" they barked in unison, as if it were a military cadence. They drank heartily, passionately, as if it were a matter of honor. Adamans did the same. *What the heck? Have they got genetically enhanced hearing?* As they slammed their empty glasses and bottles onto the tables and bar, they shouted one word: "Service!" Most nodded at him.

Even with the explanation he had provided, Adamans had succeeded in keeping the Fidelis' past a mystery. But one thing was for sure. The Fidelis were loyal to The Republic. Rather than trying to get more information about their past, Erbe chose a different tack.

"This custos. He's your leader?"

"He is that and more. He is the past and future of our people."

"How many custos have you had?"

"He is the only one." Kristoff considered that statement, and realized it was the first tangible thing he had been told by the Fidelis warrior. But even though it allowed him to guess at a number of years this might indicate, it still gave him no clear ideas as to the true origins of these people. *I wonder how old this custos is?* Time for another change of subject.

"I understand that you train in every military role."

"We do. My specialty is a light BattleMech, but I prefer duty in the artillery."

"Once we have a chance to pilot a 'Mech, very few of us are willing to turn back to the life of a groundpounder."

"We believe one cannot truly appreciate the gift of a 'Mech unless one understands every other role in the military. We study the ways of the technicians because being able to repair gear damaged in battle makes us better warriors. We study vehicles as Jägers, learning everything about them and how they perform. We fight as infantry, as Superstites, to know what it is like to stand unprotected on the field of battle."

"Your training is impressive," Erbe responded, taking a long swig of his beer.

"We are prepared to fight and, if we must, die for The Republic." Conviction rang in Adamans' voice.

"Let's hope that death is not part of this."

"I do not seek death. None of us do. At the same time, I do not fear it. I know that my children will carry on my legacy. They will one day see the reading of the Unopened Work. If I do not fulfill our destiny, they will."

"You haven't mentioned your wife," Erbe pressed.

"I do not have a wife," Adamans said, finishing his beer.

"But your children . . ."

Adamans stared at him impassively. "You have not heard how we reproduce, Sir Knight?"

Kristoff wordlessly shook his head.

Adamans guffawed and slapped the knight on the shoulder. "I am joking, Sir Erbe."

"You have a wife, then?"

"More than one," he replied. His wide smile seemed out of place on a Fidelis warrior. "We all have our duties and service to perform for our people. Some requirements are much more pleasant than others." He cocked an eyebrow.

Kristoff Erbe was not sure if the Fidelis trooper was still joking.

Price of Service 4

Breezewood, Kwamashu
Duchy of Andurien
Fortress Republic (+858 days)

Chin stood in the old processing facility and looked at the massive stacks of chemical drums stretching as far as the eye could see. This was one of the buildings he had told Sir Mannheim was off-limits, and the knight had dutifully stayed away. Jeremy had counted on his obedient nature.

The last few weeks had been a mix of boredom and keeping the vigilant Fidelis and Hunter Mannheim out of his private work in the plant. They had simulated the reactivation of the industrial complex. Fires burned in old incinerators, sending smoke into the air. Trucks drove around the city loaded with empty crates. Mannheim had concentrated on their defenses. Jeremy had concentrated on preventing him from snooping around too much in the old plant.

Thousands of drums had been stacked here over the years, in some places up to the ceiling. Some had developed leaks, especially those on the bottom. Pools of chemicals mixed. There had been attempts of varying effectiveness to contain the leaks over the years, but most of those attempts had failed by now. Jeremy was familiar with all the chemicals stored in this facility. Better yet, he knew about the other, more dangerous substances stored elsewhere in the complex.

He carefully planted the remote charge against one of the barrels, something he had done a hundred times already over the last few weeks. The placement of each charge was carefully planned. He had broken out some of the windows in this and other buildings to ensure a good flow of oxygen.

The hard part had been doing it without Mannheim or any of the Fidelis catching him—or finding his hidden cache of charges. In fact, Chin had found it disturbingly easy; just like everything else in this operation. He truly believed it shouldn't be so easy to do this . . . thing . . . that he was doing. Even if he was just following orders. "I just don't understand why taking lives is so simple," he muttered.

Chin paused. "Oh, great. Now I'm talking to myself."

His dialogue with himself was interrupted by a chirp from his wrist communicator. "Chin here."

"This is Rook." If Mannheim had switched to his call sign—"You need to report to HQ"—then there was . . .

"Trouble?"

"Double-time it."

"It's on the local media as well," Mannheim said, pointing to the portable holovid unit. "They came in at a pirate point and are two days out." The troopers in the room hung on his words. He surveyed their eyes for a long moment: Fidelis, Republic, it didn't matter—they all bore a look of determination. This moment was what they had planned and trained for. The air in the old office seemed to take on the heady smell of sweat and energy that Hunt associated with battlefields. This room, with its peeling yellow paint, broken furniture, dust and dirt creeping in at every corner, was not an office anymore—it was a command post, and this was war.

"Designation?" Chin asked.

"Our satellites picked up the insignia on the DropShips at long range. They are from the Oriente Protectorate," one of the Fidelis troopers answered from his post at the surveillance monitors.

"Ships?"

"Three," the technician replied. "All are *Union*-class."

Hunter looked at Chin. "The plan was that they would time their attack closer to the announced completion of this facility. We should have had another few weeks."

The younger knight shrugged. "Luring an enemy is an imperfect science."

"We could have used the extra time."

"That doesn't change the fact that they are here—now."

"We will need to discuss coordinating our efforts with Colonel Daum. Especially since we're suddenly outnumbered and outgunned. They are bringing in a battalion—at best with our force and the local garrison, we number two companies."

"I'm not looking forward to that conversation," Chin muttered under his breath. Mannheim had noticed in the last month or so that Chin had developed the habit of talking to himself. *It must be how he deals with the stress of a mission.* "Is there a problem with the local garrison commander?"

Chin shook himself out of his thoughts. "No. Just thinking to myself. Colonel Daum raked me over the coals pretty well when we met. I've contacted him twice since we landed to give him courtesy updates, even invite him to dinner. He's ignored me—refused to speak to me directly. I'm not sure, but I don't think the man likes me." The sarcasm had returned.

"I find that hard to believe," Mannheim replied with a faint grin.

"I know."

Finally Mannheim could enjoy the banter. Now hostile forces were arriving, and his force, disguised as Duchy of Andurien troops, would finally get into battle. They would have to lure the enemy into battle near the plant, blow it up, record the detonation in detail and get off-world intact. The footage would be released with false casualty numbers for both sides. It would be the spark that would ignite a war. That part he didn't dwell on. What mattered now was the battle itself, and this was his forte.

"We'll talk to him together."

"Just remember, you're an officer in the Duchy's armed forces."

Hunter looked at the patch he wore on his shoulder. It was the outline of Duchy-controlled space set against a map with a deep purple background. A sword ran down the center of it. *Whatever patch I wear, I am fighting for Stone and The Republic. The uniform doesn't matter. What matters is what I feel inside.*

Sir Chin, wearing his disguise as Lieutenant Colonel Gelder, and Sir Mannheim met with Daum at the fortified front gate of the industrial complex. On either side of the gate were sandbagged bunkers with Fidelis troops manning the weapons. Colonel Daum had come in his staff car, tiny flags mounted on the front fenders designating him as garrison commander. The way he moved, the efficiency in his stride, the way he shook hands marked him as a seasoned combat veteran. Chin observed him closely. *I will have to remember how he moves and acts in case I have to play that role someday.*

"We can cut through all the damn pleasantries, Colonel," Daum replied when Mannheim invited him inside for a cup of coffee. "As I told your Lieutenant Colonel"—he jerked his thumb at Chin—"I knew your presence here was going to bring trouble. Now a lot of good men and women are going to get hurt or die because of it."

"We all have our orders," Mannheim said coolly. "I go where they tell me and I do what I'm told to do—just like a good soldier." Chin would have been impressed by how well Mannheim faked his role, except that he was really just being himself with a different name. He knew Mannheim had the right idea by appealing to the common ground between all military men when he saw Daum's acknowledging grin.

"I hear you, Colonel."

"Let's cut to the chase," Mannheim suggested. "We've got three bogies incoming, a battalion of troops. You know they're going to head this way: This plant is the prize. What can we do to work together?"

"I can't leave the planetary capital undefended." Daum started with his primary constraint. "But I can use my militia to cover the city. The enemy's going to come at this plant. The plains to the west of the city, where your DropShips are, would be the most logical place for them to land. Plenty of open space, flat terrain, straight run into Breezewood."

Mannheim nodded. "I was thinking the same thing."

Daum put his balled fists on his waist. "I'll send the bulk of my forces out to the western plains as soon as we are sure that is their vector. They'll remain under my command, and I'll send you our communications channels. I will not turn over my forces to your management."

"I wouldn't ask you to, Colonel."

Colonel Daum looked Mannheim up and down. "No, I guess you wouldn't. Alright then, Colonel, I'll see you on the field in two days." Daum shook Mannheim's hand and glared at Chin, who saluted as the garrison commander got back into his staff car. He looked at Mannheim.

"Told you he was a little stiff."

Mannheim grinned. "He seemed like a perfect officer and gentleman to me."

Fortress Republic (+860 days)

Chin found Mannheim in the fake assembly plant watching the final loadout on his *Shockwave*. Jeremy watched him for a moment; Mannheim was half-leaning on the leg of the 'Mech, peering up. "He looks like a recruiting poster," he muttered. He seemed totally comfortable with the 'Mech, not at all intimidated. *I doubt I'll ever feel that casual near them.* Even with all of his training, piloting a BattleMech was not his first love. That was why when The Republic had recruited him as a ghost knight he'd leapt at the opportunity. It was much better to fight battles in bars and dark alleys than to stand in the open and face direct fire.

He was dreading this conversation, and realized he was allowing his thoughts to wander rather than deal with it.

Jeremy tugged at his uniform shirt, pulling it taut. He walked over to Hunter and together they watched the rack of long-range missiles being slid into place. Jeremy wasn't afraid to tell Hunter what he needed; he just didn't want to deal with the response he knew he'd get.

"Alright, Sir Chin, tell me what's on your mind." Hunter spoke without even shifting his gaze from the loader team above them.

"How do you know I'm not just here to wish you good luck?"

Hunter gave him a wry smile. "We've known each other for a couple of years now. The only time you voluntarily come into the 'Mech bay is when you can't put off your regularly scheduled training. Yet here you are."

"Point taken. You're right. I have come down here for a reason."

Jeremy looked away, then met Mannheim's gaze. "Once the fighting starts, I'll need to borrow a squad of Fidelis for a secondary mission."

Mannheim physically jerked away from Chin. "Please tell me this is one of your little jokes."

Jeremy shook his head.

"Damn it!" Hunter spat. "Those Protectorate forces outnumber us just by landing. Now you want to pull out a squad of our best troops at the last minute?"

"These are my orders from Redburn—no, from Stone himself. This is a necessary part of our mission here."

"Orders?" The older knight's face got red. "Orders from people who are not here. I have to deal with the situation at hand. We don't just have to fight these Protectorate attackers, we have to disengage them in battle—one of the hardest things you can do in a fight. You know that. You take off in your Fox and strip me of a squad, and you've cut me down by half a lance. I need those troops."

"You'll get them back," Jeremy said. "I just need them for a little while."

Hunter banged his fist on the leg of the *Shockwave*. "What if I say no?"

Chin had not considered that Mannheim might be defiant. It caught him off guard, and he actually stuttered for a moment, searching for words. "Redburn told you the ghosts have orders that supercede your mission objectives. This is one of those orders. I don't like it either. I met with Redburn and tried to find another way, but he's hung this on me, and I don't have a choice."

Mannheim said nothing for a heartbeat. "I like to think we always have a choice."

Chin didn't know what else to say. Then he remembered Hunter's conversation with Colonel Daum. "Hunter. You're a knight, and a soldier. You know we all have to follow orders."

Sir Mannheim closed the distance between the two men with a single long stride. He stood eye-to-eye with Chin, their faces only a few inches apart. Jeremy felt fear for the first time since the operation had begun. It was exciting and scary in the same instant. "I'm a good soldier. I'll cut the squad loose. You do whatever it is you have to do and get it done damn fast. I need you and them back in this fight. Do you understand?"

"I do."

"Good." He executed a sharp about-face and walked away. Jeremy watched him as he strode across the 'Mech bay. There was something in the way Hunter walked, carried himself, acted, that Chin found himself admiring. He closed his eyes for a moment. *If he's this mad with me taking a squad from him in battle, how will he react when he sees the full extent of our mission here?*

Interpretation of Duty 13

Brandenburg, Callison
Former Prefecture VIII
Fortress Republic (+38 days)

"**S**ir?" replied the voice of Captain Natel, coming over the speakers in the hard-shell field dome. "Say again."

Cheryl leaned over the portable communications unit and made sure her voice was crisp and clear. "You heard me, Captain. This is Midnight Angel to all units. The Light Horse is ordered to stand down. Authorization Alpha, Kappa, Psi, Zero, One. Disengage and fall back to your staging areas."

Fires still burned in the battle zone. The fighting had been focused on the warehouse district, and that's where the damage was the worst. She saw trails of smoke—gray, black, some white—twisting in the light breeze. Each a funeral pyre for the men and women who had died in the fighting there.

I could have struck sooner . . . maybe I should have. She shook her head. There was an even larger fire burning opposite the battlefield. Reports had been flooding in for the past hour that someone had bombed the governor's mansion. The flames were much higher than those on the battlefield. She could see the flicker of emergency-vehicle lights in that section of town. The mansion, perched on the high ground over the city, was fully engulfed. She had heard the rumble of collapsing timbers on her way back to the command post.

Other news reports were coming to her, not as commander of the militia but as the director of internal affairs. The Directorate investigators strongly believed the governor may have been killed in the fire. The lieutenant governor was missing, and she knew his loss would not affect the government. He had been a meaningless cog in the bureaucracy on Callison anyway. *It will be a long time before they find his body.* She should know. . . .

Her cease-fire orders to the Light Horse would quickly end the fighting. There were still a few things she had to wrap up. Switching to the broadband channel, she transmitted in the clear so that every member of both militaries would hear her words. "This is Cheryl Gunson, acting commander of the Callison Light Horse. I have ordered my troops to disengage. Sir Erbe, I request an immediate cease-fire. I additionally request a formal parlay."

She paused. There was no reply for a long few moments. Impatience began to rise. She had lied to the governor about him dying in order to meet with her—and kill her. Now she wondered if perhaps Kristoff Erbe had not survived the fighting. If not the knight, then what of Adamans, the Fidelis officer? Was she too late?

"This is Kristoff Erbe. I accept your cease-fire."

"I need two hours, Sir Erbe," she replied. "Then let's talk." It would take some time to be sworn in as governor—she would need to find a judge, and confirmation of Governor Stewart's death would have to be broadcast to the public. Formal assumption of the reins of power took time.

She met with Kristoff Erbe in the governor's offices in the city. The media covered this event with the same fervor they had shown for the chaos that had torn Callison apart. Cheryl greeted the knight in front of the media with a firm handshake, and escorted him personally into the governor's office. She took her seat behind the desk. Both of them still wore the dirt of the battlefield, though she had changed clothes for the hasty swearing-in ceremony. Her hair needed to be washed, but had been combed into a semblance of order. Her honored guest, Knight Errant Kristoff Erbe of The Republic, had pulled on an olive-drab jumpsuit stained with sweat. Neither of them cared. Both were so tired that for a long moment they said nothing. Erbe stared at her intently, then examined her blackened eye. His expression contained only curiosity.

"I saw the broadcast, Governor Gunson," he finally said, shattering the silence.

She allowed herself a tiny smile. "What happened to Governor Stewart was tragic. We have been looking for the lieutenant governor; if he can be found, I will step down and he can assume control of the government. In the meantime, under the law of Callison, I am forced to accept leadership of this world."

"They aren't going to find the lieutenant governor, are they?"

"I suppose it's possible. But I suspect it will be discovered that his health has failed him as well."

Erbe absorbed her words. "You have overthrown the government."

"I have done as I was ordered."

"Redburn ordered this?" Disbelief rang in his voice.

"My orders were to ensure that Callison remained a safe world, loyal to The Republic. I have interpreted those orders in this manner."

He was stunned. "I'm sure that Redburn never intended for you to seize control of the planet."

"My orders did not specify how I was to accomplish this goal. I was given full discretion as to how to proceed. Even the ghost paladin refused to advise me on how I might complete my mission."

"You staged a coup."

"I fulfilled my orders to the best of my ability, as did you."

"But why would you do this?"

"For Callison. For The Republic. Devlin Stone's message to Redburn said Callison is crucial to the survival of The Republic. We don't know why, but we couldn't risk it not being in Republic hands—I couldn't risk it remaining in the hands of Governor Stewart. Who better than a Knight of the Sphere to control the world and ensure that its people remain loyal and supportive of our cause?"

"People here hate The Republic." Governor Stewart had done a good job of turning public opinion against The Republic.

"People have been lied to," she reminded him. "In a few days, evidence will surface pointing to the deaths of the governor and lieutenant governor as part of a Marik-Stewart Commonwealth plot. I will tell the people that The Republic is our best hope for safety against their plans. I will tell them that my predecessor was misled by agents of the Commonwealth into thinking that The Republic had deserted them. In reality, The Republic is our future. In the end, most people hate change."

"I don't believe you're going to do this."

"Your belief is irrelevant. These were my orders to fulfill, not yours."

"You still don't know why this world was so important to The Republic's future?"

"No, but I have a guess. It's clear that our people will need a haven. Knights protecting the worlds outside of Fortress Republic will need a home, a place to rebuild. Callison can be that world. We will step up our armaments production, and over time institute a draft. The knights will be welcome here under the auspices of rotating in to protect us. The people—*my* people—will feel comfortable with that. It will buy us time to find out the truth as to why Stone felt this world was so damned important." She knew she was tired by her slip in using the word "damned" in reference to Stone's plans. She stretched, sliding against the leather of the massive chair. She realized that she must look even shorter than usual in the oversized office chair. *I guess I can have this replaced. I've changed everything else in the government.*

Kristoff studied her. "You're sure about this, m'lady? What can I do to help?"

She smiled. They were still peers, despite her new title. "I appreciate the offer. For what it's worth, this isn't exactly the solution I would have preferred; but it's the best I can do."

He leaned back in his own chair, the one she was used to sitting in. "For what it's worth, your solution is so unique it might just work."

"It has to."

"You have my support."

"Good," she replied, her eyes half-closed. "I have bent and broken enough rules for a week."

Sir Kristoff Erbe watched as the prime haulers maneuvered the DropShip engines to the *Redball Express 13* and began loading them into the transport. Across the tarmac, the remaining Fidelis and Republic troops loaded their equipment aboard the *Onondaga*. The midday sunshine poured through the clouds, and for the first time he found himself basking in the sun of Callison.

The media had turned Cheryl Gunson into a planetary hero. She used plain, simple terms to explain to the citizens how the Marik-Stewart Commonwealth had plotted to turn Callison against The Republic. Even Governor Stewart had been fooled, and when she uncovered the plot, Commonwealth agents had her killed. Those who had bought into Allison Stewart's carefully crafted anti-Republic message protested at first, but their opposition quickly died out when polls showed overwhelming support for The Republic. Kristoff assumed the polls had been doctored, but said nothing. Governor Gunson ruled Callison now, and he himself had publicly pledged to support and defend this world.

Adamans came up to him and handed him a note-puter. He surveyed the data. Their losses had topped thirty percent—fairly significant. The badly wounded would stay on Callison under Colonel Adamans' command; Erbe accompanied the DropShip engines to the rendezvous point. Adamans had shown no emotion when Kristoff related what he knew of Ceresco's actions. The Fidelis commander had simply crossed his arms and listened.

"I have received word that our people have arrived at this Fort Defiance. It is in rough shape, but can be repaired. We will begin work while you are gone." Fort Defiance was a mothballed military base in the Belvoir Plains. During the Jihad, it had served as one of Stone's many military bases. It had been empty for decades when Governor Gunson announced that she was turning it over to the Knights of the Sphere for their use. It might not be much now, but over time it would become a home. It had to be. The real home of the Republic troops was on the other side of the invisible wall of Fortress Republic. *Home is where we make it.*

Ceresco Hancock had altered Erbe's orders regarding the Callison militia materiel. In her role as governor, she was willing to provide the hardware to The Republic, but it would stay on-world and be moved to Fort Defiance. Related to this decision was the governor's stated intention to immediately increase the production of military hardware. Callison had both enemies and allies, and they would need all the gear they could lay their hands on. This decision ensured that the Light Horse would be refitted first with new gear, and it made the local population feel secure.

"We should be back in forty-eight days. Until that time, you are in command, Colonel," he replied.

"Very good, Sir Erbe. I will endeavor to serve well in your absence." He bowed his head.

"I know you will. Coordinate with the Light Horse commandant for supplies; find out if there's anything he can spare."

"If he cannot, I will avail myself of our mutual ally," he replied gravely.

"Will you and your troops be alright?"

"We will be fine. We have already salvaged much of the gear damaged in the battle and have begun repairs. We can replace all but the dead."

"Remarkable, Adamans."

"No, sir. We are simply doing what we were created for."

His words sent a chill down Kristoff's spine. "Very well," he replied, saluting the Fidelis officer. Kristoff headed toward the *Redball Express 13*, then paused and looked out past the spaceport. Beyond the hustle and bustle around him he could see the scars of the fighting. On a hill above the city stood the charred remains of the governor's mansion, a ruinous monument to the chaos perpetrated on Brandenburg.

If it happened here, what has happened across the rest of The Republic? He felt the chill return to his spine, and this time it stayed.

Price of Service 3

Breezewood, Kwamashu
Duchy of Andurien
Fortress Republic (+798 days)

"Welcome to luxurious Kwamashu," Chin said, extending his hand to his fellow knight. A chilly breeze stirred the air. Sir Mannheim accepted Chin's hand and shook it firmly. Their landing at the spaceport outside the city had been met with no fanfare or even interest on the part of the locals. Mannheim, per instructions from Chin, had marched his "Duchy" garrison unit along the outskirts of the city and into the designated industrial complex. It was a parade with no one watching.

The industrial complex was impressive even in its present run-down condition. At one time it had been tooled to assemble large industrial machines. There was a tank farm on the outlying edge of the complex sprouting a maze of pipes that served the two dozen buildings that made up the complex. The fence was mangled in some places, where someone searching for something of value had obviously attempted to break in. At one point it looked like it had been used as a dumping ground for abandoned vehicles, their rusted hulks dotting what used to be the employee parking lot. The moist air was filled with dust, and a suggestion of mold stung Sir Mannheim's nostrils. His company was assembled inside the largest of the buildings. The BattleMechs and a handful of vehicles had been fanned out to secure the perimeter.

"It's quiet."

"Breezewood is what you might call economically depressed. It never recovered from the beating it took in the Jihad; half the city is deserted, and the occupied half does not shelter the best citizens of the Inner Sphere," Chin replied, sarcasm twisting his voice. "The good news is that if you're into prostitutes, especially ugly ones hooked on drugs, this is the place for you."

Mannheim winced at the unsavory image conjured by Chin's grim humor. "I assume from the signal we received on approach that the local garrison commander believes your cover story?"

"More or less. He's not likely to be inviting us to dine with him anytime soon, but he has accepted my explanation of our presence here."

Mannheim didn't care if the man was happy with him being on Kwamashu or not. What mattered was that he believed they were part of the Duchy of Andurien's armed forces and that the local garrison would stay away from Breezewood. "Very good. What about the civilian population?"

"I hired a good-sized crew to clean out this portion of the plant. Most of the facility is in total shambles, but we got the roof repaired here and the offices are usable." He pointed to a staircase rising off the massive production floor that led to a balcony and office space beyond. "We finished up a few days ago."

"Was it wise to involve the locals?"

Chin smiled, his expression clearly stating "I have this under control, old man." Mannheim had only been separated from the ghost knight for a few weeks, but he'd gotten used to the lack of constant irritation he had felt when they were together. The younger knight just couldn't resist showing off. "This is part of my side of the business. Getting the locals in here, paying them with wages above the norm, circulating the right rumors about what we're doing here—it's all part of getting the attention of any intelligence operatives on the planet. Word will spread fast, especially from poor people who suddenly have money in their pockets."

It was worse than his usual cockiness: He was right. It was a good move. "What about billets for our troopers?"

"There's an office building adjacent to this structure, a yellow four-story building you passed as you entered the complex. The first two floors have been cleaned and set up for use as barracks. I wouldn't drink the water that comes from these pipes, but it's tested fine for showering."

As Mannheim looked around, he realized how far they were from home. Even though their JumpShip remained at the zenith jump point, rigged with a Duchy of Andurien transponder, with orders to recharge, sit and wait, it would take days to reach the JumpShip. And when they reached the JumpShip, they were still three jumps from the nearest prefecture.

We are strangers in a stranger land. It had been a long time since a Republic force had operated behind the lines of another government. If they ran into trouble, there was no one to come and help.

He quickly abandoned that line of thinking and turned his mind to the task at hand. They had already established a security screen around the complex. The next step was to create the illusion that work was being done to reactivate the plant.

"I studied the map of this facility on the way here, but it's obviously dated. Do you have anything current?"

Chin pulled out a datacube and tossed it at him. Mannheim had to scramble to catch it. "That gives you a full inventory of the assets at our disposal. For safety reasons, there are a number of the buildings that I marked as off-limits on the blueprints. They've been used to store stuff that may pose a biohazard if disturbed."

"Will they pose a problem when we create our simulated disaster?"

Chin looked away and shook his head. "No. Not at all."

Chin felt most comfortable wearing everyday working clothes. Ratty dungarees, a grubby maroon T-shirt and two days' worth of beard made it possible for him to blend in anywhere. Not bathing for a few days simply added an aromatic touch to his cover. *The key to successfully blending in is taking into account the little details.*

He had come back to New Bedford to plant rumors. He had been in several bars over the last two nights, letting the local grapevine pick up on the arrival of Mannheim's troops. While nothing had appeared in the local media, the word-of-mouth network was talking about it. He'd mention that he was in town from Breezewood, then the questions would start to fly. Flashing money and talking about his great new job refurbishing the assembly plant there also attracted attention.

He had a dossier of the government agents known to operate on Kwamashu, though he was quickly confirming how woefully out of date that list had become with the loss of the HPG network. Even working with old information, he was confident that he'd identified three or four potential spies. The real problem was that he couldn't be sure they were still in "the business." His job tonight was to follow up on one such case he'd identified a few days earlier, a man named Francis Kaff. He blended in pretty well with the bar clientele, nursing a dirty look and a half-empty glass of cheap whiskey. Chin slid onto a wobbly barstool two down from the potential spy, then spent a moment worrying that the stool wouldn't hold up.

The bartender provided Chin a drink for which he overpaid generously, enough that it caught the attention of the chronically uninterested bartender. "You plunkin' that down to keep the drinks flowing?"

He shook his head. "Nah, it's just a tip. I came into

some money recently. Might as well share the wealth."
He took a sip of his drink while the bartender eyed the
money cautiously, as if he suspected it was counterfeit.
Then he topped off Chin's drink, a gesture meant to
loosen up some more cash.

Chin held up his drink to toast the barkeep and made
eye contact with Kaff. He chugged another gulp of the
whiskey and felt the heat pulse through his body from
his stomach upward. Kaff nodded genially. "Come into
some cash, eh? Somebody die in your family?"

Money always worked as bait. Kaff was his: Only one
person could play off a spy so easily, and that was another spy. "Nope. I landed a job in Breezewood a few
weeks ago. The pay was incredible."

"Really," the Protectorate spy replied. "I heard there
were some jobs up in Breezewood, but figured it was
just the usual rumor mill."

Chin took a small sip of his whiskey and licked his
lips with mock satisfaction. "You heard the truth, bud.
They paid me four times the going wages for just a
week's worth of work, cleaning out parts of the old industrial plant up there. They told a bunch of us to come
back in three weeks and we can apply for jobs."

"Sounds like a sweet deal." Kaff figured that he was
the one doing the fishing and had just got a tug on his
line. That was the part that made Jeremy feel so great.

"It is at that." He practically beamed with pride. *No
need to rush and spill the beans early. Let him work for it.*

"I thought that old factory complex was being used
to store industrial wastes?"

"Ah, that was just rumors. In fact, they've moved in
some heavy equipment that came by special DropShip."

"What are they going to be building there—holovid
units?"

There it was. He had him. Chin was practically sweat-
ing with pride. His fish had been caught and had no
idea. "The supervisor up there said it was some sort of
military assembly plant. From what I saw of the military

units that arrived when we finished up, I think he was on the up-and-up."

"Wow. I wonder why they're building a tank assembly plant here?" Chin knew this ploy well, he had used it many a time: Jeremy hadn't mentioned tanks at all. Secret Agent Kaff was tossing his line a little farther out, hoping for a nibble.

"I don't know anything about tanks. What I heard was BattleMechs—that's one thing for sure I know they're planning on putting together there. I saw the gantry parts in crates myself."

"A 'Mech factory, huh?" Kaff pressed. "If they told you there'd be jobs, they must have some idea when they want it to go operational."

Badly overplayed, but Jeremy Chin didn't mind. "Yeah, as a matter of fact, they did say when they expected to go live." He finished his drink and clacked the glass on the bar. The whiskey burned as it went down. "You know, bartender, another round just might be in order."

The Protectorate spy threw back his own whiskey and emptied his glass. "I'll get this round, one for both of us." Jeremy figured he was good for a few more drinks before the dance was over, but the hard part was already done. He loved this part of his job. Given what he was going to have to do in Breezewood—no, *to* Breezewood—he relished this moment. This might be the last fun thing he got to do.

Sir Mannheim studied the layout of the factory complex and contemplated the task he faced. The old chair he sat in squeaked as he leaned over the former plant-manager's desk. Outside, he heard the beep-honk of a hovercar and the sounds of the ever-present wind whipping paper and trash up against the chain-link fence. Breezewood may have had charm, but it was decades in the past. The city, like the factory, had been left to rot. The locals he had met took their cue from his uniform and the colors of his 'Mech and assumed he led a Duchy military unit. They didn't offer him any particular respect. Some panhandled from his sentries while others attempted to apply for jobs that didn't exist. They were turned away. One tossed a bottle at the guards.

None of those things meant they deserved to have war brought to them.

If all went as planned, he would be blowing up this city within the city when the Oriente Protectorate landed and made its move on Breezewood. His command was going to have to make a good fight of it despite their intention to fall back and blow up the mock plant.

Even defending the abandoned factory was going to take some doing, if only for a short time. Urban combat was the worst kind of combat, and since he needed to keep attackers out of the plant until he could evacuate it and blow it up, he needed special defenses. His combat engineers from the Fidelis had begun to construct roadblocks to restrict movement into the plant grounds. Bunkers were being put up to provide defense. Mannheim ordered a few key roadways open so that he could get his troops out—but without knowing from which way the attack was going to come, setting effective defenses was going to be difficult.

The door to the office opened, and within a second the night breeze cut the room's temperature in half. Jeremy Chin stepped through the door. Mannheim could tell instantly that he had been drinking. His eyes were half-closed and his cheeks were red, and not from the wind. He caught a faint scent of whiskey as Chin swayed into the room and slammed the door shut behind him.

"Out celebrating, Sir Chin?" He was fiercely glad for his opportunity to be sarcastic.

Chin frowned. "No. I was out doing my job."

"Ah. Your job must include getting drunk, then."

"It *is* part of the job when you are planting information," Chin replied, flopping into an old office chair. The back on the chair was only loosely attached; he tipped dramatically backward but caught himself at the last minute.

"The life of a ghost knight is obviously more difficult than I imagined."

Chin contented himself with an evil-sounding chuckle in response. The drunken happiness faded to a grim expression. "Trust me, Sir Mannheim, you don't know the half of it. What are you doing up, anyway?"

"Going over the plant layout, double-checking where I've posted sentries."

"Just like a good Boy Scout," Chin replied curtly. "I'm sure that Devlin Stone would be proud of you."

"Don't talk ill of Stone. If it wasn't for him, we wouldn't be here."

Chin didn't seem impressed. "True enough. And it was his vision that brought us to Breezewood, the fat flapping hairy-ass armpit of the Duchy of Andurien. Damn wannabe government. Another freaking Marik-in-the-closet."

"You would be wise to hold your tongue. We're bringing war to these people. Whatever you think of this planet and the Duchy, no one deserves that."

Chin's face clouded with anger. "Don't lecture me. I'm not one of your kids. I know what we're doing. I know a lot more about what we're doing than you do."

Chin made a mistake by mentioning Mannheim's children. Hunter rose to his feet. "Watch your mouth, boy. You may be a knight, but that doesn't mean you're exempt from good manners. I turned my back on my family, my children, to be here."

There was an awkward pause as the two men glared at each other. Jeremy Chin looked away first. "Forget it, Sir Mannheim. I didn't mean anything by it. It's just been stressful. I haven't been in the field in more than two years."

There was something more eating at the younger knight, that much Hunter could see. Something even the alcohol couldn't pry out of him, though it had come

close. "I'm tired, too. I have to admit that I'm not en-
joying this mission myself."

"You'd better try to enjoy it now. It's going to get
much, much worse." Chin rose and waved his hand. "I'm
outta here. See you in the morning." He flung open the
door and another ice-cold breeze cut into the office until
the door closed on the night.

"What in hell do you mean by that?" Hunter Mannheim asked the closed door.

Interpretation of Duty 4

Light Horse Barracks
Brandenburg, Callison
Former Prefecture VIII
Fortress Republic (+16 days)

Riots are ugly things that rarely start out as a raging mob. They usually start as a peaceful gathering that cascades out of control. The riot outside the Brandenburg barracks of the Callison Militia started as a peaceful protest, with a few picketers carrying signs that said BETRAYERS! and TRAITORS! There were verbal taunts of the Light Horse infantry who protected the garrison in the middle of the city. One of the protesters had simply mooned the guards, to a roaring laugh from the crowd.

The barracks was a small city within the city covering ten blocks near the center of the planetary capital. It was walled off by a thick battlement that seemed more suited to an earlier time; a determined MechWarrior taking well-placed shots could blast through the wall in a matter of minutes. The buildings beyond the wall, redbrick construction with metallic roofs painted dark green, were very old, most dating back to the Star League era. Ivy grew up the walls of the structures and on the white pillars of some of the buildings. There were five gates leading into the complex, each of which gathered more infantry as the mob outside grew. Cheryl had visited the complex once during her rapid rise in the Directorate and had come away with the impression that she had visited a living museum.

The crowd continued to grow. Cheryl knew that some of the people joining the protest were being paid by the government—unofficially, of course. She knew this because she had organized the covert payments herself. The people she had hired were mostly criminals or police, both groups prone to violence. They mingled with the ordinary citizens gathering outside of the barracks, slyly escalating the crowd's anger and frustration. Some planted rumors that Legate Leif was planning a coup now that The Republic had collapsed. Someone brought an effigy of the legate hoisted on a tall pole so that the crowd could see it. The life-size mannequin was lighted on fire to the rising cheers of the audience.

Cheryl cringed. This had not been part of her instructions. Someone in the audience had taken initiative and it was working, whipping the crowd into a full-fledged angry mob. She stood across from Gate Three of the complex on M Street and adjusted her sunglasses. With a scarf pulled over her head and the largish sunglasses, no one would identify her as anything other than an ordinary bystander. She looked like anyone else on the street. Only she knew that looks were where that ended.

She heard the BattleMech stir inside the barracks before she saw it. She was intimately familiar with the sound of a 'Mech's metal feet on ferrocrete, the low rumble of each step. At first, the crowd didn't hear it. By the time they realized what they were hearing, it was already in full view. Cheryl knew that under typical circumstances, the crowd would back off at the sight of the *Hellion* stepping into view. There was a moment's hesitation. Then a hail of bottles and rocks flew through the gate and fell on the infantry on the other side.

The infantry produced riot shields and pulled back a meter or two. Glass shattered as bottles hit the ground and the shields, but they held their ground. A handful of citizens stepped forward, grabbed the steel gate and began shaking it. Soon there was a mass of humanity pressed up against the gate.

A prime hauler, a flatbed truck used to transport 'Mechs, rumbled out next to the *Hellion* and stopped. High in the truck bed stood several infantry, rifles at the ready, and Legate Leif. He wore his full dress uniform and carried a bullhorn to address the crowd. "Please step away from the gate. This is a Republic military installation. Disburse immediately." His sentences were to the point.

They did nothing to mollify the crowd.

Boos roared as he spoke, drowning out his final comment. The legate was far enough back that the thrown bottles, rocks and other debris didn't reach him, but it was obvious his appearance and orders would do nothing to dispel the mob. The crowd continued to rock Gate Three, and she heard a metallic grinding noise; they had damaged the gate's control mechanism.

From her position kitty-corner across from the gate, Cheryl watched. The riot would reach a crescendo soon. She could feel it. More people showed up as the news media broadcast the event. Most simply showed up to see what was happening. Some got caught up in the emotional reaction and were suddenly part of the yelling and throwing. Others who wanted to leave couldn't. She watched a media VTOL sweep along the street from several hundred feet up, filming the event as it unfolded. She adjusted her scarf over her head. Anonymity was important.

Cheryl didn't see where it came from, but caught a glimpse of flame in mid-flight. A Molotov cocktail. The wine bottle with its flaming cloth wick flew over Gate Three and shattered in front of the line of infantry, followed by four more. Wine splashed onto riot shields and they were momentarily sheeted with flames. The infantry reflexively dropped them and retreated a few steps, seeking cover behind their comrades. The entire line of infantry took a coordinated step back as the flames ran along the ground and black smoke swirled upward. The shouts of the mob increased at the sight of the smoke and glimmer of fire.

Someone in the militia pulled out a high-power hose and hit the fire then sprayed the protestors at the gate. There was no follow-through, and she assumed it was just one soldier who thought that the hose would solve the problem. For a moment, it seemed to have an effect. The gathered wall of humanity at the gate reeled back. Some people fell. There was screaming. Others who couldn't see jumped to the conclusion that the infantry was opening fire on the protestors. Cheryl's heart began to race. Using the fire hose on the crowd would definitely make things worse.

"I order you to disburse immediately," boomed the voice of the legate.

Cheryl saw a club drift past her field of vision, then another. Someone was bringing in the material necessary to turn the mob into a full-on riot. She wasn't surprised; she only wondered why she hadn't seen them earlier, given the mood of the crowd. Larger objects were shuffled forward. The hose was shut off as a new wave of rocks and bottles rained down on the infantry.

"I call on you as loyal citizens of The Republic to please leave this area now." Cheryl heard the worry in his voice, though she wondered if anyone else recognized the change in his tone.

A battering ram made out of a lamppost appeared out of nowhere. She saw the back end of it through the throng and heard the metallic clang of it hitting the fence. Cheryl could see the top of Gate Three and watched it rock under the impact. Each strike rocked it farther away from its hinges. A continuing onslaught of thrown rocks kept the infantry from reinforcing the gate on the inside.

She heard the distinctive cracking noise of a gunshot. The crowd must have thought it was the gate breaking, because no one appeared to panic. With a metallic thud the gate dropped, and she heard more shots ring out. The mass of humanity at the gate flooded through like liquid when a bottle is uncorked. People rushed the squad of troopers; the protestors who tried to turn around when they heard the gunfire were caught in the mass of people pushing forward. She heard cheers and saw puffs of smoke rising from the area near the gate.

The *Hellion* stepped backward, probably the last time it would be able to move without risk of crushing the protestors. The crowd began shouting. Clubs were raised. She saw one man with a pistol in his hand charge forward.

The Brandenburg barracks had been breached. She lost track of the legate in the chaos, but saw people scrambling onto the prime hauler. The Republic flag dropped nearly to the bottom of the flagpole, then was sent back to half-mast in flames. Ash flew away in the afternoon breeze; when the remains fell, a cluster of enraged protestors stomped them into the dust. It tore at her. Was this what was happening across the rest of The Republic? How could people so easily turn against Stone's vision? She turned away to avoid looking at the charred remains of the flag on the ferrocrete.

The shooting stopped when the crowd spread out as it rushed into the barracks complex. The sound of windows breaking accompanied screams of rage. Cheryl repeated to herself that all this was necessary for the survival of The Republic. She clung to that fact. What was occurring at this moment would pass.

A body dropped to the ground in front of the destroyed gate. The mob milled around it, hitting it with clubs, kicking it, spitting on it. The dark green uniform was soaked with blood. Cheryl didn't need to step forward to see who it was. The hostility of the rioters told her that Legate Leif was dead. It didn't matter whether he had been shot in the rush on the gate or bludgeoned to death by the mob. The riot had accomplished its heinous goal, the public murder of an official leader of The Republic. Guilt roiled in her stomach.

Turning away from the carnage, Cheryl melted into the press of bystanders on the edge of the mob. She heard the rotors of the media VTOL thumping above the scene as she walked away. They would have what they wanted, a story, an image for the news. Events here today would shock some, but others would cheer. For a moment Cheryl Gunson, ghost knight of The Republic, despised herself.

She tossed her scarf into a public trash container on the way back to her office. She discarded her sunglasses on a public bench; she knew someone would pick them up and take them. Her coat went into the donation box for the local branch of the Common Relief Agency. Nothing remained to tie her to any image that might surface from the riot.

The agency was swamped with calls. The riot was being shown on all of the public-area monitors. The police had managed to contain the crowd, and had broken up the riot once word spread of the legate's death. Two of the larger barracks buildings had been set on fire, but the Republic troops already had the situation under control. No deaths other than the legate had been reported, though many rioters were being treated for minor injuries. She personally contacted the precinct captain nearest the barracks to help ensure that the military hardware stayed with the Republic troops. The last thing they needed was a petty robber using a shoulder-launched SRM to commit his crimes.

She assigned two of her top infiltration experts to begin reviewing footage of the riot, demanding that they come up with the names of those responsible for inciting the peaceful protest to become a mob. This was a necessary lie. In reality, Cheryl had no need to be told the names of those responsible for the riot, because she was one of them. She wouldn't have been surprised to learn the governor herself had made arrangements regarding the mob. The fact that the protestors were provided with clubs, guns and a battering ram indicated a certain level of organization typical of managed riots: She had coordinated these types of events herself in her work as a ghost knight, and so she knew that the necessary equipment would always show up, even if she didn't arrange for it herself.

What had she expected? She slumped into her chair and closed her eyes. She had paid for people to prod the crowd into a riot. A part of her had hoped that it would be the Light Horse militia that overreacted: If they opened fire on the crowd and massacred innocent citizens, the media would have a field day. Cheryl couldn't be sure at what point matters had taken on a life of their own.

Cheryl sighed and massaged the bridge of her nose, realized that it didn't matter whose plan it had been. Ultimately, it didn't matter who paid whom to shoot whom. It didn't matter that the lives of innocent and not-so-innocent people were destroyed. *What I've done, I've done as part of my orders. What I've done was necessary for the survival of The Republic.* She repeated those two phrases like a mantra, but it did nothing to soothe her headache.

Her screen beeped twice, indicating a priority call. She sat up in her chair, her eyes burning and her face deeply lined with fatigue. She activated the monitor, and the image of Governor Stewart appeared. The portly woman's face revealed no emotion as she stared at her director of internal affairs.

"The incident at the barracks was unfortunate." If her words were recorded, they would not reveal her own involvement. *Many hands are bloodied that were never at the barracks.*

"I was in the area when the riot began and saw the tragedy for myself," Cheryl said, choosing her words equally carefully.

"It is unfortunate that Legate Leif was killed in the fighting, but we must feel glad that his was the only fatality." The governor sounded neither sad nor happy.

"The police have restored order, and already my people are looking into this event."

"Which is as it should be, Cheryl. I appreciate your attention to detail today. I always reward people for showing initiative, and I value your actions."

Valued actions. The words swam in her head. "I only did what was necessary, Governor" . . . *for the survival of The Republic.* "Nothing more, nothing less."

Overture 3

New Earth
Prefecture X, Republic of the Sphere
Fortress Republic (-91 days)

The room was just as Damien Redburn remembered it—eclectic. Most people would have described it as a museum rather than a greeting chamber. It was a domed room with white walls broken up into pielike segments by deep arches made of some dark wood. The high ceiling created the sense of a churchlike space. There were a few unmatched chairs, each one distinct enough to mark it as an artifact of some sort. The back of one was emblazoned with the up-thrust fist of the Lyran Commonwealth. On the walls were war trophies, many of which would evoke memories of anger and hate in any viewer.

There were battle standards, flags taken from command 'Mechs or vehicles. Many bore the symbol of the Word of Blake. A bent and mangled sword bearing the emblem of the Federated Suns hung above a pristine dress dirk marked with old paint that was distinctly Capellan. A battle kilt, Black Watch Pattern Number 2, hung with distinction in a case, bloodstains still showing on its fringe. There was a piece of a 'Mech, a chunk of torn and blasted torso armor, that bore the painted emblem of the Star League, the Cameron Star. In a small wall case were the codexes of several Clan warriors, obviously wrenched from them in battle. There was a burned banner taken from a Word of Blake reeducation camp mounted under glass on one of the wall segments. The words on it were eerie: TRUTH THROUGH UNDERSTANDING. That was the last thing the Word of Blake had been interested in, understanding. It was signed by the warriors who had recovered it—or had they raided the camp, or had they lived there and been rescued? Redburn didn't remember the details of the story as he had been told before.

Given the past of the Fidelis, he knew he shouldn't have been surprised to see the artifacts of the Jihad and times previous. The Fidelis had been through a lot, more than nearly any other people. They had a right to this room, their greeting chamber, as a memory to that proud past. Stone had struck a dangerous bargain with them, and now Redburn knew the time had come for him to collect on it.

The custos of the Fidelis came into the room slowly. He had a limp that had gotten worse since the last time Redburn had visited him. The custos wore a black military uniform strained by the massive frame it covered. His head was bald, eliminating the gray hairs that Redburn remembered in his sideburns last time they had talked. One eye was gone, replaced with a metallic socket and bionic replacement. The same with one arm. It appeared roughly human, but the color of the skin no longer matched the wearer. The custos wore a cape as well, black with a gray lining. Behind him walked an aide-de-camp with noteputer in hand. The other officer seemed dwarfed by the leader of the Fidelis.

He reached out and shook Damien's hand. The former exarch felt as if his hand were dwarfed in his host's grip. "It pleases me that you have come to see us again, Exarch Redburn." His voice was deep and did not betray his age. "On behalf of my people, I tell you we are honored."

Redburn bowed his head in respect. "I am no longer the exarch, Custos."

"I know a new man holds that mantle," the man in black replied. "But there is no such thing as a former exarch in my mind. The title is yours for life, at least in my eyes."

Damien allowed himself a smile. "I appreciate that. I'm pleased to see that you stay current with the affairs of The Republic outside your sanctuary here." He waved his hand to indicate the room but symbolically spoke of the entire island where the Fidelis lived. It had been given to them by Devlin Stone. New Earth had been hit early in the Jihad by a bioweapon that had killed hundreds of thousands; afterward, no one wanted to live on Mopelia Island. It had cities, factories, farms, ports—everything needed to support a culture, but the ghosts of that bioweapon struck fear in the citizens of New Earth. The island had proven a safe place for the Fidelis. They could live there and take advantage of a massive infrastructure and not bother with the rest of the world.

The Custos offered a wide smile. "That is how I know you have not come on a social visit. But where are my manners? Would you like something to drink? As I recall, you prefer tea. If matters are what I think they are, you may ask for something stronger. Northwind Scotch, perhaps?" His aide stepped forward, but Redburn waved him off.

"I appreciate the offer, Custos," he replied. "As with so many things lately, time is of the essence. To be blunt, I am here on the authority of Exarch Levin to formally request the assistance of the Fidelis." Reaching into his jacket pocket, he pulled out a datacube and offered it to the custos.

"If that is a confirmation of your orders from Exarch Levin, I do not need to see it."

Redburn withdrew the cube, and his host continued.

"You would not lie about such a thing. No man would dare." He chuckled, and Damien understood. To cross the Fidelis was to toss one's life away. "If you say the exarch needs us, then it is so."

Redburn knew their past and was always caught off guard by their trust in him. *After what they have been through, you would think he'd demand an audience with Levin to confirm.* This was the famed resolve of the Fidelis, that bond to The Republic that even he could not fully comprehend.

"What I am asking for is a great deal." Redburn phrased his words carefully.

"We are bound to our oath. Our lives are forfeit if necessary to fulfill our destiny. Tell me what you need and you will have it."

"Troops and equipment," Redburn said without hesitation. "The exarch has assigned me a role in which I will be commanding several knights on missions to ensure the long-term safety of The Republic. I am in need of combined-arms special operations forces that can integrate with loyal Republic troops. They will operate with little logistical support in a wide range of theaters of combat."

The custos' single human eye widened in excitement, as if he wanted to go himself, but the gentle tug of the years restrained his enthusiasm. "The Fidelis are suited to these missions. As you know, our warriors train first as technicians, then they are elevated to infantry and eventually to armored infantry operations. Our next level is the Jägers, vehicle operations. They are trained to perform every role in a crew and gain experience on a wide range of vehicles. Only then are they trained as MechWarriors. Then they may take assignment anywhere in the Century."

"Century?"

"Our Century is our one hundred best warriors plus their augmenting trainees. We always have a Century ready for service to The Republic. The Century consists of two Battlegroups, consisting of three Umbras each."

"Your organizational structure is different from the Republic ranks."

The custos waved his beefy hand as if to dispel the concern. "We will adapt. Adaptation is something the Fidelis understand and embrace. Indeed, it is the ability to change to fit the environment that has allowed us to survive as a people. An Umbra is similar to a Company of 'Mech forces and combined arms. It will not be an issue."

Redburn understood the comment. Stone had told him the history of the Fidelis, and he appreciated the meta-morphosis they had endured to remain a cohesive collective. A part of him wished he could have shared the story of the Fidelis with Jonah Levin, but he knew that would have been the wrong choice. Levin might be hesitant to use these people, given that past. It was best that he didn't know the *full* truth.

"We will need the appropriate hardware and DropShips as well, Custos," he said.

"We are fully equipped. However, you must understand that Fidelis warriors personally configure even their sidearms. Most of our BattleMechs have been highly modified to fit each warrior's fighting style and skills. Such is the nature of special forces. If you can advise me regarding the types of missions you are planning, I can ensure you get an equipment mix that meets your needs."

Redburn pulled out a noteputer and handed it to the custos. On the previous occasion when he had visited the Fidelis, he had been given a tour of their facilities. Their 'Mech and vehicle assembly plants were small but achieved an unsurpassed level of quality. He assumed Stone had given them access to technology and tools that had been demilitarized elsewhere. *It makes you wonder what other capabilities they have.*

The hulking figure of the custos carefully read through The Republic's requirements, his bionic eye narrowing as if he were concentrating a beam on the noteputer. The Fidelis leader poked at the controls to scroll down.

"I see," he muttered, handing it back to Redburn. "It appears that The Republic is entering a time of change."

"Our strategic goal is to keep our would-be enemies focused elsewhere for awhile," Damien answered.

"Admirable," he replied. Turning, the custos motioned for his aide-de-camp to come forward. The aide stood firmly at attention next to the towering custos. "The Venator Battlegroup is most likely the best choice for these operations. Contact Group Commander Adamans immediately and tell him to begin mobilization of his forces. I will bring him the details when I'm done here." The aide clicked his heels in salute, bowed slightly and left the room.

"There is more," Redburn said cautiously.

"Of course," the custos replied, as if he already anticipated the request.

"I know that you have a WarShip in storage. The exarch has need of it. He gave me a set of coordinates where the ship can go to receive its assignment."

"*The Flatus* is a significant asset. You would not have asked if times did not demand it. Very well. Provide me with the coordinates, and I will have her reactivated and readied."

"I thank you, Custos," Redburn said, bowing his head again. "There is more, though, something that exceeds the requests I have made for hardware. This is about the people. It is something I cannot tell you in detail but must make you aware of to the extent I can."

"You have piqued my curiosity," the massive man replied. "That is no small achievement. Tell me more."

"Times are about to change in The Republic," Redburn said carefully. He and Levin had covered the details for Fortress Republic in detail. A decision had been made about how much he could tell the leader of the Fidelis. He would have to be vague; a core competency of a politician.

"The troops that go with us will suffer losses. Circumstances may arise where it is impossible for me to have them rejoin your community here. I wanted to tell you this before you assigned troops to these missions."

"For some of my officers, this will not be an issue. Family is more of an abstract concept to them. Only the Fidelis are *true* family. I will meet with Adamans and ensure that those who go are strong enough to withstand separation from us. This does, however, open another point. So far, you are my only contact with The Republic. If you cannot return to us, how will I continue to serve the exarch?"

"I have told Exarch Levin about you, but nothing of your origins. I have told him where you are and given him some of the security protocols necessary to contact you. If he has need for you in the future, he will contact you directly."

The custos held his chin in thought for a moment. "We have only met twice before, but I have come to know you as a friend. From what you say, you will not be returning. This, then, is good-bye, is it not?"

Redburn recognized the farewells that he carried and spread like a plague carrier. He had seen that message in the faces of the knights he commanded. *Fortress Republic has that effect on people.*

"I'd like to think we'll see each other again, but I believe that will not be the case," he said. "The changes coming to The Republic are dramatic." It was an understatement—another political skill Redburn found himself tapping.

"I am old," the custos said. "Some might say beyond my years. I have seen good men and women come and go. I should be numb to it. In my youth, I was. I sent many good fighters to their death, and at the time was proud of my actions. I will miss you, Damien Redburn. You inherited a nightmare in the offing and came through with dignity. I will miss you."

Redburn felt his face tinge red. "I am glad to be here now. I'm glad that I'm the one who has set you on your path to freedom. When the Fidelis complete this task, you are free of your bond to The Republic. The past will be buried once and for all. Ever since Stone told me of the ordeal of your people, I hoped secretly that I would get this chance. I just wish it hadn't come at such a price."

"My people will be able to step into the light. That is all I live for," he said, with conviction that seemed to come from his very bones. "Our bond is still in place. Our duty is to protect The Republic, and we will do this, even if it is to the last man or woman. The Fidelis will fulfill the destiny of the Black Book. My people will one day achieve that for which we were created." He reached out and again took the hand of the former exarch.

"You are setting us on the path to freedom. I thank you."

BOOK 2

Exarch Jonah Levin's Address to the Citizens of The Republic
1 October 3135

In the past few years, The Republic has been on a slow, steady slide toward the edge of an abyss. The catalyst for this slide was the loss of the hyperpulse generator network, and thus the loss of interstellar communications—lifeblood to any star-spanning nation.

Chaos, created by the Blackout, was compounded by our own fears, our prejudices and especially by our greed. Weaknesses we thought we had vanquished. Weaknesses we deceived ourselves into believing could ever be eliminated from human nature.

During this time of trials and tribulations, we have all witnessed the best and worst that everyone—anyone, citizen or resident, peerage or proletariat—had to offer. We found greatness. And frailty. We discovered new allies, new enemies and the depth of our own resolve to take a new and stronger hand in our own lives, our futures and our destinies.

And if there was a failure, it was our failure. The failure of those of us entrusted to safeguard Devlin Stone's great legacy.

And now. And now . . .

There is nothing more to say, nothing more to endeavor, that we have not said or attempted in the last ten months. So it is with great sorrow but firm resolve that we put to you, the people of the Republic of the Sphere, that the time has come for drastic and irrevocable action.

To save what we can for the future.

With this goal, by the authority vested in me as exarch of the Republic of the Sphere, in accordance with the War Powers Act of 3082 and the Emergency Powers and Crisis Management Amendment of 3107, I have committed this nation to the following course:

First: Prefecture X is expanded, by decree, to include worlds on the list appended to this transmission. These worlds will sever immediately all economic and political ties to their former prefectures. World governors and military legates of these newly attached systems will consider themselves under the direct control of Terra and the exarch or his appointed representative.

Second: All military forces able to be safely recalled and mustered for the ensured survival of The Republic have been relocated within the borders of Prefecture X and will not be forward-deployed until such time as is deemed appropriate.

Third: Following this final address, there will be no further contact, by transmission or transport, between Prefecture X and *any* outside world or power. This self-imposed interdiction will be enforced by the most severe military means necessary.

Fourth and last: Full faith and sovereignty of the Republic of the Sphere is now invested solely within Prefecture X. All other prefectures are released to the full and sovereign control *of their people*, to decide for themselves how best to weather the coming storms.

These commands, by design and effect, do hereby constitute a New Republic Territory, under the direct and complete aegis of Terra.

And formally dissolve the Republic of the Sphere.

I cannot help, in this dark and uncertain time, but to think of what we all have lost. To imagine the terrible and far-reaching consequences of this day's actions. But there is nothing more we can do, for now, except to pray that we may yet persevere and preserve the light that has guided us for so long; to hold onto the faith that has carried us so far.

The Republic was more than a dream of utopia. It was an ideal. One which we were challenged to live up to each and every day. That bright fire may have been reduced to a guttering flame, but it shall never be extinguished. And the fire shall return! The Republic may be absent for a time, but know this and remember it well:

We are all Keepers of the Flame.

Price of Service 2

New Bedford, Kwamashu
Duchy of Andurien
Fortress Republic (+787 days)

New Bedford was only a hundred and twelve kilometers from Breezewood, but the cities were light-years apart in the degree to which they'd recovered from the Jihad. New Bedford had undergone a renaissance; lush green parks and plant-bordered walkways lined the roads leading from the spaceport to the heart of the city, and there were signs of economic recovery everywhere he looked. From what he knew about Breezewood, it was considerably more run-down.

Chin adjusted his uniform. Made of a rather stiff material, it was a lighter green than the infantry uniforms of The Republic. The advantage of this uniform, however, was that it was a uniform of the Duchy of Andurien. He wore the rank of lieutenant colonel; that and the uniform, along with the fake set of orders he carried, was all he needed. Everything else was merely part of the show, an act he would put on for those he met. It was the part of being a ghost knight that he liked the most—creating the illusion of being someone else, living in another identity. He smiled, then the grin faded as he realized that with the mission orders he had to fulfill, he would most likely live under a false identity for the rest of his life.

It had taken some work to obtain the uniform and falsified identification papers. The character he was playing, Lieutenant Colonel Thomas Gelder, hadn't existed until a few weeks ago. Now, he possessed a rich and detailed history in the military databases of the Duchy of Andurien; life details and background that Chin had thoroughly memorized. The real test would be selling his character to the planetary garrison commander.

The hovercab pulled up to the military headquarters, and Chin paid his fare. He got out of the car and walked briskly to the building, just like any other officer reporting for duty. Guards stopped him at the door, checked his ID and scanned him and his dull brown leather satchel. He was unfazed by this activity. He presented his falsified orders and was delivered to the planetary garrison commander, Colonel Daum.

A sergeant escorted him through a maze of gray corridors. He was taken down an elevator, dropping at least four stories underground, and through more twisting, poorly lit hallways before reaching the colonel's office. The receptionist's desk was empty. The sergeant knocked on the interior door and stood aside for Chin to enter at the colonel's invitation. *So far, so good. The ID held water, since they didn't lead me to a holding cell.*

Colonel Daum was as expected based on his profile in the ghost knight archives. He had lost more hair since the last holoimage of him had been placed in the file; the top of his head seemed to shine in the dull fluorescent lights of the windowless room. He was skinny, in his mid-fifties, and had a firm handshake. They exchanged the usual pleasantries and introductions. Chin sat down on the far side of the dreary government-issue desk that was covered with piles of papers and forms awaiting the garrison commander's attention. Jeremy handed over his orders to the colonel and watched him read through the materials.

"Command is really going to do this to us?" Daum asked, laying the forged orders on his desk.

"Yes, sir. I probably don't have to tell you that everything about this mission is classified, including your orders regarding it."

Daum seemed unmoved. "Why am I only now being told? We're going to be reconstituting a BattleMech assembly facility on my planet and I only get word of it now? Seems a little strange, doesn't it, Lieutenant Colonel?"

For the first time since he had taken on this role, he felt challenged. Chin's experience and training kicked in, and he responded calmly. "Sir, I think we can both agree that military secrets are some of the hardest to keep, and Kwamashu is positioned very near the Oriente Protectorate. How do you think they would react if they knew we were going to open this facility?"

"I know how *I* would react."

"There you have it. We need to establish the facility quickly, so that by the time their spies pick up on what we are doing, it will be too late for them to interfere."

"Sounds like a neat package, all wrapped up, easy for you and the rest of the upper command staff," Colonel Daum said, leaning back in his chair.

"I'm not following you, sir."

"Of course not. You're coming here to execute a little sea gull leadership: You fly in, crap all over the place, then leave. That's all I ever get from high command. Meanwhile, I'm left here with this new factory and, as you so kindly pointed out, the Protectorate ready to pounce on Kwamashu. Bottom line, Lieutenant Colonel Gelder: It's my people who have to defend this world and pick up the pieces long after you are gone." By the end of his speech, the colonel was leaning over his desk and tapping a blunt finger on Chin's orders. He was angry; Chin heard years of experience and bitterness in his voice.

"I understand, sir."

"Do you?" Daum challenged. "Based on your age, I

doubt you've had the experience to really understand."
Anger still tinged his words, but Chin had other concerns. *Does he see through my cover?*

"Sir, that is precisely why a company of special troops is being sent down to garrison Breezewood and the assembly plant. For security reasons, they will remain in Breezewood and will not intermingle with your force. The last thing we need is for word to leak out prematurely about the plant. They will provide local security in Breezewood and be available to coordinate with you in the event of an attack by a hostile government."

Daum flicked the edge of the orders and the paper slid across the table toward Chin. "I saw that in the orders. I notice that no one saw fit to have these troops actually report to me in the event of hostilities. This 'coordination' that you assume will happen will be tricky. The priority of these special troops is to protect that plant. My responsibility is to the people of the Duchy who live on Kwamashu."

"Sir, this new assembly plant is a key piece in the future of the Duchy. Defending Kwamashu and defending the plant are one and the same."

Daum grinned. "Junior officers. You all see it the same way. So simple on paper. Tell me, Lieutenant Colonel, have you commanded men in battle?"

His cover profile said that he had led troops in battle only once. It was not an impressive part of his character's background. "Yes, Colonel Daum, I have."

"How many times?"

"Once, sir."

"Pahh—" He brushed the air dismissively. "You're still wet behind the ears. I've led men and women into battle a dozen times. I've learned that orders like these, left to interpretation, will cause more problems than they solve. If the Oriente Protectorate does come, mere coordination isn't going to be enough. And you can tell your superiors that I will do what is necessary to protect the people of Kwamashu—regardless of this assembly plant."

Chin heard the message loud and clear. "That won't be necessary, sir. I doubt the Protectorate will even dare strike at us here."

Colonel Daum cocked his eyebrow. "Then why bring in additional troops just to protect the plant?"

"Point taken, sir."

The Duchy commander seemed satisfied that he had gotten his point across to the younger officer. "Very well. Per the orders you delivered, I will not do anything to attract attention to Breezewood; you and your forces will land there, set up this plant and garrison it."

"Thank you, sir," he said, rising.

"Don't thank me yet," Daum replied. "You've never been to Breezewood, have you?"

"No."

Daum chuckled. "You'll see that you have your work cut out for you."

"Sir?"

"That abandoned industrial complex you're planning on reactivating? It's the worst part of Breezewood, which enjoys a reputation as the armpit of Kwamashu. After the Word of Blake's bombing runs destroyed the city during the Jihad, most of it was left to rot. We've been shipping our industrial waste down there for years and storing it in that plant. You'll have your work cut out for you getting it operational again."

"I appreciate the heads-up," he said, offering a salute. Daum returned it.

"Don't take this the wrong way, Gelder," the colonel added as Chin reached the door. "But I hope I don't see you again."

"Sir?" he turned back.

"If I do, that means the Protectorate or someone else has landed on planet."

"Yes, sir," Jeremy replied. "Let's hope that never happens."

Training Center Opal
Bernardo
Former Prefecture VI

Sir Mannheim watched as the Sylph battle-armor troops came swooping down on the *Locust*. It was only an exercise, but he was consistently impressed by the focus and effort the Fidelis put into everything they did. He had seen Sylph armor in action before, but these troopers handled the flight-capable armor with a degree of skill he would not have thought possible. Two of the Fidelis troopers landed right on top of the moving *Locust*, their augmented hands scrambling to find something to hold on to, ripping at armor to get a toehold. They planted simulated charges on the cockpit and hovered away. The other pair dove in low and fast, skimming the ground and firing dummy rounds into the 'Mech's birdlike legs. It had turned to pursue them when the charges on the cockpit blew. The battle computer coordinating the exercise powered down the *Locust*. It was out of the fight.

Score one for the Fidelis.

He walked over to where Lieutenant Joseph Henzel, formerly of the Third Triarii Protectors, studied the events unfolding on the grass-covered slopes below. The Third Triarii contributed one BattleMech, a *Spider* that had to be gutted and rebuilt before it was of any use; a Po tank, an APC and two power-armored infantry squads to his company, and most of those troops were replacements getting a crash course in combat tactics. The Republic had suffered great losses in the last few years, and this was all the regular army could spare. The rest of his force was made up of the Fidelis, for which he was grateful. They had done an outstanding job of getting the green troops up to speed and ahead of the curve in terms of skills. *I'm lucky to have both them and the Republic veterans. I hope they know it.*

Lieutenant Henzel acknowledged Sir Mannheim and continued to watch the exercise through his enhanced binoculars.

"Impressive, aren't they?" Mannheim made it more of a statement than a question.

"They're more than impressive," Lieutenant Henzel replied. "It's like they've been training on this equipment since they were born. I spoke to one of them, a Lieutenant Carver, and he was able to quote the statistics on BattleMechs faster and more accurately than the warbook. They're bred for battle, that much is for sure."

Mannheim had had similar discussions with the Fidelis. He once had worked with Republic special forces troops, and every one of the Fidelis exceeded the skill level of those troops. They were not talkative, not engaging, but they were highly effective. *Imagine what I could do with a few hundred Fidelis in the right gear.* It was a seductive thought.

He stared at one of the Sylph battle suits and it seemed different than the others. A Fidelis MHI Hawk Moth gunship roared past his hillside, blasting their observation point with a rush of hot air from the pair of massive turbofans that kept it in the air. It lacked the usual twin weapons pods slung on either side of the cockpit. "They changed that weapons mount—again."

"Yes, sir. It took me awhile to get used to the way they customize every single element of their gear, right down to their personal sidearms and ammo loads. I spoke with one of them about it a few months ago. He told me that they always refine the weapons platform to fit the strengths of the individual warrior. I have to believe that the first time we use them in battle, their equipment will drive the enemy nuts. That battle suit, for example"—he pointed to the one Hunter had been watching. "They've created a disposable pod carrying an advanced targeting system. They use it, lose it and actually increase the speed and range of the Sylph by 20 percent. I saw one that was mounted with a disposable SRM pack—six missiles, all inferno. These troopers sure know how to take out a 'Mech."

"What about the Hawk Moth?"

"They pulled off her armaments and swapped them for pulse lasers and a better targeting system."

Mannheim chuckled. "I should probably have them crawl over my BattleMech and make some suggestions."

"You should consider asking them, sir," Henzel said seriously. "Each one of them is trained in repair, salvage and modification. They're incredible."

"Incredible and mysterious." Mannheim still was not comfortable with the fact that no one knew where the Fidelis came from. "We've been with them for two years now, training side by side, and I know less about them now than I did the day they were assigned to my command."

It was Lieutenant Henzel's turn to laugh. "The latest I heard at mess was that they are the survivors of the Minnesota Tribe—Clan Wolverine—the infamous Not-Named Clan. You know how the troops love to talk, and the Fidelis are so tight-lipped it only fuels the rumor mill. Another favorite theory is that they are survivors of the Black Watch. Apparently they have a standing order never to leave their dead on the battlefield, or else the Clans would figure out that they were the descendants of the Wolverines and come after them. Of course, none of them will even comment on these theories. The Clan angle does make a little sense if you consider that Devlin Stone used them in the Jihad like his private spec-ops force."

Mannheim said nothing for a moment. It made as much sense as any of the scenarios he had heard around the training post. In the end, where they were from didn't matter as much as the results they produced. For now, it would remain just speculation.

"Rumors are for the NCOs," he said lightly. "We're officers. Now, I have a task for you once this exercise is done."

"Yes, sir."

"I need you to coordinate repainting our gear. We are going to lift off in four days, and I want every piece of our gear painted to these specifications." He handed the noteputer to his officer.

Henzel studied the schematics then looked up at Mannheim. "The Duchy of Andurien, sir?"

"Our advance man is already in place," he said, thinking of Jeremy Chin. "Say nothing. If our men love rumors, this will really give them something to talk about."

The monastery of the Order of ꕊØ ꞁ was set into the stony face of a sharply rising plateau, and it looked as if a building was attempting to emerge from the dull tan rock. Half-pillars rose four stories tall, and there were two balconies, complete with railing, all carved out of the plateau with no visible seams.

The ground level of the monastery boasted a large, lush, semicircular-shaped garden enclosed by an old stone wall. In contrast, the ground looked like desert for a hundred yards outside the wall. Jeremy studied the low-tech structure, and after a few moments realized the wall was crowned by a string of sensors, many of them partially covered by thick vines. *Strange thing to see at a monastery.* The name of the monastery's order was posted on a small brass plaque outside the main gate, a massive metal barrier. He struggled to pronounce it. "Tempih Whya?" he muttered. "I knew I should have spent more time learning Russian." Jeremy had run the name through his translator, which gave him "Darkened Souls," which was probably not quite right. *Must be hell to recruit new members with a name like that. . . .*

From his perch behind a cluster of boulders situated a kilometer from the monastery, he considered the site and shook his head. The two monks he could see wore faded gray robes. As he studied them, a third man emerged from the interior carrying an assault rifle. *What kind of monastery has an armed defense force?* Even those that were known refuges for MechWarriors or veterans didn't offer armed protection.

What he saw wouldn't have made sense without the inside knowledge he possessed, courtesy of Devlin

Stone's notes. The settlement was just over ten kilometers from the edge of Breezewood and dated back as far as the first Star League. It was a small but prosperous community outside a city in which poverty was the largest commodity. Obviously, the armed guards deterred people from trying to rob the place, but they certainly didn't fit with the monastery being a place of worship.

He annotated the information about the monastery stored on his noteputer. *I'm coming here for a creepy reason already, and now I have to worry about bringing enough manpower with me to take care of the guards.* The presence of the guards meant one of two things: They were there either to keep the members of the order in—or to keep other people out. Damn if Devlin Stone wasn't right. The Anduriens *were* hiding something there. And Stone's notes said that artifact was his objective.

How did it end up here? Was this where *he* died? Or is this simply where he ended up? The historians would have a field day with what he was going to take, if he ever told one. Then again, who would believe him?

Chin folded up his binoculars and stuffed them in the bag slung over his shoulder. *Alright, Order of* ßØ ﻻ —*however you pronounce it—we'll have to see if you are still holding the little surprise that Devlin Stone claimed you had.*

Interpretation of Duty 2

Brandenburg, Callison
Prefecture VIII, Republic of the Sphere
Fortress Republic (-30 days)

It had been an interesting few months for Ceresco Hancock.

She was using a cover identity established years ago by the ghost knights, a common strategy the organization used on worlds throughout The Republic. In this case, she had assumed the identity of Cheryl Gunson, a mid-level manager in the Directorate of Internal Affairs. Since the collapse of the HPG network, Governor Stewart had been slowly evolving the Directorate into her own private spying organization. It was the perfect platform from which Ceresco could launch her meteoric rise to power.

The real Ms. Gunson had been on The Republic payroll even before she entered the Directorate. She was a mousy woman, easily overlooked even by her immediate manager. She was the same physical type as Ceresco. The biggest differences were her long, jet-black hair and green eyes—superficial differences, and easy enough to resolve. As soon as Ceresco was sufficiently prepared, the real Cheryl Gunson was given a new identity and

Ceresco took her place. The real Cheryl took a well-deserved vacation; when she "returned" after two weeks, she had a dramatically different hair color and style, which she simply explained by saying she felt the need for a change. It was common wisdom that changing her hairstyle also changed the shape of a woman's face, so the only disguise necessary was colored contact lenses.

When she took on the role of Cheryl, that was who she became. The ghost knight was no longer Ceresco Hancock. Her thinking, responses, attitude—everything was now Cheryl Gunson. It took tremendous mental discipline to step into a role so fully.

Other changes began to emerge in Cheryl Gunson. In a rare display of independence, she provided intelligence on a Lyran agent operating on Callison. Cheryl found no need to reveal that the information had come from the files of the ghost knights. The very public capture of the spy began to bring about the collapse of a network of agents on Callison, with new agents being uncovered almost weekly. Cheryl's work earned her the first of many promotions and the attention of Governor Stewart, who awarded her the Callison Medal of Freedom. In a few short months, she had risen from obscurity and gained the respect of a prominent political entity.

Naturally, her manager chafed at her sudden rise. So she manufactured evidence that he was siphoning Directorate funds for personal use. It was easy, really—a few hours on the network, and she had cracked his bank accounts and moved the money. Cheryl Gunson, the Directorate ristar, uncovered the plot and informed the governor directly, wisely avoiding official channels. She had planted the evidence expertly, and her manager was soon being whisked off to jail.

Thanks in part to Governor Stewart's influence and her own ingenuity, the shake-up of the Directorate of Internal Affairs put her in the top position in the space of a few months. Cheryl had achieved her goal, but it bothered her that it was so easy. Clearly, with the information to which every ghost knight had access, they could carve out a piece of any world for their own. So much power, and she had ignored it for so many years. It was painfully simple. It was seductive.

Governor Allison Stewart was a formidable woman who had already sipped from the cup of power. Cheryl had studied her carefully. Her ties to the nearby Marik-Stewart Commonwealth ended with her last name: Any connections to her family in the Commonwealth were tenuous, at best. No, what made Allison Stewart so dangerous was her personal ambition and drive.

The woman was only slightly taller that Cheryl, but wide. She was stocky, with a swimmer's muscular chest. Her legs were like stubby tree trunks. She did not possess the personal charisma most people would assume was required to hold her office. Her power came from within. Cheryl admired that aspect of the governor's personality: Stewart didn't rely on good looks to get ahead, but ruled by the authority she held.

Standing in the alcove outside the governor's office was becoming a familiar occupation. The governor was in her office and Cheryl was on time—early, in fact. Governor Stewart always made her appointments cool their heels to remind them who was in charge. She also had lowered the guest chairs by a full inch, another way to remind visitors of their position.

The administrator finally opened the door, a good ten minutes after the scheduled start time, allowing Cheryl to enter the office. It was an unexpectedly modest office. There was no paperwork on the desk, only a single flat monitor and well-disguised access to the government's network. The bookshelves in the room were made of rich Callison cherrywood and filled with countless books, many antiques. Cheryl wondered if they were for show, or if the governor actually read them. The floor was wood, accented by a round, deep blue rug with the seal of office woven into the center. She noticed that there were no elements of The Republic in the room. Those had all been carefully removed over time. She understood the message. *The Republic ends at this door. Inside is only the intention of the governor.*

"Good to see you, Ms. Gunson," the governor greeted her, gesturing to the chair opposite her desk. Cheryl took the seat, sinking deep into the low leather seat. The governor returned to her own chair and leaned forward on the desk. She loomed over her guest.

"I'll cut to the chase. You're my Director of Intelligence. What have you learned regarding the rumors we discussed last week?" the middle-aged woman asked.

"Three JumpShips have passed through our system since we talked. I have interviewed the executive staff of each of them. The rumors we have been hearing seem to have validity. Numerous personnel changes are being made across The Republic, many being governors and legates. Units are being transferred from local militias to regular army units and are being relocated. Some militias are simply being stripped of their hardware and gear."

"Relocated where?"

"A variety of worlds," Cheryl replied, handing over her noteputer for the governor to review. "Ordinarily, troop movements like this are made in response to a full-blown invasion. That would make sense except that the enemies of The Republic seem to be the same that we've been facing for the past few years. The worlds they are being sent to are concentrated around Prefecture X, which does not indicate that they are expected to face a known enemy."

Governor Stewart studied the report for a full minute in silence. She handed the noteputer back across the desk. "What is your interpretation of the data?"

This was a delicate line for Cheryl to walk. She knew the truth, knew about Fortress Republic. Damien Redburn himself had revealed the plan to her and the other knights on New Earth. What her intelligence reports had uncovered was the preliminary groundwork to Fortress. Her gut clenched at the thought of telling Stewart what was really unfolding, because it was obvious that this woman had her own agenda and would use Cheryl's information for her own ends. On the other hand, if she played out this data correctly, Cheryl knew she could use it to get even closer to Stewart's inner circle.

"In my opinion, The Republic appears to be circling its wagons. They may be hunkering down in Prefecture X in hope of making a last stand there."

"Against whom?"

"Does it matter?" she shrugged. "The Jade Falcons are pushing Skye around. The Draconis Combine is driving into The Republic. Even the Capellans are biting out chunks. Everyone is smelling blood and moving in for the kill. Perhaps this new exarch, Levin, plans on digging into Prefecture X."

"And what about us? What about those of us who are not in Prefecture X?"

"It's difficult to say what will happen to the rest of The Republic. I can only provide you with an educated guess of what *may* be happening. It is entirely possible that I am wrong." She said the words, but there was no conviction in her voice. For a moment, even she wasn't sure if it was Ceresco or Cheryl talking. She was suddenly terrified that her cover had slipped.

"You don't think you're wrong though, do you?" Stewart probed.

"No, Governor. I don't."

"Are we at risk?"

Always the people first. "Doubtful. The Marik-Stewart Commonwealth seems to have no interest in us. There have been signs of troop movements in the Lyran Commonwealth, but I doubt we are their target. Our prefecture is relatively quiet. I would say that for the time being, our risk is low from other powers."

"You misunderstand my query. What is the risk of The Republic taking action in this prefecture?"

She's very good. She's sensing opportunity. Time to show her just how smart I am. "It is difficult to guess at this point, but I believe that if we face a risk at all from

The Republic, it would be from them coming to strip away our militia's hardware, and perhaps other materials they might need for the war effort." This was not a guess. She knew Sir Kristoff Erbe's orders in full. She knew why he was coming to Callison, and more importantly, she knew exactly when. But revealing that knowledge would tip her hand.

"That could prove interesting," Stewart replied. The governor smiled a predatory grin. "Who knows," she continued. "Perhaps they will arrange a new assignment for our legate at the same time." It had become obvious over the last month or so that the governor and the legate were not seeing eye to eye. But Cheryl Gunson knew that change of command was not in the cards at the moment.

"Yes, ma'am," was all that Cheryl Gunson replied.

"I would like you to implement a new precautionary measure. I want you to intercept all communications from JumpShips arriving in our system. If there is a change coming to The Republic, I want to know about it before the general public. I want to ensure that the message is properly explained to them."

Translation: She wants to deliver her version of the message.

"I understand, Governor," she replied. "This change will be implemented immediately."

"You've proven quite insightful, Ms. Gunson. I appreciate your service and support."

"My duty is to Callison, ma'am," she replied. It was not entirely a lie. Cheryl was following orders. Damien Redburn had told her that Callison was to play an important role in things to come. Callison was part of The Republic. Her duty *was* to Callison. But her orders were open to interpretation.

I know I am doing the right thing. Why do I have so much doubt?

Altar of Freedom 2

Training Facility Lion
Northern Mopelia Island, New Earth
Prefecture X, Republic of the Sphere
Fortress Republic (-38 days)

As she had requested, the dinner table was set for a formal meal. This would be their last night in The Republic for God only knew how long, and as such the occasion deserved some recognition and respect. Synd had ordered a formal meal to be prepared for the rest of her troops as well, but this table was set for her and her command team. *Tonight is our last night under these stars, perhaps forever.*

She had invited Paladin Redburn to join them, but he had politely declined. His own JumpShip was recharging and he was preparing to leave New Earth in a matter of hours. She had met with him privately, but only for a few minutes. His questions were focused on making sure she was ready for her mission; when Synd expressed her concerns, he gently redirected the conversation. When she tried to tell him the details of what she was going to have to do on Ryde, Redburn had responded only that she was to fulfill her orders in the best way possible with the resources at hand. It had hurt to hear him be so casual about the loss of innocent lives, but as he turned to go she saw the gleam of tears in the corners of his eyes.

I am not the only one who knows that I'm being asked to do a great deal beyond the call of duty.

Tonight would be the last time she could savor being inside what would become Fortress Republic. One quick jump, and they would be on the outside. While the rest of the Inner Sphere had no idea what was truly unfolding, Lady Synd understood the implications, and she hated knowing. The ignorant had nothing to fear. Knowing what was going to happen, the not-so-subtle changes that would take place, made her long to erase her own memories of the last month or so.

She stood at the head of the table with her hands on the back of the tall cherrywood chair and surveyed the dinner settings. A white linen cloth embroidered with the logo of The Republic on each of the corners was perfectly pressed and hung precisely over the edges of the table. Two candles burned brightly, their lights flickering on the crystal water glasses and the polished silverware. The Fidelis appeared frugal and austere, but they understood the requirements for a formal dining experience.

Captain Paulis came in first, followed by Boyne. Both wore gray dress uniforms. Paulis' was adorned with several campaign medals and the patch for the Tenth Principes Guards on his shoulder. In contrast, Boyne's uniform revealed nothing about him or his past. It was a blank slate, decorated with his acting rank of captain and nothing else. Synd smiled wryly when Sir Jayson Greene entered the room; his uniform was the same as Boyne's, showing only his acting rank. With a gesture, she invited them to sit, and silence reigned until the waiters came in and poured a crimson wine into their goblets, the filled glasses adding a burst of color to the table. The wine was from Terra, an obscure winery in western North America.

Lady Synd broke the silence. "I have ordered a case of this wine to be taken to my DropShip."

"In order to celebrate when we're done with the mission, m'lady?" Paulis asked.

"No. Quite the opposite. We are leaving The Republic. In the months and years to come, we must remember what we have left behind. We will toast our friends and families, those we cannot be with, and those who have died along the way. This wine will be used to commemorate what we left behind and to salute the future." Her words set the tone for the intimate gathering. *Optimism in its purest form.*

Crystal reached out and took her glass, gently swirling the wine, then lifted her glass in a toast. "To The Republic!" Sir Greene's face wore a faint smile. Boyne offered no change of expression. Paulis seemed happy that the silence had been broken. The men reached out and joined her in the toast. In unison they took a sip.

"I appreciate the offer of dinner, Lady Synd," Captain Paulis began as the waiters again entered the room. Soup was carefully ladled out, with a slight clang of china being handled. He paused until the waiters departed, closing the doors behind them. "We finished getting the troops ready for departure at 0700."

"Good. Because tonight is our last night in what will be known as Fortress Republic, I felt that dinner together was important. How often in life are you aware that you are facing an event of galactic historical significance? We do not know when or even if we will be back. We should reflect on that, and relax, if only for a few moments."

Sir Greene stirred in his seat. "I prefer to think of this as a beginning, not an end. What we are doing is the best course of action. It has become impossible for The Republic to defend all its worlds. The exarch is doing the right thing by entrenching and defending the worlds we *can* defend."

"To Exarch Levin," she said lifting her glass again. "And to Damien Redburn." She realized that adding the paladin sounded like an afterthought, but toasting Redburn was getting harder. She had spent the last week reviewing and re-reviewing the plan of battle. *He is ordering me to lead my troops into death. The Falcons are not to be toyed with. He's assured me I'm doing something important for our future . . . but how can I be sure he's right?*

She turned to Boyne, who did not seem to be drinking much of the wine. "Captain Boyne, have you ever been outside of Prefecture X?"

He shook his head. "No, Lady Synd. The Fidelis have been on New Earth since the Jihad. No exarch has recognized a threat to The Republic like that which we now face. We only go when called to serve."

Paulis barely managed to keep from smiling. "Must be strange for you, never having actually fought in combat. Now you're leaving your home and shipping off to do some real fighting."

"My father died in combat."

"But there was no fighting on New Earth. What battle did he die in?"

Boyne smiled in return. "Not all training exercises for MechWarriors are performed using dummy ammunition. Part of our training requires life-fire experience. He was serving as a Lead Jäger of the First Umbra when he was killed by a precision artillery barrage."

Paulis had the grace to blush. "My apologies for your loss."

"No apologies are required. He died doing his duty, training another generation of the Fidelis. I have been told that he was smiling when he died. I like to think that he would be proud of me going on this mission." For a moment, his expression changed, and he looked thoughtful.

Synd decided to change to a less solemn subject. "Major Greene. Part of our mission is to convince the Jade Falcons that we are from the Lyran Commonwealth in hopes of increasing tensions between their two governments. You haven't told us your plans for achieving that."

"Correct, m'lady. This deception requires no action until we are on the ground."

"Will we be camouflaging our gear as Commonwealth equipment?"

"That won't be necessary. No matter what we do, the Jade Falcons will assume that we are attempting to deceive them. We will remain marked as Republic of the Sphere units. Using open communications channels when we land, we will send out some prerecorded German commands. After we depart, they will analyze their intel data and assume that we were a Lyran troop disguised as a Republic of the Sphere unit. If that plan doesn't work, I have a few other tricks up my sleeve that will convince even the most hardened intelligence officer; we can use any of these ploys once we recover the scientists."

Paulis shook his head. "So we fool them by not fooling them at all?"

"That's the plan."

Boyne joined in. "I trust the squad you have chosen for your extraction of the scientists meets with your satisfaction, Major Greene?"

A firm nod. "Yes. Their combat engineering skills are going to prove invaluable. Though I prefer to think of this as a rescue mission more than an extraction."

"But they have not asked to be saved. To be a prisoner, you need to recognize that fact first, correct?" Synd wasn't sure, but she thought this might be a hint at Boyne's sense of humor.

"The Falcons invaded Ryde. In my eyes, everyone there is a prisoner living under their rule," Greene responded.

"I meant no offense, Major Greene. It is simply that in my people's past dealings with the Clans, we have learned that what is known and what is assumed are two different things."

Greene tried to shift the focus of the conversation. "Your personnel in the unit are also proving quite talented, Captain Paulis." Paulis had no response. He only had two men in that squad, and he had let Synd know that they found working so closely with the Fidelis a little frustrating. The Fidelis were very efficient, but did not thrive on the camaraderie that Republic troops—that *most* troops—were accustomed to. It had been one of several friction points in integrating the Fidelis troops. The Fidelis, however, had not complained, not once. It was the regular forces that seemed to chafe at their presence. *It would be easier to respond to the complaints if the Fidelis weren't so effective.*

They sipped their soup for a moment in silence, and the salads were delivered and they began eating them before the conversation picked up again. Greene launched a personal topic. "I don't have any family that I will be leaving behind. What about you, Lady Synd?"

She hesitated. "My brother Albert just entered training on Northwind. I have sent him a written letter that will take weeks to reach him. By the time he receives it, there will be no chance to respond. I prefer it that way. Albert is the only family I have left. He is training as a MechWarrior and will understand." *I hope . . .*

"And you, Captain Paulis?"

Paulis wiped his mouth with the corner of his napkin before he spoke. "Major Greene, I have a large family, but have been away from them for the past two years. My brothers and sisters and their children will receive a holovideo that I prepared, but it will not ship until after we leave. My sisters will have a meltdown, but they'll accept my choice after some time has passed."

"And you, Captain Boyne? What about your family?"

Boyne shrugged. "I will be with my family."

"You have family in your command?"

"No. The Fidelis *are* my family. As long as one Fidelis lives in my command, I am with my brother or sister."

"A band of brothers, eh?"

Boyne was obviously puzzled. "I am not familiar with that phrase."

"Shakespeare," cut in Crystal. "*Henry the Fifth.*"

The Fidelis officer shook his head. "On the Road of

Pain, my people lost much of the literature that was not of a technical nature. We have little in the way of entertainment that is not martial in nature."

Road of Pain? It was a clue, but to what, Synd was not sure. Like so much else about the Fidelis, this clue was shrouded in mystery. She knew the troops in her command were running several pools guessing at the origins of the Fidelis, and she had to admit she was as curious as they. But this was not the time for probing into this mystery. This was an occasion for remembering the past and hoping—no, praying—for the future. It was best to change the subject before Paulis pressed further.

"I have completed my review of the attack plans, specifically your suggestion, Captain Boyne, to destroy the two buildings along the John Cabin Parkway to obstruct the road." She cradled her wineglass and stared at the last sip of liquid for a moment, then drank it. "After much consideration, I am going to approve your suggestion, with a few caveats."

Boyne seemed amused. "I am pleased only because I believe it will help ensure our success. What restrictions are you contemplating, m'lady?"

"You must evacuate those buildings before they're destroyed."

"I believe that will be impossible to accomplish—not in the time frame we have to work with."

She shook her head. "This is not subject to interpretation or debate. It will take a minimum of twenty-five minutes to place the charges on the right structural points to drop the buildings in the direction you want. You can activate the fire alarm and let the people evacuate the building while you're setting the charges."

"This may tip our hand to the Jade Falcons."

"I contemplated that possibility. It is a risk we will have to accept." The waiters came in and refilled the wineglasses, creating a pause in the discussion of the operations on Ryde.

Major Greene spoke up as soon as the door closed. "M'lady, I find myself respectfully siding with Captain

Boyne on this. Even if you evac those civilians, they might end up in the wrong place when the charges go off. Anytime you drop a skyscraper there's dust, debris and death, in that order. You'll have rescue equipment there on the scene and some of those people will be killed, too. It may prove too problematic to be practical."

She refused to accept that saving lives should be labeled as "problematic." She lightly tapped her fist on the table for emphasis. "I swore to protect the citizens of The Republic. That includes citizens under occupation by the Jade Falcons. Some will die: I understand that and accept responsibility for that. I am a knight, and there is no shirking the duty of our mission. We have a responsibility to reduce the loss of life as much as humanly possible. This mission may force me to compromise some of my beliefs, but I will not cross the line and become a cold-blooded killer. I owe that to The Republic—owe it to myself. We all do."

A tense silence followed her declaration. She made eye contact with each of the officers. Boyne bowed his head. "It shall be done, Lady Synd. By doing so, we honor Devlin Stone. I will give the order as you have requested: I also find waste of life distasteful."

"I appreciate that, Captain." She regarded them solemnly. "Gentlemen, even with the extreme measure of destroying property, we are still outnumbered and outgunned. This action will buy us time that we will desperately need. Our losses are going to be high. I have reviewed the terrain and the force we are taking in, as well as those we will be facing, and there is no way I see to mitigate our losses any further. This will be a bitter fight." Paulis bowed his head for a moment at her words, Sir Greene gave a single slow nod of understanding. Boyne regarded her steadily. Again, she found it strange that he was the one to break the silence.

"All I ask is for your orders, m'lady."

"Service! She is mad . . . asking for the evacuation of these buildings." Morella slammed her fist into the table, but Boyne was unmoved by her gesture. He had seen it all before, the tantrums. It was what held her back in her service to the Order. Even in the small conference room buried in the bowels of the training facility, he knew her anger reverberated.

Moreover, he discovered that he did not agree with her. He was beginning to know Crystal Synd, Knight of the Sphere, and found her *interesting*. Boyne understood her. She was upholding her vow, just as he upheld the vow he had taken as a warrior of the Fidelis.

"She is our commanding officer, and you will learn to control your words and temper," he replied in a level tone.

She growled in the back of her throat. "This knight places our people at risk unnecessarily," Morella countered. "Evacuating those buildings will cause confusion and congestion and will signal our plan to the blood-taint-accursed Falcons. It is not necessary for the successful completion of the operation. You know I am right!"

Boyne listened to her and waited. He had learned years ago that it was the best way to calm her down. "This is not about being right or wrong. She has command. Part of service is knowing how to follow orders, Morella."

"I know how to follow orders. I welcome a chance to repay these Jade Falcons for what they did to our people during the Great Betrayal. I simply do not wish to die before I get a chance to spill their blood. Needless deaths are the most feared of all—you know that." She was not afraid to die: None of those in the task force from the Fidelis ranks were afraid. They were precision tools of war and wanted to be used with the care accorded such tools.

"Our plight has been long. We are the first of our generation to serve in the Cause and we will be the ones who release our people from the bonding oath. I, too, wish to draw the blood of the Clans in memory of the Road of Pain and the Great Betrayal. To do that, I will honor the memory of Devlin Stone and his representative, as will you. We will follow her orders because that is what is required. She is a knight. I am learning that means something more than simply commanding a military unit."

Morella sneered at him with an icy glare. "I believe your feelings for her cloud your thoughts—but I will do as you say."

It was Boyne's turn to fight back a ripple of rage. How dare she accuse him of having feelings for Lady Synd? "Morella, you cross many lines. It is what holds you back. Do as she commands, as I command, and I assure you that you will find the salvation we *all* seek."

She reached across the table with her fist pointed at his heart. He curled his own hand into a fist and punched her knuckles. Solidarity. It was what had saved the Fidelis all of these years. Now it would serve them on a field of battle.

Interpretation of Duty 11

Brandenburg, Callison
Former Prefecture VIII
Fortress Republic (+37 days)

A shower of short-range missiles hit the building with little discrimination as to their target. Three found the floor where the squad had been hiding. Five slammed into the lower floors, blasting off the brick facade of the old warehouse and setting countless fires inside. A full wave of missiles hit above the floor where the infantry were stationed, sending bits of ceiling and flooring raining down. Gray dust filled the air and obscured the view. The infantry disappeared from the window, and Kristoff was pleased, because it meant they were on the move, shifting position again.

The Callison Light Horse was no longer a green militia unit led by a handful of veterans. They were all veterans of the fighting against his hardened Republic troops. The planetary militia was taking its mission seriously. The soldiers were driving back the Republic forces one building at a time, blasting and charring any structure from which they encountered resistance.

Sir Erbe maneuvered his *Hellstar* back a few steps and angled behind a building. His tactical display told him that the Light Horse was pressing hard to the west and south, ensuring that he could not attempt a breakaway rush to the spaceport. He was picking up the signature of a small craft, a Tamerlane strike sled, attempting to turn the flank. It had tried that a few minutes ago, and the Fidelis troops had discouraged it. Now it was attempting to swing around behind his *Hellstar* again. He charged his medium-pulse lasers and jerked his BattleMech out into the open.

Sure enough, the Tamerlane was charging right at him at flank speed. It had been hoping for a rear shot; now it was going to get a taste of real firepower. It opened up first with its Marlin Mini-SRM pack—a pair of short-range missiles that were more irritating than dangerous. Kristoff shrugged off the hit. Aiming just in front of the vehicle, he fired a stream of coherent light. The laser attack looked like a miss, but the hovercraft couldn't simply stop mid-charge. Sir Erbe had hoped it would turn to avoid the attack that was devouring the street and only suffer minor damage. The driver must have frozen at the controls, because the Tamerlane charged right into the center of the burst.

The laser pulses charred a series of burn scars and holes right up the front of the stubby scout craft. It dropped hard to the ferrocrete, skidding as it ground to a halt about half a block from him. He checked his fire, his eyes stinging from the sweat running down his forehead to the corners of his eyes.

The Tamerlane exploded as something inside cooked off, most likely the SRM ammo. A sickening black cloud rolled into the air.

Blast it! He was trying to not destroy the craft. He had deliberately aimed so as only to injure it. Kristoff wanted to drive it away from the fight, scare the crew, shatter their nerves. He had given his word to Lady Hancock that he would try. She had warned him that the Light Horse was going to come at him with a vengeance, and she was right. More citizens of The Republic were dead and dying. Dead and dying by his hand.

"Harbinger, sit rep." He spoke calmly into the mic built into his neurohelmet.

"Squirrel, we have armed citizens on this front. I have scattered them several times, but they are moving up along with militia troops. They have figured out that we will not shoot innocent people, and are using that against us." Colonel Adamans paused. "Do you have new orders for me, sir?"

He knew what the Fidelis officer was asking. He was asking for permission to open fire on the civilians. They were armed in insurrection against The Republic. He was within his rights to order the attack. But the citizens of Callison were defying The Republic because they had been misled by their governor. As tempting as it was to fight fire with fire, Kristoff Erbe was not going to give in to the temptation to change his orders.

"No change in orders, Harbinger. Lay down a pattern of suppression fire. Spray them with debris from the buildings and road, but do not fire directly on the noncombatants."

"Acknowledged."

Erbe sidestepped across the intersection, intent on locating a prize he knew was operating to the south. While the infantry dealt with the JESII missile carrier, he was in pursuit of an SM1 tank destroyer. While SM1 was its formal designation in the warbook on the battlecomputer, the troops in the field referred to it as a " 'Mech Buster" or "Crotch-Kicker." It had a well-deserved reputation for being able to pry open a BattleMech with only a few salvos. This one had only appeared a few times in the battle, darting in, firing and running. Its crew was using its firepower wisely, wearing down his troops. It was time the hunter got a taste of its own medicine.

Kristoff intended to take the vehicle out of the fight, and he reminded himself of that as he closed on the flank of the hovertank, now only a few blocks away. At the next major intersection they would come in line of sight and the deadly game could begin.

He came to the next roadway; the SM1 had already turned the corner and was waiting for him. Even moving at trotting speed, his 'Mech was a massive target. The SM1 unleashed its big gun, the Ultra autocannon 20. A spray of shells hit the legs and lower torso of his *Hellstar*. The 'Mech lunged back and to one side as he fought hard to keep it upright. He ignored the amber warning lights flickering on his tactical display—a stress warning for a hip actuator, a few holes in his armor and other minor damage. He paid closer attention to the indication of friendly transponders down the block near the SM1. That meant governing his fire.

He angled the large lasers in on the SM1 as it headed for the next street over—its usual game of shoot-and-run. Not this time. Kristoff fired both the large lasers, jabbing sustained beams of jade light into the hovertank. One hit the skirt and tore away a long swath as the tank moved, resulting in the tank dipping down on that side so that it almost touched the ground.

The other laser beam hit the side of the tank and burned a mark parallel to the damage on the skirt. Armor plating held but turned black, then one plate popped out of place and landed in the street with a clang so loud he could hear it. The SM1 continued its move out of the line of fire. He moved along a street parallel to it. This time when he came to the intersection, he paused. He had fallen for the trick once. His sensors were having a hard time distinguishing the tank from all the infrastructure, but he could tell that it was there; slowly, methodically making its way down the street toward him, hunting him like a wild animal.

He cycled to his secondary target interlock circuit and angled the boxy arms so that his pulse lasers were set at the right range. Kristoff's plan was to step out quickly then duck back, hopefully startling the SM1 crew into firing. They would miss, then while they were reloading, he would rip up her hide with his pulse lasers.

He juked into the street and immediately pulled back. The SM1 fired and the shells sprayed down the street and angled at his right arm. Five or six rounds tore into the *Hellstar*'s right arm. The impacts jerked back the arm hard against the actuators. The *Hellstar* didn't have humanlike arms, and the designers had not intended the 'Mech to move that way. The actuator overextended and locked up, and he couldn't pause to try to adjust it.

Jumping back out again, he fired. One salvo of energy darts struck the front of the SM1, savaging the armor there and causing the hovertank to come to a dead stop. The driver belatedly figured out that he had been tricked into the open, and now realized that he had come too far forward. There was no place to hide.

The second shot from the *Hellstar*'s badly damaged arm was almost laughable. The laser sprayed upward into the skies over Brandenburg, alerting everyone in the city to the battle—as if they didn't know already. The heat in his cockpit rose as he pulled back and assessed the damaged arm.

His comm channel activated. "Squirrel, this is Infiltrator Four. Hold your fire, we are engaging. Move out for cover fire if we fail."

It was the first pleasant surprise of the day. He paused for a moment to let his 'Mech cool slightly, then he once again burst into the intersection. Kristoff watched as the last of the Fidelis troops in Kage battle armor dropped on top of the tank. Apparently they had been moving along with him, parallel to the SM1 but at rooftop level. The stubby wings on the upper shoulders of their armor guided them right down on top of the SM1: The crew never saw them coming.

Sir Erbe knew when the SM1 crew realized something was wrong. They rammed the hovertank into the nearest building but could not shake the infantry from the roof. Two of the troopers used their chainguns to hit the driver's bubble on the right side of the tank while the others worked the hatches. He saw the flash of satchel charges going off, but still the Fidelis held on. The driver turned away from his *Hellstar* and tried to make a break for the Light Horse lines, moving fast enough for Kristoff to follow him with several running steps.

The SM1 dropped unexpectedly to the ferrocrete roadway. The thudding noise reached him in his cockpit. The driver's bubble had been compromised. He could see smoke rise inside the ferroglass bubble as something burned. Hatches opened and the crew was pulled out one at a time. They raised their hands slowly in the air as one of the Kage troops shed his armor and entered the tank.

"Good job, Infiltrator Four," Erbe signaled.

"Service! Infiltrator Four has added a new call sign, sir," replied an unfamiliar voice. "Infiltrator Five reporting for duty, sir." With those words, the SM1 rose unsteadily on its damaged skirt and turned full circle in a victory dance.

"Very well, Infiltrator Five and Four. Get those prisoners back to the base," he replied. In the distance he saw his favorite annoyance coming down the street once more—the Yasha VTOL was back for what seemed like the twentieth time. Kristoff paused for a second and stared at his damage display, which had a blinking red arm actuator. He stepped close to the nearest building and snapped his torso around in a tight turn. The boxy arm assembly slammed into the building. Bits and pieces of the old warehouse shattered and sprayed the street. The frozen actuator shifted from blinking red to yellow. He tested it, and it responded to his moves, though with some reluctance. There are some things you learn that they never taught in basic training. One was how tough a BattleMech really was, and that it's sometimes possible to bump and grind something back into working condition.

We have to be thankful for our victories, even the small ones. Kristoff Erbe fell back another block. The battle for Callison was far from over. He only hoped that the last victim wouldn't be his faith in Ceresco.

Price of Service 5

Hunter's *Shockwave* felt comfortable, like an easy chair in his home. Given how long he'd been away from his home and family, it was perhaps understandable; his BattleMech *was* home. To some the cockpit of the *Shockwave* was claustrophobic, but to Sir Mannheim it was like a womb.

He led the command lance of the company west toward where the Oriente Protectorate forces had landed. Just beyond sensor range he could see signs of battle; Colonel Daum and the local garrison were already tangling with the raiding force. He did not aim directly for the battle, but off to the flank. Conventional wisdom said to put your firepower on the flanks of a good fight, hit them from the sides and pinch them in the middle.

He commanded a lance of mixed firepower. There was a Goblin APC the Fidelis had modified by stripping off armor in favor of firepower. They called the modified vehicle a HobGoblin; Mannheim appreciated the humor and let it go. The APC was carrying a little surprise in the form of a gun nest and crew, which would have deadly range and wreak plenty of havoc when dropped off near the Protectorate attackers. The HobGoblin was shadowing his 'Mech; the Fidelis troops hoped that the signature of the *Shockwave* would draw the enemy's attention away from them.

An MHI Hawk Moth VTOL was running on his right flank, hovering right above the ground and kicking up dust in its wake. Lifted by heavy turbofan jet engines, the tiny gunship was painfully effective in a fight. On his other flank was a Kelswa tank, unable to match their speed and drifting farther back each minute.

"This is Rook to"—he checked the comm channels and callsigns Colonel Daum had given him—"Pickaxe."

"Nice of you to drop in," came back the harried but even voice of the Duchy colonel.

"You hold the center and we will move up the flanks."

There was a static-filled hiss so sharp it almost hurt. ". . . atch yourself. They've got heavies on the ri . . ." Again the static cut in.

As he crested the low, sloping ridgeline he saw the reason for the interference. The Duchy force under Daum was being swamped on both flanks, led by an assault 'Mech twice the size of his *Shockwave*, a menacing-looking *Jupiter*. He arrived just in time to see the *Jupiter* pump a burst of autocannon fire into a garrison *Firestarter*. Flames lapped up the side of the *Firestarter* as the stream of shells ripped into it and sprayed the fuel for her flamers everywhere. The 'Mech lumbered around like a man on fire and finally shut down, her 'MechWarrior trapped in the cockpit to slowly cook.

The *Jupiter* turned to face him.

"Have at 'em, boys and girls!" Mannheim ordered. He sent his *Shockwave* into a trot and the Hawk Moth kicked up more dirt as it rose from the nape of the earth to a flying gun platform, swinging wide to link up with Colonel Daum's force. "Take down that *Jupiter* as your primary."

Hunter tied his Republic Thunder autocannon Type

10 and his DO extended-range large laser to the same target interlock circuit. He heard the reassuring click of the missile load cycle completing. The *Jupiter* had taken a few hits, but not enough to even the odds. That time had arrived.

"Rook Three, deploy to the right flank and drop your cargo. I'll hold his attention for a few minutes." The HobGoblin peeled off. God bless those Fidelis troops, no complaints, no questions.

The *Jupiter* was obviously lining him up for a shot when he dropped his targeting reticle on it. "Let's see what you've got," he muttered, and fired his autocannon and laser. The temperature in his cockpit rose by a few degrees but the result was worth it. The autocannon rounds peppered the *Jupiter*'s legs, pockmarking the armor with smoking white holes where the shells had penetrated deep into the Protectorate raider. His laser lashed out with a brilliant emerald beam that initially missed the chest of the 'Mech but slowly corrected to score on the torso, searing a black scar across its chest.

The *Jupiter* fired back a millisecond later. Both its extended-range PPCs jabbed the *Shockwave* with streams of charged particles, like brilliant white-blue bolts of lightning. One shot missed by less than a meter but its arc discharge sent tiny bolts of static energy sparking up his 'Mech's right arm. The other shot hit him in the legs. The *Shockwave* rocked under the impact, vibrating wildly for a moment as the knee actuator froze and fought to break loose. When it did, he leaned hard to maintain his balance and moved the leg once again—though now with a slight limp.

The Hawk Moth gunship roared in behind the *Jupiter*, whose pilot couldn't know that the Fidelis had improved its armaments and targeting system. A crimson laser burst hit the *Jupiter* in the back of its head, and he saw at least two pieces of armor fly off. The *Jupiter* twisted its torso to look for the threat. *Good*.

Hunter squeezed the trigger of his second TIC, unleashing a salvo of long-range missiles. The wave of warheads swarmed over the *Jupiter*, and nine of the ten found their mark. The Hawk Moth peeled away, and the *Jupiter* turned to face him.

Oh, joy . . .

The Kelswa, still on his left rear, opened up with its pair of autocannons. These shells seemed to spread out more than the missile barrage, but still whittled away at the *Jupiter*'s armor. As it moved, smoke rose from holes everywhere on its body.

Mannheim heard a roar as the quad mounting of DL Ultra autocannons on the *Jupiter* came to life. These four deadly cannons sprayed a literal wall of destruction. Their target, much to his surprise, was not his *Shockwave* but the HobGoblin. They caught it dead on as it sped off to the far right flank. The shells ripped and gouged at the armored personnel carrier, tossing it wildly about. The vehicle looked as if it were going to flip under the impacts. Billowing black smoke belched out of the rear of the empty APC as it struggled to outrun the crippling assault. In the distance Mannheim saw infantry moving in to mop up whatever was left of the APC and finish it off. *Good luck. That crew is Fidelis.*

He fired another salvo with his laser and autocannon simultaneously. This time both found their mark in the battered upper chest of the *Jupiter* and rocked it back just as it fired. This volley was his to suffer.

Thirty long-range missiles tore through the space between the BattleMechs and plastered his *Shockwave* with a thunderous roar that made his ears ring. His damage display showed a few small dots of yellow where the missiles had breached his armor. He noticed a black mark on the armored cockpit glass that had not been there a moment earlier, and realized the missile had hit just in front of him.

The gun crew dropped off by the HobGoblin opened fire. Their armor-piercing rounds slapped into the *Jupiter*'s left arm and leg. It didn't seem to notice. It stayed on target and bore straight at the *Shockwave*—no surprise there. It would be a few moments before they were at pointblank range. If he was even a little lucky, he could hold off the beastlike *Jupiter*.

The Protectorate MechWarrior was no fool. Pushing his luck and his heat levels, he unleashed his quad autocannons at a full run. The shells created a storm the *Shockwave* had never been designed to take. It reeled under the assault, and Mannheim felt a twinge in his head that turned into a roaring headache with a single beat of his heart. Neurofeedback—the bane of every MechWarrior. He wanted to rip the neurohelmet off, but his training kicked in and he resisted. Staggering, he reversed his *Shockwave* and began to move slowly backward, increasing the time it would take for the *Jupiter* to close with him.

The gun crew unleashed a salvo at the flank and rear of the *Jupiter*, and the missile racks rocked on their mounts. Hunter flinched as the *Jupiter* got closer. Just enough time for one more . . .

He fired. The LRM pack emptied with a whooshing noise; the warheads had just enough time to arm before striking. This time there were no misses—it was practically impossible at this range. They exploded in a cloud of shrapnel, and he saw a slick green ooze running down the *Jupiter*'s right chest, a shattered heat sink losing its coolant. It looked like the *Jupiter* was bleeding. Hunter stopped, set the 'Mech's feet and leaned his *Shockwave* forward. *This bastard is going to run right into me, and I need to be ready to take the hit.*

From the corner of his eye he was stunned to see the mangled HobGoblin shudder into view, aimed at the *Jupiter*'s legs. It was using its last burst of speed to make a ramming attack. As expected, the Fidelis had beaten back the infantry assault a few minutes earlier.

· The *Jupiter* MechWarrior was not expecting the assault, that much was obvious. The APC caught the 'Mech's feet and it tripped. The APC flipped over twice in front of the assault 'Mech as it fell forward, right on top of the vehicle. There was a sickening crunch as the 'Mech went down, armor grinding armor. Flames burst from the APC as the ammo cooked off and leapt upward at the 'Mech on top of it. Miraculously, two Fidelis troopers scrambled out of the carnage and began running back toward the industrial plant. A hundred meters away they paused and looked back. He couldn't say why, but Mannheim had the oddest sense that they had stopped to confirm that the HobGoblin was burning hot enough to be completely destroyed.

The *Jupiter* stirred. It was down, but not out—so Hunter finished it off. A blast from his primary TIC sent a laser beam and a steady stream of autocannon rounds into the already battered rear armor. They drilled in deep. Fire broke out on the back of the 'Mech, and he saw the orange glow of the damaged reactor shielding shimmer under the ripples of heat rising from the downed 'Mech.

Occupied by the *Jupiter*, he had not been monitoring the progress of the battle. Checking his sensors now, what he saw made him sick. The Protectorate forces had driven through the lines of the planetary garrison a few moments ago. The Duchy forces had been routed, and the Protectorate forces were shifting toward Breezewood proper rather than aiming for the industrial plant.

"Rook to Pickaxe," he signaled.

"We are regrouping about two kilometers from the city. They are driving at Breezewood. It looks like they intend to hit the factory complex on the flank. I hope you boys have defenses in place." Daum's voice sounded ragged, like he'd been running.

"I want to keep them out of the city."

"I'm not the one you have to convince," Daum snapped back. "The Protectorate is acting like they suspect a trap. You need to pursue while we fall back and reform."

Mannheim twisted his 'Mech's torso and conducted a quick visual assessment. His gun crew had limited movement now that their ride, the HobGoblin, lay burning under the *Jupiter*, hissing and popping like a bonfire. The Hawk Moth was bobbing and weaving through a ground-based laser attack and took a hit. The VTOL roared away and banked in a long, hard curve then rose slightly, looking for an opportunity to move in again.

Long-range sensors indicated his second lance, designated Victory Lance, was making a controlled retreat in support of the militia. His remaining force was positioned at the industrial plant perimeter. As expected, his plan had not survived contact with the enemy, and now he had to adjust. Now there was a good chance that with the collapse of the militia forces in the center, his company might be taken out to the last man.

Damnation!

"Victory Lance, this is Rook. Move to the edge of the defense perimeter at coordinates"—he checked his tactical readout—"Delta 21. Cut into the city and try to stay on the flank and rear of those raiders. Pickaxe, I need you to reform your elements and move into the same area, swinging east. I need you to hold the line while Victory Lance pushes them into you."

"It shall be done," replied the commanding officer of Victory Lance, a Fidelis lieutenant named Carver.

Colonel Daum was not so optimistic. "Pickaxe on discreet. They are hounding me. I am going to have to fall back to the far east side of the plant. We can move through your perimeter and help shore up your defense."

Through the plant? Not with all of those explosives in place. "Negative, Pickaxe. Suggest you find another way."

"We're on the same side, damn it!"

"I know," he said, adding a lie to the numerous ones he and his people had already told. He was doing Daum a favor. When he was forced to blow the industrial complex, he didn't want any of the planetary garrison to be injured—but he couldn't say that. Still, he needed something that would drive a seasoned veteran away from a course of action. "We have sown mines. Suggest you find another way."

The channel went silent. He knew that the colonel was cursing him six ways to Sunday.

Better that than dead.

Interpretation of Duty 7

Metropolitan Gardens
Brandenburg, Callison
Former Prefecture VIII
Fortress Republic (+36 days)

The Metropolitan Gardens, or the Metro as it was referred to by the locals, was a domed botanical paradise just outside of Brandenburg. The domes had been built centuries ago and somehow, miraculously, remained untouched by numerous wars and strife, even the terrorism of the Jihad. Trees and wildlife from dozens of worlds thrived here in perfect conditions. Winding brick paths snaked through the gardens and under the arbors of flowering vines. A manmade waterfall and creek dominated this particular dome, one of the eight linked together to form the attraction.

Governor Stewart had asked Cheryl to join her here. The media had covered the governor's arrival for a private tour of the gardens exactly as they were meant to, describing the scene as "the governor choosing the peace of the botanical gardens—and the reminder of interplanetary cooperation they represented—from which to contemplate the crisis in the city, and to meet with her advisors regarding the unexpected and unwanted Republic military presence in the capital." It showed the citizens that their leaders were calm and in control, not overreacting. Allison Stewart had made only one comment on her way into the Metro: "I hope we can find a diplomatic resolution to this sudden intrusion into our internal affairs."

Cheryl had entered the Metro a short time later, and the media had grabbed shots of her as well. She had little use for the media in her role in the government and a healthy disdain for them in real life. Regardless of her personal feelings, she was closely observing Allison Stewart's technique for controlling the media and felt she was learning valuable lessons.

She passed the governor's security detail, undergoing a quick visual inspection and once-over with the weapon-sensor wands. Cheryl herself had ordered security for the governor to be tightened after the death of Legate Leif; in fact, the governor had demanded it after receiving death threats from Republic loyalists who considered her actions heavy-handed. Internal Affairs had been assigned to rounding up the loyalists in the interest of maintaining civil order. Cheryl gave the governor and the press what they wanted—an occasional arrest. She could have done more, but nothing more was necessary. Ceresco Hancock knew that often the more pressure you applied to resistance, the firmer it became.

She walked along the main path until she found Governor Stewart, who was leaning over a rosebush, carefully smelling the flowers. Cheryl slowed her approach, waiting for the governor to indicate she was ready to talk. Stewart slowly released the flower and turned to her advisor. "Thank you for joining me today, Cheryl."

"I am at your disposal, Governor," she replied quietly.

"I understand that matters have escalated with the protestors."

Governor Stewart had wondered a day ago if it was possible the protestors at the spaceport might somehow find themselves in possession of small arms that were more effective than ordinary rifles. Cheryl, of course, understood the implication: The governor wished to arrange for locals to fire on the DropShip. "Yes, ma'am. There have been no damage or injuries, but I assure you there is a psychological effect on The Republic troops."

The stocky woman crossed the path and stared intently at another flowering bush. "I acknowledge your recommendation for negotiation, and I appreciate your loyalty and capability to follow orders with which you do not necessarily agree."

"I am loyal to Callison," Cheryl replied instantly.

The governor turned to her and smiled. "As am I. Now, this knight errant seems more than willing to play a waiting game with us. From what my public relations people tell me, each day he remains here without taking action costs us support among the population."

"I understand."

"Sir Erbe has not seen fit to tell us why he is here on Callison, and that concerns me, Cheryl. If we knew his goals in coming here, that would be something we could leverage in our negotiations." She didn't say that she would use that information to arrive at a peaceful solution, and Cheryl harbored no illusions.

She must choose her next words carefully; what she was about to say would change her life forever. She had no choice if she was going to fulfill her directive. "I have learned why he is here, Governor."

"You have?"

"Yes, ma'am. His mission is twofold. He has come to secure for The Republic two completed DropShip engines that are stored here in Brandenburg. This was why he escorted a commercial transport."

"What else?"

"His additional orders require stripping the Light Horse of certain hardware for transport off-world. With the massive scope of the Fortress Republic operation, I'm not surprised they would need the hardware."

The governor paused for a moment before asking, "How did you come by this information? Has it been confirmed?"

Cheryl managed to keep her emotions off her face, though she felt sick at her complete betrayal of Sir Erbe and his men. "Governor, I hope you will accept that I cannot reveal my source and risk compromising either you or my source. Suffice it to say that this source is someone I trust completely." It was true. She trusted Kristoff Erbe. That he also trusted her was what hurt.

"They have come to loot Callison," Stewart gloated. "This is marvelous. Do you know how the people will react when they are told? Anyone believing that The Republic still supports our world will see the truth. The Republic as we know it simply doesn't exist anymore."

"Yes, Governor."

"The only thing that would make this perfect is if we knew when he was planning to make his move. If we knew that, we could have troops in position to deal with him."

It got harder. Deliberate betrayal was like that. People tended to think that once you started it got easier, but not for Cheryl. "My source also was able to inform me of when Sir Erbe plans to deploy, and where."

The governor seemed suddenly cautious. "Such good luck seems impossible, Cheryl. I must insist that you tell me how you managed this."

"I'm sorry, ma'am, but I can't say."

All at once, Stewart seemed very pleased with herself. "I think I know."

Oh, God—I hope you don't. Before Cheryl could speak, the governor continued.

"Traitor. For you to have an understanding of the knight's battle plans, you must have a traitor on the inside of his force. Someone who is sympathetic to Callison's plight. I'm right, aren't I? It's a traitor."

Cheryl held her breath; her blood sounded loud in her ears. Governor Stewart was right; someone on the inside was revealing secrets—just not whom she suspected. "It would be best if you refrained from speculating on this topic, Governor. I would hate to place anyone's life in danger as a result of our work. Let's just say that not everyone fully supports the exarch's Fortress Republic plans and leave it at that."

"But if we were to point out that even those in the military consider that Exarch Levin's course of action is wrong, it could be a public relations coup for Callison." Stewart was always thinking of the public, always finding ways to get them to see the universe the way she did: with her in the center.

"To reveal this now would place lives in jeopardy needlessly and tip our hand too early. Maybe when the dust from this affair settles, we can let people know that even The Republic military doesn't agree with the exarch. For the moment, our source should remain completely unknown."

"You are a valuable and resourceful asset, my dear," Stewart said, placing her hand on Cheryl's shoulder.

It was now or never. "I appreciate that, ma'am. You know that I have never asked for anything for myself. My duty has always been to Callison first." Those hints should be broad enough for even the dimmest politician, which Stewart certainly was not.

"But now you'd like to ask for something?"

"If I may."

"Go ahead."

"As shown in my personnel file, I served in the militia myself for a few years—junior officers training program. When we make the move against Sir Erbe, I would like to be there—with the militia, if you will allow it." Her words were sincere, practically dripping with patriotic fervor. She didn't want to overplay her hand, but she wanted the governor to think bigger, broader.

Stewart pondered the request for a moment, turning to quietly study another flowering bush before she responded. Cheryl thought she could read the older woman's thoughts. The governor would be looking for a way to turn this into something that she could use, something that she could leverage to her own advantage. "Cheryl, I know you are loyal, and I deeply appreciate that. But I cannot have you serving in the militia when the Light

Horse must defend our homeland. I'm afraid that wouldn't be right."

That wasn't the answer she had expected. *Maybe I overacted.* Governor Stewart continued. "Simply being there with them is not enough. For your service, I will turn over command of this operation to Internal Affairs. You will not simply observe or participate: You will command the operation against this knight errant."

Cheryl felt her face turn red, though she knew the governor would misinterpret the reason. "Thank you, ma'am. I won't let you down."

"I know you won't." Stewart plucked one of the flowers from a bush and drew a long breath. Then she casually tossed the flower onto the path for someone else to clean up. "Now then. Let's plan how you will crush this knight."

Her apartment was dark when Cheryl Gunson walked in. As soon as the door closed she dropped her bag and flopped onto the couch. It had been a long day. She had betrayed a man she barely knew and the people who served him. It hurt to think of it that way, but she knew it was the truth. The only thing that allowed her to stay the course was one thought: *What I'm doing is in the long-term best interests of The Republic.* In the darkness of her tiny flat, the thought offered little solace.

She was proud of one thing. Cheryl had not revealed everything she knew. Part of her training as a ghost knight had been learning that it was never wise to lay down all your cards. It was better to keep back something for the future. She was particularly proud that she did not reveal the last bit of information she knew because it would have shattered Kristoff Erbe—not as a knight errant, but as a man.

Rubbing her temples, she kicked off her shoes and lifted her legs onto the couch. Revealing his secret to Governor Stewart would have given the governor a dramatic edge, especially if she in turn made it known to the public. She felt sure that Kristoff Erbe's true past was known in very few circles. The ghost paladin had provided the information to her only because she might need to leverage it in order to complete her assignment. Cheryl was glad it hadn't been necessary.

It could be argued that the Jihad represented mankind's darkest time. Some worlds and cities were laid waste, others were terrorized. Erbe's homeworld of Towne had been occupied by the Word of Blake, and their reign of terror included both death camps and re-education facilities established to break the hearts, minds and wills of the local population.

On no planet did the Word of Blake operate alone. On every world there were those who helped them, who simply saw them as a new government, a new flag in the wind over their capitols. Those with violent or sadistic tendencies joined the Word of Blake, committing atrocities and war crimes; others served as minor functionaries and administrators under their regime. Not until Devlin Stone took up the war against the Word of Blake and shattered their core, driving them from world to world until they were crushed, was it possible to consider the guilt or innocence of the collaborators.

Kristoff Erbe's secret was tied to those events. His father, Jacob, was an Education Minister on Towne before the Jihad. When the Word of Blake seized control of Towne, they placed him in charge of a reeducation camp. He did everything in his power to behave humanely and to maintain humane conditions, but people still died in his camp. Jacob Erbe could not stop the baser instincts of the oppressors.

Transcripts of his trial showed that he did what he had to do to save the lives of his family. The Word of Blake threatened to kill them all if he didn't accept the assignment. Kristoff was four at the time. Ceresco didn't know how much he remembered of his father. She didn't want to know.

When the Jihad ended, Jacob had been rounded up along with all the others who had cooperated with the Word of Blake. In every case, the citizens called for a quick trial and an even quicker verdict, which was always death, painful and public. But it was an inescapable fact that Jacob was a minor official performing a minor job for the oppressors. His critics—malcontents all, looking for someone, anyone, to pay a price for their own inactivity during the occupation—claimed that he actively supported the Word of Blake administration. Jacob Erbe faced a board of inquiry and gave his testimony. He hid his family during that time, facing his accusers alone. Ceresco knew firsthand that such measures truly were necessary: Her own mother spoke of those times, but rarely.

Jacob Erbe never was formally charged with any crime associated with the occupation, but the damage had been done. He carried a mark on his name and soul. It became impossible for him to get a job; he had no hope of survival. He never left Towne; she assumed it was because he felt he had done nothing wrong. She considered his attitude admirable but stupid. She would have left. If he had gone somewhere else, he would have had a chance at a new life.

Three years after the inquiry, Jacob Erbe committed suicide. It was barely mentioned in the papers. His funeral was private. He was survived by Kristoff and his wife, who killed herself two years later. Ten-year-old Kristoff was adopted by an aunt and uncle who were not named Erbe, but Kristoff never changed his last name. He didn't hide who he was. Ceresco admired that, and cursed it: It meant he would be stubborn, determined not to do what his father had done.

Yes, Cheryl Gunson was glad she had held back this nugget of information. *One betrayal a day is enough for me; should be enough for anyone.* She closed her eyes and prayed for sleep that never came.

Interpretation of Duty 10

Brandenburg, Callison
Former Prefecture VIII
Fortress Republic (+36 days)

The staccato of fire off to the west told Kristoff that his attack force had reached its objective. The Po tank on Bagley Avenue had done an admirable job of keeping his Republic forces bottled up. Every time he attempted to shift his troops, the tank would appear at the exact worst moment and make its presence known. He had suffered four casualties so far from the Po, not to mention a sabot round that had almost penetrated his Morgan assault tank's turret. The impact had been so violent that two of the crew had been knocked unconscious. The gunnery officer had held things together enough to force the Po back into hiding, but it was frustrating Sir Erbe enough that he decided to take more drastic action.

Ask any soldier, and they would tell you that urban combat was the worst kind of fighting. Cover was everywhere, and if you needed more, with a few well-placed shots you could create your own. He would not have chosen to fight in the city, but rarely in his career had he been given the choice of battlefield.

Colonel Adamans led the attack force of two squads of infantry: shock troops and PAL-suited troops. Using the maps Ceresco had provided, they navigated the sewer system as skillfully as rats. The tunnels were dank, dark and foul beyond description, but the Fidelis troopers said nothing and simply accepted their duty.

Their route was not quick or direct. They had to snake through the ankle-deep ooze of rotting human excrement some four blocks out of their way to reach the rear of the militia, and would exit the sewers into a small sewage-pumping facility. If the sewer plans and their intel were accurate, they would exit just to the rear of the Po's area of operation and hit it when the crew's guard was down—hopefully when they were breaking for dinner. Kristoff checked his chronometer again and saw that the optimal window was an hour gone: Either the team had run into delays or was simply biding its time. He had given complete control of the mission to Adamans, so he had no way of knowing the reason.

"Squirrel, this is Harbinger," Adamans signaled. "Target has been neutralized. We have recovered two crates of expendables and are returning. Please inform the sentries."

"Good work, Harbinger. Pickets will be informed." He sent word down to the defense perimeter that their troops would be returning in a captured tank. It was a small success, but one of the few in the mission so far.

The image of Ghost Knight Ceresco Hancock, Knight of the Sphere, defender of The Republic, sitting in a cockpit and firing on Republic troops was etched into his brain. He wanted to come up with a good reason for her behavior, but couldn't—other than her mysterious mission objectives. *What kind of mission could require her to turn on her own people?* He knew that as a ghost knight she lived in a world of backstabbing and betrayal. Perhaps she was running her own game—perhaps her orders had nothing to do with her actions. Had she turned rogue, and begun carving out a position of power for herself? *No!* He suppressed that thinking. Knights, even ghost knights, answered to a higher calling. They defended the vision of Devlin Stone.

None of this explained her opening fire on the people she was supposed to defend. Kristoff realized that the only person who could answer his questions was Lady Hancock, and she was currently at the other end of a barrel aimed at him and his troops.

"Identification sequence initiated," the computer voice stated.

"We're running with the shadows of the night." Cheryl lifted the right arm of the *Hellion* and performed several twisting gestures that the computer would recognize as her code. Combined with her voice it was what unlocked the BattleMech to her sole control.

"Voiceprint and move sequence authorized. Welcome aboard," the battlecomputer replied. The fusion reactor under her cockpit throttled up automatically and the rest of the cockpit controls came online. The muscles in her jaw ached inside the neurohelmet; tensing them was a nervous habit, and she was plenty nervous lately.

She had thought things through. The next two days were going to be quite busy, and she knew that she was going to be hard-pressed to pull off everything she had planned. Certain supplies had to be secured and hidden away for later use; that had been easy, given that she had nominal control of the Callison Light Horse militia. The explosives had been much easier to secure than the ingredients she needed for her other planned operation.

Cheryl knew that it was critical that she reach Sir Erbe—which was now going to be quite difficult, with her forces laying siege to his position. At this point, both sides were doing little more than sniping at each other. The most significant event of the day had come in the early evening. Somehow Erbe had gotten a force behind the lines and had taken out the Po tank she had posted to the west. She added "sneaky" to her long list of Fidelis traits; they had an urban infiltration finesse matched only by the elite troops of the Federated Suns. She had augmented the cordon with ad hoc militia— police units and volunteers armed with everything from small arms to shoulder-launched short-range missiles. These were the kind of units that would drive Kristoff Erbe crazy. He wouldn't want to fire on them since they represented civilians.

She angled her *Hellion* out into an open street that led to the west and the warehouse district. The *Hellion* had made several forays into the battle. She had fired on the Republic troops, usually misdirecting her shots and doing what she could to minimize damage to the "enemy." These people were not her enemies. If Erbe had done what he was supposed to do, he would be at the spaceport right now, peacefully negotiating terms for his safe passage off Callison.

But he hadn't. She had miscalculated; she had been wrong. That line of thinking irritated her like a nasty, unreachable itch, so she avoided it. Erbe's choice to hole up in the warehouse district had forced her to accelerate her plans, but it had also brought Governor Stewart's real plans to the surface. Matters were quickly coming to a head, and she needed to make sure that Kristoff Erbe was working with her. The time for killing—killing in the streets, at least—was coming to an end.

She moved along the right side of the street, keeping close to the buildings for cover. Officially, she was on patrol, keeping the pressure on The Republic forces. Unofficially, her mission was to reach Sir Erbe and secure his cooperation.

Her tactical display blared a warning. She saw the foe two blocks ahead and winced; she had hoped for something less imposing and deadly than a Mars assault tank. She needed to give observers a good fight but avoid being killed. Locking onto the tank, she fired her medium lasers. The green beams stabbed the narrow rear profile of the tank near the missile racks. Armor seared and peeled back from the hit. One of the warheads in the racks went off in a sympathetic explosion. Otherwise, the Mars shook off the attack as if it was an annoyance.

Then all hell broke loose.

The Mars mounted three Crossbow long-range missile racks, fifteen missiles each. With plumes of orange and red, the forty-four surviving missiles rose from the racks in a unified wave of carnage, all headed right at her. The gauss rifle fired at the same instant. She could see the co-mounted laser had been stripped off and the caliber of the gauss beefed up. Another mark in the Fidelis win column.

Most of the missiles found their mark on some part of the tiny Light Horse BattleMech, and the *Hellion* was not designed to take this kind of punishment. It rocked under the missile impacts, pushing her torso around just in time to see a silvery slug from the gauss hit her missile rack. Warning lights flared as she twisted and stumbled back, fighting to keep her footing. She recovered her balance and glanced out of her cockpit at the missile rack; it was half gone. The damage diagram indicated that it was semi-operational. *That was like saying someone was 'sort of pregnant.'* It either worked or it didn't. She locked her targeting reticle onto the Mars and fired the launcher.

One missile slid out of the tube and dropped to the ground, sputtering somewhere off to the side of the *Hellion*. The remaining five missiles found the Mars tank's front glacial plate, rattling the tank and kicking up chunks of the ferrocrete road. It wasn't a killing blow, but to anyone observing, it was clear she was putting up a fight.

She moved diagonally across the street to close the distance between her and the Mars tank. The tank had other ideas—as she was sure it would. This time the missiles came flying at her in a sputtering stream of twos and threes. Some missed and hit buildings in the distance. Others blasted into her already-torn armor. The *Hellion* rocked and quaked with each thudding blast.

Smoke, black and gray, wrapped around her cockpit. Her hand swerved across the control panels to the handle. It was time. Red warning lights screamed for her attention, but her focus was elsewhere.

Cheryl leaned the *Hellion* forward at the waist just as the Mars fired its gauss rifle a second time. She pulled the handle. There was a flash, and her cockpit canopy blew up and outward. A rush of cool air enveloped her, and she felt a grinding pain in her back and buttocks as the ejection seat fired. Something hit her neurohelmet hard, jerking her neck and head to the side. She felt as if she were in a thunderstorm of noise and light. A wave of dizziness came over her, and she went limp as the parachute deployed. She had to concentrate to open her eyes, and the moment they did, her seat slammed onto the street only thirty meters from the Mars.

The infantry was on top of her before she could move. Four or five pairs of hands jerked her free of the seat. Someone pulled off her neurohelmet and she saw the source of the impact she had felt; a shard of armor plating had lodged in her neurohelmet. Another few pounds of force and it would have cut into her brain and killed her. She looked back at the fallen *Hellion*.

"Like I planned it," she muttered faintly as the infantry dragged her behind the Mars and into their custody.

"I hope you can give me a reason why I should not hold you for treason." Kristoff Erbe kept his voice just below a shout. He stood in a corner of the weakly lit room off the main part of the warehouse, looming over Ceresco Hancock. He could hear the anger in his voice, and he wanted to make sure she heard it, too. What he wanted even more was an explanation.

She shifted. Her hands were bound behind her, and she sat in a small wooden chair that had been scrounged for her interrogation. Kristoff had ordered everyone out of the room except for Adamans. At this point, he trusted the Fidelis officer more than his fellow knight.

Despite her bruises and a little rough handling, the

ghost knight did not appear to be mentally shaken by her situation. In fact, she seemed almost pleased to be captured, and that irritated him. "I think treason is a little strong, Sir Erbe. True, I fired on Republic troops, but only in pursuit of my mission objectives."

"Bah!" he cursed as he paced in front of her. "You have been using your secret mission as a shield since we met. Tell me your orders, so I can judge if you are a traitor or not."

"You know I can't do that. And while you may not believe this, I took my 'Mech out into the street today in hopes of reaching you. You don't really think I'm stupid enough to tangle with a Mars in a frigging *Hellion*, do you?"

He had to admit it wasn't a very bright move, but deception was part and parcel of the ghost knight's life, and he didn't know what to believe. "I don't know what your motivations are. That's the root of the problem here. You tell me that you are loyal to the Republic, but at the same time you are leading an attack against us."

She frowned. "If you hadn't been so stubborn as to drive on this warehouse, we could have resolved this whole thing with only a few shots being fired. You were supposed to fall back to the spaceport. And as for my leading the attacks against you, I'll have you know it takes a lot to manipulate a leader as shifty as Governor Stewart into putting me in charge of the fight." He heard a note of pride in her voice, but that didn't make sense.

"You are killing people you are sworn to protect."

"If I wanted to wipe you out, I could have. I wouldn't have provided you with the schematics of the streets or even the location of your precious DropShip engines. I could have kept all of that from you. I could have used my knowledge of the city against you. If I were a traitor to The Republic, I would have used the sewer system to kill or capture you. I didn't. Grow up, Kristoff. You of all people know that what people think isn't what's important. What matters is what's true."

"What do you mean by that?" he demanded.

"You know what I mean," she said in a low tone.

"If you are trying to judge me by the actions of a man I hardly knew, you are making a huge mistake."

"Why do you think you were chosen for this mission? Did you really think this assignment was so simple as to land on Callison and pick up some DropShip engines and military hardware? I spent time with Redburn before this mission. I know that Callison is important to the future of The Republic: Devlin Stone said so. I'm going to make whatever that is possible. For that to happen, you have to trust me."

He stared at her. "You certainly don't make it easy."

"I never do," she said in a confessional tone. "Regardless—you have to trust me, or a lot more people are going to be hurt and Callison will be cut off from The Republic for years to come."

Kristoff considered what she was saying. Her words made sense from a certain point of view. At the same time, the image of her in the *Hellion* cockpit filled his vision. He was angry; at himself, at her, at Damien Redburn for putting him in this situation. *What can I do? Who can I trust?* Knights were not supposed to take up arms against fellow knights. His universe was changing too much with Fortress Republic. He wondered how many other, similar choices were being made throughout The Republic at this moment. How many of those decisions were going to be wrong?

He studied her face. Levin, Redburn and the ghost paladin had chosen her. They trusted her. They chose him to work in conjunction with her. They obviously knew something he didn't. He realized, if he couldn't trust his leaders, the leaders of The Republic, then the Republic was already dead. She might betray him, but he could not betray himself or the oath that he had taken. It was that oath, that knighthood, that his mind embraced as he stared into her eyes.

He moved behind her and cut the straps binding her wrists. She rubbed her hands and stood up. "What changed your mind?"

He hadn't been sure until she asked him. "I'm a Knight of the Sphere. If I can't trust another knight, then The Republic has ceased to exist—and I refuse to believe that, not yet."

"Me either." She offered him her hand, and he shook it without hesitation. "Here's the situation. The governor has ordered a full-on assault. I want to reduce the risk of casualties as much as possible, so I'm going to need your troops to hold back. The last thing we need is more dead."

"I'd offer to surrender, but I doubt that would be favorably received."

He saw the answer in her face. "The governor expects me to obliterate your force. She wants your annihilation to stand as proof that The Republic is dead. No survivors, no hostages, no prisoners." Her words rang ominously in his ears.

"What a bitch!"

"Trust me, you don't know the half of it." She gave him a flat grin.

"We could launch a breakout. With you in command of the road to the spaceport, you could feign the defense and pull back. We could reach our DropShips."

"It won't work. We've placed mines and set ambush points all the way to the spaceport. No offense—I know you're a good MechWarrior, but you wouldn't stand a chance."

"So what do you want?"

"Fall back. Make us work for the ground we have to take. I can't order my troops to pull their punches: They will do their best to root you out because that is what the governor has ordered. I can mitigate some of that, but damned little. Understand this, however; I am *not* going to fulfill the governor's orders. What she has asked me to do is wrong. I have to put up a fight, but it's just to buy me time."

"Time for what?"

"Time to strike. My mission is left to a fairly broad interpretation. I need an audience with the governor, and the fastest way to get that is to continue fighting and tell her I need to update her on the situation."

"Then what?" he pressed.

She hesitated. "I'll do what I have to." Kristoff knew that no amount of probing would make her reveal anything more. Very well. He wrapped himself in the veil of her trust.

"Adamans," he said, turning to the man standing in the shadows.

"Yes, Sir Erbe?"

"I trust that your troops can get her through the lines so that it will look as if she escaped."

"We can."

Erbe turned back to Ceresco. "I was going to punch you in the face when I learned you had betrayed us. I just thought you should know."

She straightened to her full height, a head shorter than him, and gave him a coy smile. "I would have done worse to you if the roles were reversed. I tend to be a kick-in-the-groin kind of fighter." Her face became sober. "I will need to show that I got away, and that it wasn't easy. The last thing I need at this stage of the game is for the governor to question my loyalty to her."

"What are you saying?"

"Take your best shot, Sir Erbe. God knows I earned it."

Nothing was said between them after that. His knuckles throbbed as Adamans helped her up and toward the door.

As a mortar round went off just a few buildings up, both Adamans and Lady Hancock ducked. A layer of dust from the building next to them drifted down and coated them like fine snow. The Fidelis warrior held his assault rifle at the ready, covering their progress.

"We're in position," he said, pressing flat against the building. "Your forces are just across the street. I've ordered my troops to hold their fire so that you can make a break for your lines."

She eyed the Fidelis trooper. One side of her face pulsed with pain from the punch she had taken. He had watched her as they moved through the warehouse district, but had said nothing, offered no interpretation of events. Adamans was a closed book to her, as were all the Fidelis. She had left New Earth without getting to know them. The only thing she knew for sure was that they were incredible fighters. They had caught her Light Horse forces off guard in nearly every encounter.

"No guarantee that my own troops won't fire on me," she muttered, surveying the street ahead.

"We all must assume some risks. Sir Erbe assumed a risk in letting you go. I believe you are capable of assuming a few yourself."

"What about you? What do you think of all of this?"

Adamans kept his focus on the street, on the rooftops, on the sounds of battle nearby, the popping of gunfire in the distance. "I don't trust you, but I don't know you. My duty does not always allow me to question such things."

"You're hiding behind words."

He turned and made eye contact with her. "You are correct."

"So why didn't you say something to Erbe?"

His icy stare cut deep. "It is not my place. My people learned their place a long time ago. We came to understand who we are by what we lost. Now we understand."

"Where are your people from?" she said, leaning toward him.

"Your nightmares," he replied with a sinister grin. "And if you have lied to Sir Erbe, sleep carefully knowing that the Fidelis will avenge him."

She knew beyond a doubt that his words were not an idle threat.

Altar of Freedom 5

New Dearborn, Ryde
Jade Falcon Occupation Zone
Fortress Republic (-18 days)

"What's that lunatic doing?" barked Paulis.

She stepped over the shattered, still smoldering remains of the *Gyrfalcon* she had managed to enfilade by moving through the confining New Dearborn streets. The *Gyrfalcon* had been moving methodically up the street in pursuit of her forces when she came down a narrow alley at its side. The buildings and infrastructure had masked her signature. The Falcon had gone down hard, in the process putting three good volleys into her *Templar*. Her attacks, combined with a barrage from one of her tanks, forced the *Gyrfalcon* to finally succumb.

"Who?"

"Boyne. He charged up Georgia Avenue with a lance of infantry. Those bloody damn Fidelis troops are following him to their deaths. He's heading right smack into the Falcons."

You've answered your own question. She checked her sensors and could barely make out the IFF transponders of her units and those of the advancing Falcons, even a short distance away. Captain Paulis was right, though,

Boyne was charging into the center of the Jade Falcon force. Fidelis or not, this was a bold move that would result in a bloody engagement. In fact, he had almost no chance of surviving. She refrained from vocalizing any of her thoughts.

"He's buying us all time," was all she said.

"They'll be wiped out," Paulis countered. "We need to fall back to the DropShips and use them for cover."

It wasn't that she hadn't thought about that. The turrets of the *Aurora*-class ships would offer a nice umbrella of fire, but retreating now would surely prevent Sir Greene from linking up with them. Boyne was doing what was necessary; he was doing his duty. If they fought alone, his force would die, and that was not right. *When I became a knight I promised to defend The Republic. This is another opportunity to live up to that oath.*

Boyne wouldn't die alone . . . not if she had any say in it.

"Form up on me. We'll go up to—" She checked her tactical display. "Thirteenth Street and cut over. That should bring us out right where he's at. If he can hold on long enough, we can reinforce him."

"M'lady . . ."

There wasn't time for argument, so Synd aimed for Paulis' ego. "Captain Paulis," she said sharply. "Captain Boyne understands *his* duty. If you're afraid to fight, you should surrender now and hope that the Falcons are taking bondsmen today." Anger rang in her voice.

"Whatever is left of Strike lance, form on me and move up to Thirteenth Street," Paulis ordered after a moment of silence, bitterness evident in his voice. Lady Synd had no way of knowing whether she or Boyne had shamed him into continuing to fight. In the end, it didn't matter. She wasn't proud of what she'd done, but she was pleased with the results.

She had to buy time for Sir Greene. Damien Redburn had made it clear that the objectives of the ghost knights took precedence in these operations. Greene had a mission to do, and her job was to ensure that he had the time to get it done. She wanted to signal him to hurry up, but she assumed that by now the Falcons would be monitoring their communications channels and could track him down.

Hurry, Jayson. Time is running out. A Morgan tank appeared on her flank as she moved down the street and rounded the corner onto Thirteenth. Three blocks down, the gates of hell were opening up.

Sir Greene pushed the office chair back from the monitor, rolled a meter or so, and then popped to his feet. The cube in his hand held the data that the Falcons had been researching. They would have backups and techniques to recover the data he erased, that much was sure. What they wouldn't have was the scientists to replicate the work or to warn the Falcons about the viruses that he had planted in their network to corrupt the backup data over time, eventually damaging all of it.

He had seen the data as it dumped to the cube: images, research papers, schematics and so on. He was not an engineer or scientist, but he knew a space defense system when he saw one. And this material had an extra element that he found disturbing: It appeared that the Jade Falcons were looking at the technology of automated space drones—leveraging a design that the Word of Blake had used in the Jihad. At this point in the game what they were doing was pure research, but the potential scenarios were scary, nonetheless. What he found even more disturbing was that The Republic would go to such lengths to obtain these scientists and their data. *Are we willing to taint ourselves to leverage something the blasted Word of Blake was so eager to use?*

He stuffed the cube into his pocket and secured the flap so that it wouldn't fall out. Reaching into another pocket, he pulled out a button and tossed it on the floor in a conspicuous location. A uniform button from the Lyran Commonwealth Armed Forces; specifically, one of their elite strike forces. The Falcon Watch would comb the research facility carefully, looking for any intel about the attack force. On the surface, everything would point to the Republic of the Sphere. That would be too easy. Digging deeper, they would find little bits of evidence that pointed to the Lyran Commonwealth. The Falcons would certainly find that to be more logical. Hopefully, their frustration would turn against their old foe rather than The Republic.

Greene checked his chronometer and winced. *Damn.* It had taken much longer than he had expected. Until this moment, he had deliberately ignored the time and focused on his tasks. Now, time was everything. He wondered if he was going to be able to make it back to the DropShips—or if the DropShips were even still there. There was only one way to find out. He began to run down the hall of the research facility. It was a long way to Veterans Park.

A Jade Falcon JESIII missile platform skidded to a stop and fired a second later. The missiles, nothing more than streaks of twisting gray smoke, hit the side and rear of her *Templar* with a sickening roar, like a thunderstorm breaking loose. Lady Synd heard metal tear away and the moaning of her *Templar*'s internal structure. The sound sent a chill down her spine and made her teeth throb. She fought the impact and managed to keep her 'Mech upright—barely.

One of her ATV squads, consisting of Fidelis and Republic troops, opened up on the JES, giving it just enough punishment to make it back around the corner in hopes of blocking line of sight. The Fidelis had tricked-out the ATVs, modifying some with a single flight of long-range missiles, others with portable camouflage gear. . . . Hopefully the changes were just enough to confuse the Falcons' sensors. A pristine Falcon *Phoenix Hawk* stepped up to take its place. Its brilliant emerald paint made it look like a deadly stalking predator.

The ATV squad sped off after the JES, but the *Hawk* wanted nothing to do with them . . . it was after her. Hoisting its arm-mounted laser, it aimed and fired before she could move. The brilliant green beam sliced like a hot knife through butter, slashing at her already mangled torso armor plating. A glob of molten armor splattered onto her cockpit canopy and sizzled as it melted into place. There was no way she could ignore it.

But she did.

She focused on the *Phoenix Hawk*. Synd had one working PPC; the one on the left side had been turned to a mangled and twisted chunk of salvage by a missile barrage a few minutes earlier. The targeting reticle seemed to fight her efforts; either the battlecomputer was straining from damage or the heat, or the weapon system itself was damaged. It didn't matter. She had to make this work.

As the reticle drifted over the *Hawk* she fired, not waiting for a weapons lock tone. She felt her cockpit temperature spike again as the cobalt beam of charged particles stabbed at the Jade Falcon. The beam tore a gash from the shoulder blade of the 'Mech and traveled upward, hitting the cockpit and an overhanging portion of the jump jets mounted on the rear of the *Hawk*. A trio of short-range missiles from one of her squads slammed into the Jade Falcon as well, hitting the legs and leaving black circles where they had pitted the armor. Not so pristine anymore.

The Falcon MechWarrior was obviously unimpressed. He fired his jump jets and headed straight at her. The narrow street, now lined with burning civilian hovercars, restricted her movement to forward and backward. Synd attempted to move her 'Mech backward but hit something; she wasn't sure what.

The *Phoenix Hawk* came down on her from an awkward angle. Death from above was like that. On holovid shows it was neat and clean: In real life, it was a dangerous move that was as risky for the MechWarrior executing it as for the victim.

She heard a terrible *crunch*. Her *Templar* groaned and dropped down on its left side. The restraining straps in the cockpit dug deep into her shoulder blades, and somehow her coolant vest had been torn and was spewing a thin, sticky stream of light green coolant into the air. Lady Synd wondered if she had broken a rib in the fall.

The damage display of the *Templar* showed that it was still functional, but most of the torso armor was gone. Her fusion-reactor shielding must have been fractured when she fell, because the heat warning indicator was rising quickly. Nothing about her situation was pretty, but she still could fight—and still had the desire to. Rocking the pedal controls, she levered the *Templar* up to its knees. The *Phoenix Hawk* was in the street in front of her.

The Jade Falcon warrior was struggling to get his 'Mech upright as well. His 'Mech was less damaged than the *Templar*, but she could see that the 'Mech's left side was crumpled like a hovercar that had been in a bad head-on collision. She charged her functional PPC as she rose. This warrior was good. This warrior had to go down.

Before she could get off a shot, a squad of Fidelis warriors, along with a lone Republic soldier, appeared at the knees of the *Phoenix Hawk* and immediately went on the offensive. She watched two Fidelis scamper up the side of the *Phoenix Hawk* and lash satchel charges to the area just below the cockpit. These were not normal charges but shaped explosives that detonated in a cone configuration. They would fire a jet of superheated metal into the target, a blast that could penetrate even the toughest armor. The Fidelis warriors moved away, and the MechWarrior in the cockpit of the *Hawk* could do nothing. He had to be able to see the charges, and his only option was to punch out.

Synd wanted him to punch out. He didn't. The charges went off and the cockpit filled with death. The *Phoenix Hawk* slumped to the street, ripping up the ferrocrete as it dropped.

She hoped the fight was over, but those hopes shattered when a *Stalking Spider* emerged through the smoke. It fired down at her *Templar*. Fresh into the fight, her new foe came at her with the ferocity she had come to expect from the Falcons. Lifting her PPC, she prepared for the next wave of death and destruction.

It came far too quickly.

Interpretation of Duty 5

Munich Spaceport
Brandenburg, Callison
Former Prefecture VIII
Fortress Republic (+33 days)

They arrived on a cold, windy day. The *Onondaga* was an *Aurora*-class DropShip, a relative lightweight as DropShips go, and the atmospheric turbulence added a new dimension to the return of gravity; Kristoff Erbe felt a jolt of nausea with every bump. He was glad to be watching their approach from the bridge rather than making a hot drop into a combat zone.

Their sister DropShip was a merchant transport named the *Redball Express 13*, and it landed a few minutes after the *Onondaga*. The *Redball* would take charge of the DropShip fusion engine assemblies, the retrieval of which Kristoff Erbe considered the easiest part of his mission. The trickier part would be meeting with the legate and governor and arranging to obtain and take off-world a percentage of the Callison militia's hardware. After he completed this mission, he would follow Paladin Redburn's orders to make a rendezvous in the Talitha system.

It had been a sobering trip for Sir Erbe and the rest

of the crew. The day they jumped, a message had been broadcast to their JumpShip from Exarch Levin himself via Damien Redburn. The walls of Fortress Republic were going up. The knights and their troops would be jumping out of The Republic per their existing arrangements, and they would not be coming back. Redburn had relayed the message from his own JumpShip, the *Hartford*. The phrasing of the message strongly implied that he, too, was leaving The Republic.

Erbe watched as his troops listened to Levin's address to the Inner Sphere. The handful of Republic veterans were shaken. They had known that their mission would take them away from The Republic, but actually hearing the words that dissolved the ideal they served deeply moved them. Erbe saw more than one man crying.

The reaction of the Fidelis troops surprised him. He studied their faces as they listened to Levin speak. He had half-expected them to show no emotion at all—they generally appeared to be completely stoic. One by one, they bowed their heads as if in prayer. The gesture caught him off guard: It was as if they had come face-to-face with a prophesy. He thought back to his discussions with Damien Redburn, and realized that the paladin had been right: Faith was an important aspect of this mission.

Adamans broke the mold of his fellow Fidelis. He had a ready, dry sense of humor. Erbe and the Fidelis commander enjoyed a drink together each evening, and Adamans relaxed, telling stories of the Fidelis military training. After a while, Erbe decided he seemed perfectly normal—except for his refusal to talk about the history of the Fidelis. Kristoff soon stopped asking questions. *We all have something in our pasts that we don't want to discuss. I understand better than most.*

As the DropShips settled onto their landing pads, Sir Erbe issued the standard orders for military ships arriving on a planet. Though he carried a company of troops, he expected to have no need for them, since his mission required only discussion and negotiation. Still, things had

changed since they left New Earth. He assumed that
Callison knew about Fortress Republic; the news broad-
casts were filled with stories of changes in The Republic,
but he had paid them little attention.

He was a Knight of the Sphere on a mission for the
exarch, and that title had always commanded consider-
able respect. It was somewhat concerning that the news
reports didn't portray the citizens of Callison as supporting Fortress Republic, and there were discussions of "the
unfortunate incident at the barracks" that caught his attention. In light of this uncertainty, Erbe chose to err
on the side of caution. He ordered Colonel Adamans to
deploy a light security screen around the DropShips and
coordinate with spaceport security forces.

As soon as Adamans left to organize the security detail, Erbe attempted to contact Legate Nehemiah Leif,
whose profile he had reviewed en route. His call did
not go through to the legate's office; he was abruptly
transferred to a number of different government agen-
cies. That struck him as odd, since standard operating
procedure for the arrival of a Republic military force on
any planet required immediate communication with the
planetary legate. When he became annoyed with the
runaround and demanded an explanation of why he was
not being immediately connected, the channel was cut
off. Apparently the Callison Light Horse was not taking calls.

Minutes later, Colonel Adamans requested his presence on the forward personnel ramp, and Sir Kristoff
Erbe realized that his mission on Callison was not going
to be a milk run.

Adamans pointed at the perimeter fence nearly half a
kilometer away. Munich Spaceport was an urban facility,
situated on the east edge of the city, surrounded by
warehouses and bustling city streets; a completely ordinary arrangement for most planets. What stood out here
was that the fence was lined with ranks of protestors.
Some held up flags of The Republic that had thick red
tape pulled diagonally across the insignia. Others held

up protest signs that he couldn't read. The sound of angry yelling and chanting floated across the ferrocrete. It was an impressive gathering.

"What do you make of this?" Adamans asked. "I have deployed our security forces under the landing struts to take advantage of the available cover. These residents are not behaving as expected; in addition, I have been informed that the spaceport authority has refused to provide us with any services, including supplying us with potable water and fresh food. They say they have orders to deny us access to their facilities. They were . . . curt."

"You informed them that we are on a mission for The Republic?"

"They did not seem impressed. One of them used a derogatory term regarding Exarch Levin and his birth mother; I will not repeat it for you." Erbe caught a fleeting glimpse of Adamans' dry humor. "I think it is safe to say they were not impressed or intimidated by our presence."

Kristoff surveyed the protestors again. "Alright. Adamans, keep all troops beyond the security detail on board the ships. Prep our 'Mechs and vehicles for rapid deployment. Inform all personnel that we are on a heightened state of alert. Make it clear that no one is to fire their weapon unless they are directly fired upon. No one is to leave the ship without your personal authorization."

"Understood, sir," the Fidelis trooper replied. "What do you plan to do?"

"I need to talk to someone in authority," Erbe said. "There is some sort of misunderstanding here that I need to sort out." As he watched the protestors, he saw a Morningstar command vehicle move just behind the mob. *A militia vehicle, supporting the protestors, monitoring the spaceport. Something has gone seriously wrong.* His first reaction was that Legate Leif must have turned traitor—or something worse. *This kind of behavior toward us cannot be ignored or tolerated. This is still The Republic!*

*   *   *

From the bridge of the *Onondaga* Sir Erbe watched the sleek hoverlimo move through the mob and onto the spaceport tarmac. He used the bridge viewscreen to magnify the image. The crowd seemed to treat the hoverlimo with reverence; no one pounded on the hood or doors as it passed. Governor Allison Stewart clearly held her people under control.

It had taken several hours to get through to her office, and Erbe was not allowed to speak directly to the governor. She apparently was too busy dealing with the civilian unrest at the spaceport to talk to him. He convinced her administrative assistant to arrange for him to meet Governor Stewart, but he was not allowed to go to her. She would come to him.

He recognized that it was all part of the media ploy. The image of Governor Allison Stewart bravely driving without guards to the heavily armed DropShip would play well with her image in the press. He didn't mind. In the hour prior to her arrival, he had seen several other Light Horse vehicles mingling with the mob at the perimeter fence, including a massive *Mangonel*. Governor Stewart was making it clear that Callison was not a friendly place if you wore the uniform of The Republic.

Adamans escorted the governor to Erbe's stateroom. There were more comfortable rooms on the ship in which to conduct this meeting, but Erbe decided that since Stewart possessed all the advantages so far, it wouldn't hurt to try making her a little uncomfortable. She was waiting for him when he entered the cramped gray space in the bowels of the ship.

Kristoff was surprised by her appearance. She was short, stocky and not very physically appealing. He was of average height, yet he towered over her. He immediately understood that she must be a crafty politician in order to wield such power without physical charisma. He understood that she was tricky and dangerous.

He extended his hand and she shook it courteously.

"I am Kristoff Erbe, Knight of the Sphere. It is a pleasure to meet you, Governor Stewart."

She gestured for him to sit. "I wish this meeting could have taken place at a more opportune and peaceful time, Sir Erbe."

"I could not help but notice the gathering that is protesting our arrival, Governor. I expected that the arrival of a representative of The Republic would have received a more cordial reception."

Her face betrayed no emotion. "We have had an unfortunate series of events take place here on Callison, Sir Knight. When word of Exarch Levin's abandonment of our prefecture reached Callison, a series of protests broke out."

"Abandonment?" he replied, his voice filled with apparently sincere distress. "I heard Exarch Levin's speech myself, Governor, and it was clear that The Republic has not abandoned this Prefecture or Callison. He is making a strategic move necessary to preserve The Republic. I fear someone has misinterpreted his message."

"I suggest you reread the transmission the exarch released. Your version of events does not match my interpretation, nor is it what the majority of my constituents believe. They see only that the exarch has retreated, holed up to save himself and a mere fragment of what Stone was able to create. Levin has turned a blind eye to us."

"This is a distortion of the facts."

She flashed a short smile. "The facts are that we are alone here, and are likely to be alone for some time to come."

"How does Legate Leif feel about all of this?" He asked this question quite deliberately: While waiting for the arrival of the governor, he had studied the recent media reports. It seemed obvious to him that the rioting that had occurred days earlier was organized and the legate targeted. He had been the only fatality of the event. *I have to assume she was involved.*

The question didn't fluster her. "I am afraid that the legate was killed during the outbreak of violence. Per Exarch Levin's instructions, I have assumed direct control of the Callison Light Horse."

Sir Erbe paused. "I noticed that the militia was deployed in support of those people at the fence, Governor Stewart."

"Strictly as a precaution. We could not predict your intentions. We do not want violence, and the Light Horse ensures that order is maintained without suppressing the rights of the people to free speech. Which brings me to an excellent question: Why *are* you here, Sir Erbe?"

She finally had cut to the chase. "I have come under orders from the exarch. Given the current state of relations between Callison and The Republic, I am reluctant to reveal those orders. Suffice it to say that the present matters here and the loss of the legitimate legate leave my orders in question." He chose his words as carefully as she had.

She faked puzzlement, clearly an expression she assumed for his benefit. "I don't understand, Sir Erbe. In the past, many governors have assumed leadership of the military—until a replacement can be named, of course—when legates have been killed. I have simply fulfilled my role as outlined by The Republic. And as to our state of relations—I am unaware that we are at odds. Are we not part of the same government?"

"Those protestors tell me differently. I have landed at your spaceport peacefully, only to be confronted with BattleMechs of a Republic militia and an angry mob picketing my presence. Surely you must accept that I would be somewhat apprehensive at revealing the nature of my mission."

"The militia is there to *protect* you, Sir Erbe," she said warmly. "Given the protests that resulted in the death of the legate, I simply wanted to make sure that these protestors did not exceed their legal rights."

Perhaps kill me as well? "I hear what you are saying,

Governor Stewart. But I must interpret your actions with the safety of my troops in mind."

"I'm sorry that you feel you cannot trust me, Sir Erbe. I find that disappointing. It is a sad day when a Knight of the Sphere must operate under such conditions and terms." She paused. "I would ask that any actions you undertake be coordinated with the militia and through me. I would hate for military movement on your part to be misinterpreted by the people of Callison. The exarch's speech has caused turmoil, and I would hate for you or your personnel to suffer from the chaos." Kristoff heard the threat veiled by the diplomatic doublespeak.

"Governor Stewart, sleep well tonight knowing that we have come at the exarch's request. If matters get out of hand and you are unable to control your people, we stand ready to assist you."

She gave him a curt nod, and they stood at the same time. A Fidelis trooper, a tall woman, escorted the governor off the ship. Adamans entered the tiny room and stood next to the knight. "I trust that your negotiations went favorably?" His eyebrow lifted as he spoke.

"For a Fidelis, you sure are sarcastic," Kristoff replied.

"The results of poor upbringing, I assure you," Adamans replied with a grin.

"They did not go well at all."

"What are your orders, sir?"

Kristoff paused. "Adamans, let me give you the situation. The planetary legate has been killed in rioting that was supposedly spawned by the formation of Fortress Republic. Governor Stewart is boldly using this opportunity to seize complete power of Callison, including the military, which is now under her control. The local population has turned against The Republic. I am supposed to work with a ghost knight who hasn't made contact and apparently has done nothing to stop the current situation from escalating. We're alone, cut off from reinforcements or aid and surrounded by potentially hostile forces—people I have no desire to injure or kill. With

Fortress Republic in place, we have no where to retreat."

"Sir," Adamans replied, as if to acknowledge their plight.

Nothing in his training or past experience would help him in this situation. Erbe said nothing for a moment. "My orders are 'sit and wait.' Stewart wants us to react—to overreact. Not yet. When we act, it will be on my terms. We still have a card to play. That card is a joker named Ceresco Hancock."

Altar of Freedom 7

DropShip **Excelsior**
New Dearborn, Ryde
Jade Falcon Occupation Zone
Fortress Republic (-18 days)

Lady Synd was jerked into consciousness by a nearby explosion. The troopers carrying her fell from the blast concussion, and she jarred awake at the impact and the pain that flooded her body. She moaned, making a sound she had heard on countless battlefields—an uncontrollable cry of agony. She was embarrassed for a second. *I'm a Knight of the Sphere. I'm supposed to set an example.* Her fingers dug into the grass and she pushed hard to turn on her side. In a way, she was glad for whatever it was that had brought her pain. She had regained consciousness, and that meant she had control again . . . of her command and her fate. She clung to that thought.

Boyne rolled her over. Dull red droplets of blood, probably not his own, splattered his brow and cheeks. "Are you alright?"

"Define 'alright.'"

He grinned. "That will have to do." Hoisting her up, he laid her over his shoulder like a personal kit. It hurt, but she fought the urge to complain. He walked as smoothly as possible up the ramp of the DropShip *Excelsior*, then laid her onto a medical cot. Immediately a medic began to check her over. She waved him off. Synd was lightheaded, but it was still her battle to win or lose. "Sit rep," she commanded.

"M'lady, you are in no condition—" Boyne began.

"We can talk about me later. Sit rep, Captain."

His brows went up in silent amazement at her perseverance; it was a significant indication of respect from the Fidelis commander. "We are falling back. The Falcons have regrouped and have entered the park. Our rear guard caught the worst of it. The Jade Falcons are closing on the DropShips and we are using the turrets for covering fire. We should have everyone on board in less than a minute."

"Greene?"

"He's on the bridge. Our guests are aboard this ship as well."

"Let's get out of here." The mission would still be a failure if the Jade Falcons managed to take the DropShips. As if in support of her thought, the *Excelsior* shook as it took a hit, replying with the whine of a nearby turret discharging its lasers. She drew a deep breath, and her chest ached as if to remind her of the extent of her injuries.

Boyne's wrist comm buzzed. He activated it, and she could hear the voice of Major Greene. "Boyne, we need to take off. The Falcons are practically knocking on the door to get aboard over here."

Boyne moved his wrist so that the comm unit would pick up Synd's voice. "Mongoose here. Order the *Pontchartrain* to take off immediately, Major. We'll be right behind them."

"Mongoose, it's good to have you back. We are dusting off now."

She looked at Boyne sternly. "I have lost enough people on this mission." She relaxed onto the cot and deliberately closed her eyes. It was out of her hands now. As the DropShip engines roared to life beneath her, she knew the fight was now in the hands of the DropShip captains and their crews. Her people had already paid their price.

Outbound to Nadir Jump Point
Ryde System
Jade Falcon Occupation Zone
Fortress Republic (-15 days)

"We were told that our families would be with us," Doctor Andrew Brunner shouted, pounding his fist on the table. "This man lied to us." The doctor stabbed a finger at Greene, who seemed unmoved by the gesture.

"One of my primary objectives was to retrieve you and your team from Ryde. I did and said what was necessary to accomplish that goal." The ghost knight did not apologize. She and Sir Greene had debriefed each other, and she had spoken with him at length about what he had done. She felt that she would have found another way to achieve the goal rather than lying to the scientists. But when she thought about it, she wondered if that were really true. *Would I have traded honor to achieve the objective—especially if achieving the objective meant saving lives?* She didn't want to answer that question. What had changed in The Republic was forcing her to make decisions based on new criteria. And it bothered her that she believed he had done the right thing.

"I understand that you are upset. I would feel the same if I were in your shoes. However, *we* did what was necessary to preserve the future of The Republic. Our mission was to recover you and your data, and that is what we did." A part of her wanted to say "we were just following orders," but far too many crimes had been committed throughout history under that guise.

"You don't honestly think we'll work for The Republic after what you've done to us, do you?" Brunner's voice was filled with venom. In the tiny dining room aboard the *Excelsior,* his voice seemed to dominate the very air.

It had been a long three days since they had lifted from Ryde. Two harassing attacks by aerospace fighters had nearly destroyed the morale of the survivors of the raid. Her own emotions felt raw, and her body was in constant pain. Sir Greene opened his mouth to attempt a rebuttal, but Synd cut him off. "Doctor Brunner, I don't know or care what you do from this point forward. Once we leave disputed territory, we are going to take you to the rendezvous point and transfer you off this ship. What happens to you then and what you choose to do is not my concern."

"We didn't want to be rescued. We never asked you to come for us. The Falcons left us alone to do our work, but now our families will pay the price for what you've done." Brunner's voice broke. "New Dearborn is my home. We all have friends and families there. You have ripped us away from our lives. Damn you to hell."

"What we did, we did in the name of The Republic. It was necessary." *If it wasn't necessary, we wouldn't have done it—wouldn't have lost so many good people.*

"You are an evil person."

She should have let that go, but she couldn't. "Don't you dare say that." Anger made the blood rush painfully to her face. "Taking you away from the Falcons cost the lives of thirty-eight good people—thirty-eight people who died to ensure your well-being and the health of The Republic. You're upset because you're worried about your families. That's fair. But because we have accepted this mission, my troops may never see our families again either. We've all sacrificed our way of life for you." She took a deep, shaky breath. "Evil? I assure you, Doctor Brunner, you have no idea what evil is." With those words she nodded to the guards, who led out the former Falcon hostages. Aside from Sir Greene, the only person who remained was Boyne. He had stood in the corner during the entire conversation, arms crossed, observing the exchange but contributing nothing.

"You are not correct," he finally said.

"About what?"

"Master Sergeant Franks died a few hours ago. There are now thirty-nine dead."

Greene shook his head. "Does one more death make a difference?"

"It does," Boyne replied, "if you are that person." Greene shook his head once more, rose to his feet and stepped out of the room, leaving Crystal Synd alone with the Fidelis warrior.

She closed her eyes. "You hide your emotions well, Boyne."

He surprised her by sitting down across the table from her. "From your perspective, I am not showing my emotions. But do not take my lack of expression as not caring. I have not slept since we left Ryde. At night, I see the faces of those who fell. Know this, Lady Synd: I believe they died the way they hoped to; fighting for The Republic."

"It sounds noble, Boyne, but the truth is most people would prefer to die of old age, at home with their families, after a long and joyous life."

"Not the Fidelis."

"That sounds like a Clan attitude," she replied.

He chuckled. "I am sure that the Jade Falcons would not appreciate the comparison. We do not fear old age: In fact, we have come to appreciate it a great deal. The difference is that you rarely get a choice in this life as to whether you see old age."

"I hope this mission was worth it."

The Fidelis nodded. "It was. We fulfilled our objectives."

Synd cringed. "I wish I had your faith. How can you ignore the dead and wounded? This mission cost us more than seventy-five percent of our troops. I have two operational 'Mechs remaining, and a few vehicles that may never see combat again. This unit may never be combat-ready again."

Boyne waited for a moment before responding. "What matters is the mission, correct? You and I are military personnel. We know that losses occur. We understand that some men and women will not come back. In this case, our mission went as planned. Our objectives have been achieved."

He spoke so confidently, with such self-assurance, that it was hard not to agree with him. She accepted that every military engagement ended with the loss of soldiers—but the losses she suffered on Ryde were so far beyond typical that they staggered the imagination. Most military units lose ten to twenty percent of their number and are rebuilt. "We achieved the mission, but the cost in blood was too much."

"You knew what the cost would be before we left New Earth," Boyne stated flatly, but not unkindly.

It was true. She had warned Damien Redburn what the cost was going to be. "You're right. I did know going in. But I have been fighting as a knight for many years, and in those years I've learned how to minimize losses. What happened on Ryde—that doesn't jibe with my understanding of The Republic." Afraid that she was beginning to sound petulant, she stopped talking.

"The Republic has entered a new era with these Fortress plans. Very soon, we will be sealed off from The Republic we knew. Soon, it will change, and we will be forced to change as well. My people have had to embrace change many times; but in the end, who we are in our souls never changes. Our goals as a people have never changed." Boyne's words were mysterious, almost mystic.

Synd thought for a moment. "I think I understand. Even though The Republic may change, I remain a knight; I do not need to sacrifice what was good about The Republic. I don't need to compromise who I am."

Boyne surprised her again. "Then The Republic lives on." She saw the flash of a smile and felt a glimmer of hope. He was right. If they believed in it, then the spirit of The Republic survived.

She decided to change the subject. "What you did back there with Morella. What was that?"

"It is the Blessed Release. Each one of the Fidelis has

this device implanted in their left shoulder. When the vial is activated, it releases a chemical agent that corrupts our DNA. We leave nothing behind that will allow our enemies to identify us."

"But many Fidelis troops were killed in the fighting."

"I have checked. All received the Blessed Release. All of them achieved their final hour."

"Why do you do this? Why is it so important?"

"There are those who would come for us if they knew our true origins. The very fact of our existence would ignite hate that should be dead and buried. You are a knight. You know the power of hate and prejudice, and how those emotions can rally even good people to a wrong cause. The Fidelis also understand this. We have no desire to relive our past. Those fires are best kept smothered."

"Where are your people from?"

Boyne grinned at her. "Does it really matter? When The Republic needed us the most, we answered the call. If we were not here, your mission would have failed. Our origins do not define who we are, only where we came from. As a knight, you know this well yourself. Your family history does not define you. What defines you in my eyes is what you did on Ryde. I saw you fight. You risked death alongside my men and women. You have not compromised what you believe is right. Even now, with all of our losses, you have not changed who you are. That describes us as well."

"You understand our curiosity?"

"I do. Despite my personal desires, I cannot tell you. My word is my bond."

She leaned back in her chair and pain surfaced, aches that had been lurking for days but remained dormant as long as she didn't move. Her leg throbbed as she shifted. The blast that had taken her out had given her a broken ankle. Now the medics had her in a cast up to her thigh—she had probably compounded the damage by trying to walk on it during the evacuation. She used the pain as a reminder of the loss of her 'Mech and most of her command. She didn't fight the pain, but instead tried to master it.

"You know, Boyne, I was thinking. We need to go back to Ryde; you and I, and Greene, too. Someday Ryde will be free and part of The Republic again. When that day comes, we need to go back to Veterans Park."

"I am intrigued," he replied. She thought his tone sounded deliberately casual. "Why?"

"We left our dead there. We need to remember them and honor what they did. We have no choice but to let the Jade Falcons bury them, but they served The Republic: They deserve commemoration and honor. Do you agree?"

He nodded thoughtfully. "The dead always deserve remembrance. I will come with you if I am able. Meanwhile, I will honor them in the way of my people, by fighting for The Republic."

She reached for her crutches, which stood off to the side of her chair. Boyne reached them first and handed them to her. She thanked him and slowly, carefully, rose to stand first on her good leg. When she had them placed to her satisfaction, she looked up and saw Boyne still standing between her and the door. "Is there something else, Captain?"

Boyne reached into his right chest pocket, pulled out a small pin and handed it to her. She turned it over in her hand and saw a lone white star on a background of black. "When my squad and I were pinned in that building, you charged that *Stalking Spider*. You saved our lives. We—no—*I* appreciate what you did for us."

"I did what was required," she said. "I am a Knight of the Sphere."

"You fought like one of us. It cost you your BattleMech, but you fought like a Fidelis. We do not forget that. The pin I have given you is a symbol from our past, the only insignia that we carry with us from the before times. I have discussed it with my troops, and they agree that you are one of us." He retrieved the pin from her and attached it to her collar.

"Do you know what 'Fidelis' means?"

She shook her head.

"It means 'the True.' You have shown yourself to be Fidelis, not just with us but with yourself. You are now one of my people—a sister in battle."

"I don't know what to say."

"Say nothing," Boyne replied. "While your family of knights has been separated by these Fortress walls, you cannot be separated from your kin in the Fidelis."

The True. She thought she understood. While she didn't know what the Fidelis were true to, she knew that she was true to her principles. She had pressed herself to the limits of what she considered acceptable, but hadn't lost who she was in the process. Boyne understood all that without it being spoken.

"The True," was all she said out loud.

Interpretation of Duty 12

Governor's Mansion
Brandenburg, Callison
Former Prefecture VIII
Fortress Republic (+37 days)

This was the first time Cheryl had been summoned to the governor's mansion. She should have been surprised, especially at this time of night—but the message she had sent the governor practically guaranteed that she'd get her meeting. Cheryl had been waging a controlled war with Sir Erbe's Republic forces for hours since her miraculous escape from his clutches. As she waited in the comfortable room, she touched the tender skin around her black eye. *Miraculous, my ass.* Kristoff had punched her hard, but she'd deserved it. She had earned every ounce of his rage. She was shocked that he was actually capable of punching a fellow knight, and a female; but she found that she respected him more for hitting her.

Cheryl had crafted her message carefully, knowing that it would take an urgent message to convince the governor's chief of staff to wake her. The governor's personal security guard had admitted her to the mansion. She was still wearing her MechWarrior gear and carrying her kit bag. The guards had searched it, but quickly and not very carefully. Cheryl forgave them their sloppiness. She was, after all, a high-ranking government official. They showed her into the governor's private study and left her alone in the dimly lit room. It had a magnificent library, much like Governor Stewart's office in the city. She walked over to one of the bookshelves and pulled out a volume. Thelos Auburn's *A Study of Empires* series. She slid it back on the shelf. *Pity*. It was a good book, from what she remembered.

The governor came in wearing a robe over her satin pajamas. Her hair was arranged in its usual casual style, but it was obvious that the little makeup Allison Stewart usually wore had been removed. She gestured for Cheryl to sit as she maneuvered her round body behind the desk.

"Cheryl, it pleases me to see you alive and well," she said, staring at her bruised eye. "Your escape is just the kind of thing our director of public relations will love to have as a story when this is all over. I was quite worried when I heard from the captain that you had been forced to eject."

"Thank you, ma'am."

"How is your eye? Did they do this when they captured you, or did it happen when you ejected?"

She shook her head. "Sometimes you just get hurt by the decisions you make." She offered no other explanation.

"Well, then. I received your message—is the fighting over?"

"Not yet. There are pockets of Republic troops that refuse to budge. However, Sir Erbe has been killed."

"Are you sure?"

"Quite. I checked his *Hellstar*'s cockpit myself. He died on the field of battle." She rubbed her brow. "He fought quite bravely."

"It is sad when someone is confused and is killed for a lost cause. The Republic he was fighting for died the

day Exarch Levin issued his Fortress Republic plans.
This Fortress concept is a stillborn child. I feel bad that
you were forced to kill this knight errant."

"As you said, sometimes people are confused and
fight for the wrong things." She bowed her head as if in
respect for Kristoff Erbe.

"The media has been playing up the battle quite favorably for our side. The press still maintains that The
Republic has turned against Callison. You have done
your duty well."

"It isn't over, Governor."

"I know. You said there were some diehards out there
still fighting. You will defeat them—I know you will."

"I appreciate your confidence in me, Governor," she
said, rising to her feet. "But battles are not won on confidence alone. There are still many people who don't
support your policies."

"Well, you serve as the head of Internal Affairs. We
can ferret out and eliminate the opposition. Anyone who
can kill a knight is bound to instill fear in ordinary
citizens."

"I have to admit I had reservations about this assignment, but you have convinced me that I am doing the
right thing. I thought at first I was heading down the
wrong path, but having spoken with you, I have come
to the realization that this is the right thing to do. In
fact, it may be the only thing to do."

Governor Stewart smiled. She rose to her feet as well,
and walked around the desk toward Cheryl. The interview clearly was over. Cheryl Gunson wobbled slightly,
as if she were feeling dizzy. She touched the governor's
shoulder for a moment to regain her balance. Allison
Stewart jerked slightly at her touch, but pressed Cheryl
back into her seat before returning to her own chair.
"Are you alright, Cheryl?"

Cheryl sighed deeply. "Yes, thank you. I feel like the
weight of this world has just been lifted from my
shoulders."

The governor rubbed the shoulder Cheryl had used to

balance herself. "I'm feeling a little light-headed my-self," she said.

"I imagine you do. Then again, you have good reason to."

The governor's mouth hung open slightly, making her look a little stupid. She tried to move her head, but instead slumped limply in her chair. Her hand slid from her shoulder to her lap. Her eyes seemed glassy. None of this surprised Cheryl. She crossed her legs at the ankles and leaned forward to inspect the governor's condition.

"Sumptin wong. Wha . . . happen? Wha'ya do t'me?"

"I did my duty," Cheryl replied sadly. "You have been poisoned. Tiny prick of a thin needle when I touched your shoulder. It's a chemical compound recovered from the Word of Blake during the Jihad. Nasty stuff, really. It attacks your motor control centers and suppresses your neurofeedback. Your body right now is shutting down, starting with your extremities. I know you want to yell for your guards, but you'll find your vocal cords are constricted. There are a few things you have to give the Word of Blake; one was, they knew how to torture people."

The governor began to drool. Cheryl did nothing to help her. "I know you have a question burning in your brain, so I'll answer it for you. I am not Cheryl Gunson. She was a plant, a cover identity. I am Ceresco Hancock, Ghost Knight of the Republic. *Loyal* knight, I might add."

There—the governor's eyes flashed slightly at those words. Her body seemed to stiffen. "I was given a mission here on Callison, and I've been working on it for months. Your greed pushed matters to a head, I'm afraid. You have managed to turn some of the population against The Republic, but that is just for the short term. With your death, I will be able to counter the lies you've propagated. It will take some work, but I have learned a great deal about public relations from you."

Allison Stewart's face lost all color and a few beads

of sweat began to form. Cheryl ignored them. "I appreciate your making me the director of internal affairs. That makes me third in line for succession to the governorship. I have already made arrangements for dealing with the lieutenant governor. Your death will be most tragic, as will his. As you draw your last few breaths, know this; you have been played like a cheap fiddle. Putting me in command of the militia was a great media stunt for you, but in the end it allowed me to seize power on Callison. I will hold it for years to come."

Governor Stewart moaned, feebly. "What was that? I won't get away with it?" She filled in the words she thought the governor would say—if she could speak. "I tend to think differently, ma'am. You see, your unfortunate death will be blamed on the Marik-Stewart Commonwealth. If the people need an enemy to unite them, I will give them an enemy. The Republic was not the enemy of these people. *You* were the true enemy."

Cheryl rose and lifted her kit bag to the desk. "I would recommend that you replace your security team for missing the explosives I wove into the seams of this bag, but that won't be necessary. Most of them will be killed in the blast. Your remains will be reduced to such tiny particles that no one will find any traces of the poison. All in all, a tidy way to wrap up this entire affair."

"Wha . . ." the governor's question was a mere whisper.

"Why?" Cheryl repeated. She had to admit—she was impressed that the governor had managed to form any sort of word at this point. It testified as to just how tough the woman really was. "You want to know why. Fair enough. You deserve that much.

"I was following orders. Orders from the exarch, delivered by the former exarch. Redburn gave me orders that required me to take extraordinary steps. He asked me to do this. It wasn't until today that I realized this was the mission I had been trained for my entire life. It took the punch of an honorable man to show me how to interpret the orders I had been given."

She activated the tiny digital timer sewn inside the satchel. "I'll let the guards know that you asked not to be disturbed. Governor Stewart, wherever you end up, whatever afterlife you have, know this—Stone's Republic will exist as long as loyal sons and daughters are willing to follow the orders of their hearts."

Cheryl pushed the explosive charge closer to her former boss. "Adieu," she said, "bitch."

Price of Service 6

Breezewood, Kwamashu
Duchy of Andurien
Fortress Republic (+860 days)

The battle for Breezewood was not unfolding as Hunter Mannheim had planned. The Oriente Protectorate troops had obliged him at first by landing on the flat plains to the west of Breezewood. Once the attackers had collapsed the planetary militia, however, instead of heading straight across the open plains to the industrial complex rigged with explosives, which was masquerading as a BattleMech assembly plant, they had veered off into the city limits. This practically assured there would be civilian casualties, something Mannheim's plan was designed to avoid—or at least minimize.

Now all he had to do was regain the initiative and convince the attackers to play along.

His *Shockwave* was still in the fight. It had taken minimal damage so far, though it was running hotter than normal—an indication that a heat sink or two had been disabled. The cockpit damage display said there was no problem, but his own internal thermometer told him a different story.

The outskirts of Breezewood consisted of little more

than a string of shantytowns, wooden shacks cobbled together by people too poor to afford housing. Most were abandoned ruins, though some were occupied by squatters. As the Protectorate forces plowed into the ramshackle structures, he saw dust, dirt and debris rise into the air. A pack of dogs fled in front of the Protectorate 'Mechs blasting their way through to the more prosperous sections of the city.

The Hawk Moth attached to Mannheim's lance swept in alongside him. A string of burn holes and laser scars covered the side of the VTOL gunship, and a viscous black fluid oozed from several places. Like him, it was staying in the fight. Moving out in front of his trotting *Shockwave*, it approached a Protectorate *Hatchetman* that was turning to fight a rear-guard action. The *Hatchetman* lifted its deadly axe as if to protect its head, holding it like a sword.

The Hawk Moth juked to the right and Mannheim moved to the left of the 'Mech. The *Hatchetman* focused on the Hawk Moth, firing its Imperator Ultra autocannon at the VTOL as the flyer turned to bring its weapons pod to bear. It was a tricky shot, but the Protectorate MechWarrior was equal to the task. The autocannon rounds caught the VTOL almost square on, and the tiny gunship quaked under the rattling impact. Smoke whipped out from the starboard turbine, and the Hawk Moth spiraled toward the ground, the pilot regaining control just before the VTOL slapped into the shantytown. The turbo fans kicked up dirt and shards of wood as the pilot fought to keep his gunship alive.

Mannheim switched each of his weapons systems to a separate circuit and began to work the triggers one at a time in an effort to get the attention of the *Hatchetman*. His own autocannon rounds hit the right side of the 'Mech, including the arm that held the hatchet. The Protectorate 'Mech took a step forward as Mannheim heard the tone of his own missile lock. His long-range missile rack hissed as the salvo went downrange. Half the missiles missed, blasting the shanties around the feet of the enemy

'Mech. The others struck near the recessed head of the *Hatchetman*, leaving craterlike marks on the armor.

The Protectorate MechWarrior chose a more direct assault. He charged at Mannheim. This was the second time in the fight that a 'Mech had rushed him, and he thought again how dangerous these Protectorate forces were. The Hawk Moth rose slightly, fighting gravity, and fired a blast with its pulse laser pod. It caught the *Hatchetman*, but very nearly slipped off-target and hit him in the process. Hunter sidestepped and dropped his targeting reticle onto the approaching 'Mech.

This time he didn't get the shot.

The *Hatchetman* fired its medium laser, sending a searing blast into his already injured legs. This time the damage display flickered from yellow to red, and he could feel his *Shockwave* resist his attempt to keep moving. The three heat sinks he suspected were damaged suddenly showed up red on the display. But the biggest threat was that the *Hatchetman* was preparing to swing the huge hand weapon from which it got its name.

He fired. His large laser hit dead center of the 'Mech's torso, pouring its green beam of energy right into the chest and drilling deep. Mannheim hoped the shot had hit the engine. The 'Mech hesitated for a half-beat, then half-fell forward a step.

From his left he saw short-range missiles arc up from the ground into the 'Mech. Two shots landed on the cockpit, the rest hit in the same spot on the torso as his large laser. He could hear the patter of the shrapnel on his own ferroglass cockpit as the powerful warheads exploded. The *Hatchetman* closed in a single step and swung its axe.

The weapon hit the *Shockwave*'s right arm just below the elbow. His 'Mech reeled under the assault, tipping hard back and to the side. Mannheim tried to regain his balance by shoving his arms forward until they hurt. The damage display showed no color where the hatchet had hit: It was simply black.

Stepping back two staggering strides, he saw that the

arm of his *Shockwave* was gone, severed below the actuator. Exposed myomer muscle bundles sparked as they touched each other, fibers whipping wildly as they contracted and released. Leaking coolant sizzled on the damaged area. The *Shockwave* felt lopsided, and he had to work hard to compensate for the weight lost with the arm.

The *Hatchetman* pilot took advantage of Mannheim's scramble to stay upright to vent some heat before attacking again. In the chaos swirling around them, no one but Mannheim noticed the trike squad of Fidelis rush the *Hatchetman* and scramble up the access ladders on the front legs and torso of the 'Mech. Hunter held his fire, instead moving to break away.

The *Hatchetman* was tracking him, but the slight hesitation before attacking again would cost him. One Fidelis warrior fell to the ground as the Hatchetman twisted his torso. The other two reached the cockpit and blew the side hatch with a satchel charge. Now Hunter hesitated, watching in awe as the Fidelis pulled the enemy pilot out of the cockpit.

He locked onto the 'Mech and brought all of his weapons online. *If that thing so much as farts I'm going to pump it full of cannon rounds.* There was a crackle in his earpiece, then he heard, "This is Sweep Two. We have the *Hatchetman* under control. Please disengage your target lock while we change our transponder frequency."

Hunter let out a long sigh. "Good work, Sweep Two."

"Awaiting your orders."

"We've got to link up with Victory Lance and try to keep the Protectorate forces out of the city." What remained of his *Shockwave* lumbered forward, followed by the captured *Hatchetman*.

Chin entered the monastery with the Fidelis squad. They were methodically clearing the narrow hallways and tiny rooms and securing the egress out of the complex.

The Fidelis had only one question upon hearing their assignment. "Do we kill or incapacitate?" Jeremy knew the interior of the monastery was going to be a room-by-room fight. He made the only decision that made sense: "Kill." Using sniper rifles and unarmed combat in a coordinated attack, they had taken out four monks and five guards in the opening three seconds of the assault, eliminating everyone outside the carved-stone complex.

The rooms were literally carved from the stone cliff and furnished with little more than a single narrow bed. The monks put up a fight but were no match for the Fidelis. Two guards inside the monastery tried to hold out, but the Fidelis were in no mood for a dangerous gunfight at close quarters. Two grenades quickly—and messily—ended the fight.

Chin rounded a corner and saw a hallway that ended in a door that was not the usual rough-hewn wood. In the dim yellowish interior light, the polished bronze doorway looked like gold. This had to be it. He turned to his Fidelis squad. "Secure that room. Do not destroy anything inside."

The troopers leapfrogged down the hall, hugging each nook, cranny and doorway along the way. They reached the door in a mere few seconds and burst through it. Chin heard a single shot, then the last man through the door signaled the all-clear.

The room on the other side of the heavy door was a small chamber with a single altarlike pillar in the center. It was draped in a cloth embroidered with words he couldn't read. A half-dozen candles burned in the room, and two small white lights shined on the pillar. The air was stuffy. Lying on the floor was an old man wearing a simple white robe, now marred by a red-brown stain of blood. His hand clutched some sort of ceremonial knife. Even against armed troopers this man had tried to defend this room.

On the pillar was a small wooden box, three quarters of a meter long and tapered at the ends. It resembled a small coffin. The wood was quite ordinary, decorated only by small brass fittings on the corners and a discreet plaque where he would have expected a lock. Chin motioned for the troopers to remain where they were. He approached the pillar.

"Exactly how Stone described it in his notes," he muttered. Leaning close to the box, he examined the tiny plaque and saw that it displayed only one character: the symbol of the Word of Blake. Almost reverently, he lifted the box and tucked it under his arm.

"You sick bastard. I hope you're worth it."

"Sir?" one of the troopers asked, unsure of what he had heard.

"We got what we came for," he replied, regaining his composure. "Let's get back to Breezewood and help out Sir Mannheim." He stepped over the dead monk, leaving a bloody footprint as he walked away.

The fighting near the perimeter of the industrial complex was ferocious. The Protectorate forces had rushed the main gate and been stopped by the fortifications. They had pulled back, circled around one block and probed until they found one of Sir Mannheim's exit routes. They pushed through to the outer edge of the complex, where Victory Lance and a handful of militia infantry held firm. Mannheim couldn't guess how long they would hold. And the garrison force under Colonel Daum was nowhere to be seen.

The facts were inescapable. The Oriente Protectorate had invaded with a full battalion, which had stacked the deck against them from the start. The Fidelis troops had inflicted a disproportionate number of casualties, which had improved the odds, but the defeat of his force was still only a matter of time. Worse yet, he could not disengage from the enemy and flee the plant, because they held the key roadway he needed to use to withdraw.

A miracle was needed, and it would have to be a manmade one. He fired a stream of autocannon rounds into a building where infantry laser fire was sputtering out of the upper-floor windows. His assault blasted the entire side of the structure and set it on fire.

"Victory One, this is Rook."

"Rook, this is Victory One."

"Lieutenant Carver, we've got to drive these troops back enough to open our exit lines."

"Understood, sir. We will handle this."

"Victory One, the odds are against you."

"My people have faced much worse odds. We will succeed."

"I can't order you to do this," Mannheim said.

"We are volunteering. Service! Victory One out."

As if on cue, the lance rushed forward, reinforced by several militia squads. They did not advance to engage the Protectorate forces, but rather charged *through* them. Carver's *Panther* fired its jump jets and went over two tanks. He landed behind them and continued on up the street. The tanks wheeled around to meet that threat as battle-armored troops dropped on top of them, savaging the thin top armor with their metallic claws.

The *Panther* charged deep into the rear of the Protectorate force, targeting a Thumper artillery piece. Under an umbrella of fire, the artillery tank tried to get away, but a blast from the *Panther*'s Lord's Light particle projection cannon seared off its barrel at a lopsided angle and sent globs of melted armor splattering onto the ground.

The assault confused the Protectorate force; as they turned to face the threat at their rear, Mannheim's lance pressed them from the opposite direction. Their frontline troops were squeezed between two hostile forces. The captured *Hatchetman* rushed a Demon wheeled tank and buried the hatchet deep into its side armor. With black smoke billowing from the resulting hole, the Demon attempted to speed away, but the *Hatchetman* followed up with a crushing kick.

In that two-block stretch of road, both sides fired every weapon available. In the eruption of carnage he saw a Fidelis trike squad take a blast of PPC fire that disintegrated one man and trike. He damaged a Po tank making a break for a side street with a salvo of long-range missiles. When the smoke cleared, the tank was gone, but he could see pieces of tread on the street and knew that it was either immobile or limping.

The fury of the assault was indescribable. He caught only glimpses of the action as he kept up a steady rhythm of moving and firing: seemingly fearless Fidelis troops charging the Protectorate forces, attacking at dangerous ranges regardless of losses. One squad landed at the feet of an enemy *Arbalest*; the 'Mech raked their formation with its medium lasers, throwing up huge chunks of ferrocrete as the squad was cut down. A ruptured water main sprayed a fountain in the air. His large laser blasted the *Arbalest*, forcing it to break and run. Through the smoke, steam and raining water, he saw one of the surviving Fidelis move to each of her fallen comrades. She quickly knelt at their side and gripped their shoulder, each the same way. *What is she doing— what is this ritual?*

He suddenly realized that the hurricane had stopped. Parts of 'Mechs and burning vehicles lay everywhere. Carver's assault had taken out the Thumper, but his *Panther* was reduced to a shell. It was blackened from top to bottom, and only a few torn and twisted fragments of armor remained on its legs. At least three squads' worth of dead infantry in Gnome battle armor littered the field. The *Hatchetman* would not fight again today. The Fidelis MechWarrior who had captured the 'Mech had ejected, and so the entire head of the 'Mech was missing.

Their counterassault had shattered the Protectorate forces, if only temporarily.

A Fox armored hovercraft slid into view, covered with a squad of shock troops. It slowed as it entered the battle zone, and the squad debarked and moved for cover. Mannheim's comm unit activated. "Foil to Rook. Mission accomplished."

Mannheim stared at the undamaged Fox. It would be

needed against the next wave, and he was glad it was back. Still, he gritted out, "Took your time, didn't you?"

"Orders are orders."

"You mind telling me where you went?"

"Trust me, you don't want to know. What's our situation?"

Hunter sighed. "We need to find Colonel Daum and prepare for the final phase of this operation."

Finis 1

Contaminated Zone A1 (Previously Breezewood)
Kwamashu
Former Duchy of Andurien
Fortress Republic (+21 years)

A light breeze caressed the gathering people, who came together again as they had for the past few years on this date. It was an anniversary, a memorial to those who had gone before, a tribute to the dark times that had followed Fortress Republic. In the distance was a field of green grass and red poppies. Breezewood had been plowed flat years ago, pushed into the crater formed by the blast that had eventually laid waste to much of Kwamashu. A few cities had sprouted on the planet, places where people tried to scratch out a living on a world the rest of the universe considered a contaminated tract. Those millions who remained lived far from the epicenter of the disaster.

Pristine rows of grave markers fanned out on the grass-covered slopes away from the city; some were in better shape than others, though all were uniform in shape and size. A circular plaza of fieldstone stood just off-center, occupied by a lone sepulcher. Flagpoles marked one end of the plaza, though the flags that flut-

tered in the breeze were different than those that had
flown over Kwamashu two decades years earlier; different than any then known. Though governments changed,
respect for these dead never did.

They gathered here each year to honor the dead, and
perhaps purge their souls of the stains of their own actions. The only building visible was two kilometers away
from this spot, an old monastery carved into a rock wall.
It received a respectful look from each new arrival as
they made their way to the stone plaza. The monastery
was the home of the custodian, the man who maintained
this site.

One by one the people who gathered, veterans and
family members alike, made their way to the tomb. They
approached in silence, each resting a hand on the pink
granite, caressing the stone, mentally passing on their
respects. Some closed their eyes, savoring their memories. Other faces showed the pain those memories inflicted. Each year knights who had never made the
pilgrimage came for the first time; every year time
thinned the ranks of those who had come since the
beginning.

One man relied heavily on a cane as he limped to the
sepulcher. He came every year, refusing the fanfare and
entourage he deserved. His flowing cape marked his
rank and his weathered face mapped what he represented to each person gathered there. Time was taking
a toll on him, but as his wrinkled hand caressed the
name carved on the tomb, a flicker of a smile lit his
face . . . pride in the man entombed there.

Jonah Levin pulled his hand away reluctantly.

Damien Redburn had died years ago in the way he
deserved to die—in an epic battle that had strained their
friendship nearly to the breaking point. Jonah Levin had
ensured that his friend had enjoyed a formal state funeral on Terra, after Fortress Republic had been broken
and the great Liberation accomplished. Some dignitaries
came, though few knew of Redburn's role outside For-

tress Republic. Even fewer knew of his role in events on Kwamashu. The coffin entombed on Terra was there for ceremony only. Levin had made sure that his predecessor had been buried here, a truth known only to these veterans. It had been Redburn's last request, supported by the survivors of those dark years.

This year's speech was being given by Vergessen, a strapping young man untouched by the chaotic years of Fortress Republic. He was a stirring orator. He spoke of honoring the dead on Kwamashu, of Damien Redburn and the knights who served him, the sacrifices they made in the name of the old Republic. His father, Boyne, stood proudly in the crowd. Lady Synd, Vergessen's mother, had not attended the last three reunions. She had last come with her husband to reinter the dead they had lost in the fighting on Ryde. The older members of this gathering were fond of pointing to Vergessen and commenting that "back in the day, he would have made knight, or even paladin."

A hovercar arrived at the edge of the plaza and a woman got out. Her security people remained with the car, but carefully scanned the gathered group. She moved into the crowd, quickly blending in. Her sunglasses hid her eyes, but her face was well known. Cheryl Gunson made her way to Jonah Levin and bowed her head respectfully as she stood at his side, wrapping her trench coat tighter to keep out the cool breeze.

"I wondered if you would make it this year," he said.

"I don't miss this. Hunt makes sure I'm here, even if he never comes."

Levin scanned the crowd. "Each year there are less of us. But Hunter is here. I had dinner with him two nights ago. He just never comes to the ceremony. His children are over there."

"How could I miss them?" she said, flashing a smile. Hunter Mannheim's children had played important roles after Fortress Republic. Ron was known for his prowess as a MechWarrior, and Judith Mannheim was an up-

and-coming politician on Terra. They were in the crowd, listening to Vergessen's words. "It is a shame that I see them more than Hunt does."

"He'll come around. Even after all this time, there is a lot for him to resolve. Kwamashu's scars run deep in him and the custodian. You know that."

"Jonah, he still hasn't spoken to his children," she replied bitterly.

Levin changed the subject. "And where is Kristoff?"

"He wanted to come. This is the first year he's missed. Given the current state of affairs, though, I needed him handling matters at home." She made no further reference to events on Callison. "Plus, travel is harder on him these days."

"Has he made an honest woman of you yet?" Levin poked, the prerogative of an old man.

She gave him a wry grin. "No one can make me honest, Jonah. You know that." Vergessen's speech ended. Wine bottles and glasses seemed to suddenly appear everywhere in the crowd. The wine was part of the ceremony. It was from a stock that Lady Synd made sure was delivered each year for the survivors. Few knew the origin of the tradition, but everyone solemnly honored the living and the dead with a traditional toast.

The old man looked around as the crowd began to mingle; there was a muted shuffling as children and grandchildren pointed him out to each other, and in a moment most eyes were focused on him. He had tried years ago to avoid speaking to the group, claiming that he wasn't worthy to speak to such a distinguished gathering. That line had never worked.

"Redburn was proud of you—all of you," he said, raising his voice loud enough for everyone to hear. "Fortress Republic was a necessary and dark time for our people. You, your parents, your loved ones, all played an important role in the events of that time. This is the one place where you are allowed to honor yourselves. There are other memorials, like Fortress Wall in Genève, where the Inner Sphere honors those who fell in service to The Republic. But this is the one place where you, the knights and ghost knights who worked under Redburn to keep Stone's dream and ideals alive, can come to honor each other. Redburn held each and every one of you in the highest esteem, and in the end gave The Republic his ultimate sacrifice. He asked to be interred here, instead of on Terra, so that he could be with his knights." Someone pressed a glass of wine into his hand. He hoisted it high for everyone to see. "To the defenders of the faith."

The crowd responded with a quiet but firm "Defenders of the faith." Unshed tears brightened many eyes, but as many smiles signaled hope for the future.

Hunter Mannheim had aged a great deal over the years. His waist had grown two inches, but he was still fit enough to pilot a BattleMech. His hair was white now, his skin was weathered to the consistency of leather, and wrinkles marked the corners of his eyes. Hunt nursed his cup of coffee, looking out the window of the monastery at the gathered crowd. He came each year, the same as them, but each year he remained here, visiting his friend, fulfilling an obligation he had placed on himself more than a decade ago.

The custodian was as skinny he had been in his youth and still moved with the same speed. A hint of gray at his temples was the only sign of his age. Ghost Knight Jeremy Chin wore ordinary clothes suitable for gardening, with grass stains at the knees. Tending the memorial was his responsibility. Years after the massive evacuation of the world, the monastery he had raided on his mission to Kwamashu had become his home. No one bothered him here—the only exception being the few weeks a year when he allowed Hunter Mannheim to visit.

The rest of the time he had someone else to keep him company.

"Your children are out there again this year," Chin said, fixing himself a cup of coffee. "You should put an end to this. For Stone's sake, go and see them."

Hunter bowed his head. They had this conversation every year, and every year his answer was the same. Hunter had not seen his family since the walls of Fortress Republic went up. Even when his wife died and it seemed possible for him to see his children, to talk to them, to try to explain where he had been and what he had been doing all of these years, he couldn't face them. Each year it got harder. Until he took care of his other son, the man in front of him now, he couldn't stand to face them.

"You know it's just not the right time" was all he said.

"You're afraid," Chin chided.

Hunter glared at him. "I am no longer afraid of anything."

"You're afraid of them. You don't want them to know the truth about what happened here."

"They know what I did."

"Do they?" Chin raised his voice and slammed his coffee onto the wooden table. He closed his eyes and turned his head, but only for a second. He was on medication, but when he got excited the voice came back. He was struggling with it now; Hunter knew, because he had seen it so many times before.

The voice of Thomas Marik taunted his friend, goaded him, mocked him.

His eyes sought the small wooden box set on a low stool at the foot of Jeremy's bed.

"Come on Jeremy, you can beat him," he said in a low tone.

Chin turned his eyes back to Hunter. "I will. He hates you. It's worse at night, you know."

The box. That damned box. It was the anchor that tied Jeremy to this spot. It was a burden that only the two of them could understand or bear. Ceresco Hancock had found help for Chin early on, but the experts all agreed it would take time for him to recover. By now, it had been years. Jeremy had continued to serve The Republic with distinction, but he had changed as the dead Marik seemed to influence his actions more heavily. That was why Jeremy finally had chosen to become custodian of the memorial. Hunter had hoped things would change for the better when they returned Marik to his resting place. But it seemed to have gotten worse. All because of that damned beaten-up box.

His anger, his frustration at the years his friend had dedicated to this horrifying artifact, the pain he saw in Jeremy—it tore at him. He tore his eyes away from the box and considered the man who had been his charge all these years. The urge overwhelmed him. He leaped from his chair, grabbed the box and hoisted it above his head. Jeremy screamed in sheer terror. No one else had ever touched the box. Mannheim slammed it onto the stone floor and the wood shattered. Jeremy dropped to his knees amid the remains, moaning in panic and fear.

"You've caused enough pain in the universe, you bastard!" Hunter shouted at the splinters of wood.

The remains of Thomas Marik had spilled out among the remains of the old box. Hunter had expected to see bones. What he saw was sticks of wood, each one carved with characters he couldn't read. Jeremy, his mouth agape in shock, chose sticks at random, picked them up and examined them.

"He's gone."

Hunter pushed at the sticks with the toe of his shoe. "He was never here." Either Thomas Marik's remains had never been in the box or they had been stolen years before. The Duchy of Andurien could not have known it was a box full of fancy sticks. After Kwamashu, they had sent teams to search for the stolen remains out of fear that their government would be exposed for hiding the worst criminal known to mankind.

It had all been a lie.

He hunkered down next to Jeremy and put his arm around the younger man's shoulders, as if he were comforting a child. Chin simply muttered, "Gone," over and over.

"I'm sorry, Jeremy, but he had to go."

"He's gone."

"Yes, Jeremy," he said, helping him to his feet. "He's gone forever. He can't hurt you anymore."

Chin stared at his friend. "I feel—different."

"Good." Hunter smiled.

"He's gone."

"I know."

"I'm free. I am finally free. I don't have to listen to him anymore." He seemed younger than he had in years. His hands were shaking.

Hunter smiled. "Are you going to be okay?"

"Yes," he said. "I will be, I think. I can be free now."

"I think you'd better sit down."

"No, Hunter, I'm fine." Jeremy glanced through the window that faced the memorial. "You . . . you need to go, though. The ceremony will end soon."

"Go?"

"You've released me; now I'm releasing you. Your children are here but won't be much longer. You need to see them."

"Are you sure?" Was it really this easy?

"Don't worry about me. I feel like the weight of the world has been lifted off my shoulders. I know you've felt guilty all these years because of me. You don't have to anymore. Go see your kids. For God's sake, do it now."

"You should come with me."

"No. I can't. I want to clean up here." Chin gave the shattered box an uneasy look.

Hunter stared into his old friend's face and saw a new calmness in his eyes. He was amazed, practically giddy with relief. *If I had known all it would take was smashing that damned box, I would have done it years ago.* He clasped Jeremy's shoulders, nodded once and turned to go. He felt unusually light. As he walked toward the memorial, he glanced back once and saw Jeremy Chin in the window, waving to him.

"You've gotten better at lying over the years." Thomas Marik chuckled as Jeremy gathered the last fragments of the box and the carved sticks and set them together on the table. "He believes I'm gone."

Jeremy grinned. "You're the one who's wrong. You are gone."

Marik, his half-obscured face twisted in mock surprise, struck a dramatic pose. He almost looked heroic. "What do you mean, Jeremy? You can still hear me."

"You're in my head. I know that. I always knew it."

"So? That changes nothing."

"You've stopped me from doing what I wanted to do all these years. You've stopped me from doing what needed to be done. Now, I control you. I can ignore you."

"You don't have to do this," Thomas Marik said. Chin could hear the plea in his voice. "There's always a better way to handle things like this."

Jeremy Chin looked at the pieces of the box that had not held Marik's remains. It was as if years of bondage had shattered with the wood. He grinned. "I can do something I wanted to do all along, something you wouldn't let me do."

"No!" Marik screamed.

Chin pulled the holdout pistol and in one fluid movement put it to his temple and pulled the trigger.

Finis 2

Each step was a struggle, but he refused help. He was custos of the Fidelis, and this would be his swan song. They would not remember him as feeble. At 131, he had cheated death many times. He often joked that he would outlive Kerensky himself and was pleased that he had, but he had paid a cost over the years. One of his legs had been budded from genetic stock. One eye and arm were bionic replacements. Transfusions and genetically grown organs had replaced the originals that had failed. *I haven't felt my pecker in decades; a small price for cheating death.*

In the past ten years, he rarely rose from his bed. Today changed that. The message he had received from Levin had changed that. He had taken the drugs mixed just for this occasion. They would give him the strength to walk in, to preside one more time. The cost . . . well, it was worth it.

He took his seat at the center of the half-circle of seats that made up the Enclave, the ruling council of the Fidelis. Each member watched him, their silence marking a deep reverence for their leader. Adamans, the na-Custos, sat to his right, the battle scars on his arms marking his turning point from warrior to leader.

The custos studied his council. His bionic hand held a piece of paper. He couldn't feel it but the sensors in the arm gave him feedback indicating that the note was secure. It wasn't touch, but it was close.

"I convene this meeting of the Enclave," he said in a gravelly voice. Heads bowed to his word and will. He had sent a message to Jonah Levin, the last leader who knew of the Fidelis' bond to The Republic. He had done this without the consensus of the Enclave. While Levin's status in the government had changed—hell, everything about what had been The Republic had changed—he alone could answer the question that must be asked. The custos had met Levin after the Great Liberation; the two men had not always been friends, but as custos, he had always honored his people's pledge to Stone.

"I took a liberty within my role as custos," he began. "I sent a message to Jonah Levin. I asked him if the Fidelis had completed their duty—if we had honored fully our service in Stone's memory." He heard the murmurs, but no one dared challenge him. The custos scanned their faces and saw anticipation. Anxiety. Excitement. *All things that were becoming harder for him to feel.*

He unfolded the paper. "Levin's response was yes. The Fidelis are released from their bond. We are free to determine our own destiny." Everyone talked at once. Their voices were filled not with joy, but with fear.

"What will we do?" Hargis asked.

"What are your plans for us, Custos?" asked Jezebel from her seat at the far end of the curve of chairs. He let the questions fly, giving them nothing but a smile in response. *That must scare them. I can't remember the last time I smiled.*

"That question is for another to answer. I am done. My service as custos, carrier of the Visum, is fulfilled. Adamans is now your leader, and your questions are best leveled at him." He nodded to Adamans, who was regarding his former leader with a curious look. The former custos forced himself to a standing position. For decades he had carried the weight of his people. *I did what I set out to do. Now someone else can finish the work.*

As the Enclave erupted in a chorus of voices, he leaned over to Adamans. "When the dust settles, come and visit me. I have a few things for you." Chuckling quietly, the former custos slowly, painfully made his way from his seat for the last time.

He lay in his bed with a tube connected to his bionic arm. It was how he had eaten for the past two decades. A mix of specially prepared nutrients, vitamins and medication dripped into him. In response to the cocktail of drugs he had taken in order to appear at the Enclave in person, his body was shutting down.

His bed was angled so that he was sitting upright. He held a book on his lap, caressing it with his human hand. It had been many decades since the massive tome had been opened. In celebration of their freedom, and his release, he had opened it and read it for himself. The words flooded back to him, sparking memories he had assumed were long since gone. They comforted him.

Adamans entered his bedchamber and waited to be acknowledged. The former custos beckoned him closer.

"With all due respect, sir, I am not sure I am ready to fill your shoes."

"Bah." He cut the air with his hand. "You are more than ready. My time is over. Our people will need new leadership now. The Inner Sphere has changed again. It is time for us to have a new perspective on things. Besides, I'm an old man."

"Sir," he began, but was cut off.

"I'm dying, Adamans; my dance with the devil is almost over. Now that our people are free from their bond, a universe of opportunities awaits. Who better to lead them than you? I haven't been off New Earth in

generations, not since the Great Betrayal and the Jihad."
He sank for a moment into his memories of lost comrades. It was strange that his thoughts went to men from the Before Times. At the time, sworn foes rather than friends. *Ironic that in the end I am like you, right down to the eye.*

"I'm not worthy." Adamans' voice brought him back from his memories.

"You know, you used to have a sense of humor. You should rediscover it. The Enclave will follow you now that we are truly free."

"Follow me—where?"

The ancient man chuckled. "Wherever you lead them. The Fidelis will need to help the rest of the universe come to grips with who we really are. The present generation knows little of our origins, and most will not resent us for our past. Others, especially the Clans, will doubt us, or try to destroy us."

"What do you recommend, sir?"

"Terra," he replied. He reached for the glass on the bedside table and took a sip of water. "Take our people to Terra. It was our destiny before it was ripped from our claws. Go there yourself and feel the grass in your toes, the wind in your hair. Walk in without fanfare and claim your birthright . . . the birthright of our people."

"I will not fail you," Adamans pledged.

"Don't let our people forget who they really are, Adamans. The Fidelis must teach the rest of the Inner Sphere about our past. Instruct them in how our people have served. Allow them to see that their past also has returned." Using his human hand, he grasped the massive book, half-lifting, half-sliding it to his successor.

"This is—"

"The Unopened Work," the former custos confirmed. "Only one copy survived the Road of Pain and the Great Betrayal. It is our history, and tells the origin of those events. Now that we are free, each Fidelis should read it for himself and learn its stories. I have preserved the book all these years, but I also have added verses as our people changed and grew. It is your duty to share it; it is up to our people to write the next chapter."

Adamans hefted the book. Every Fidelis knew of its existence, but it was rarely seen. The book had the mystique of a sacred text: The Unopened Work was a critical element of many of the Fidelis' ceremonies, but only the custos touched it or opened it. This book had survived through the darkest of times of his people. Now he was charged with using it to bring them into the light.

The old man coughed hard, painfully. The sound jerked him away from his thoughts. "Custos?" Adamans asked, leaning forward.

"I am not the custos, boy, you are," he said, wiping phlegm from the corner of his mouth. "Now, I am just a dying man. Call me once by my name—not the title."

"Sir?"

"Call me Paul," he said with a smile, and closed his eyes.

He relaxed completely, and a long sigh escaped his lungs. Adamans set down the book and gently lifted the old man's wrist to check for a pulse.

The past had died. What remained was the future.

He looked at the book once more. The symbol on the cover was a powerful leaping predator—a smoke jaguar—and the image made his heart swell with pride. "I will not fail you, Paul. I will let the rest of the Inner Sphere know that the wayward children whom they damned have returned to their doorstep as their saviors."

About the Author

Blaine Lee Pardoe was born in Virginia and raised outside Battle Creek, Michigan. He holds bachelor's and master's degrees from Central Michigan University. He works for Ernst & Young LLP as an associate director in technology. He lives in Virginia and swears it is the best and most beautiful place to live in the known universe.

Pardoe has written more than forty books, including a number of computer game guides, science fiction sourcebooks for BattleTech™ and other series, the bestselling business book *Cubicle Warfare* and the highly acclaimed Great War military history book *The Cruise of the Sea Eagle*. He is a member of the Von Luckner Society, the National Maritime Historical Society and the Organization of American Historians. He wrote material for FASA for more than fourteen years. He has written several novels for the BattleTech™ and MechWarrior™ series, including *Highlander Gambit, Impetus of War, Exodus Road, Roar of Honor, By Blood Betrayed, Measure of a Hero, Call of Duty, Operation Audacity,* and *Target of Opportunity.*

Blaine has appeared as a speaker at the U.S. National Archives, the U.S. Navy Museum and the New York

Military Affairs Symposium, and on numerous national television and radio shows.

Blaine is a Civil War buff, and when he can, he hunts for relics from the war in the old camp and skirmish sites near his house. He also plays the great Highland bagpipes. Those fans who want to contact him may do so at bpardoe870@aol.com.

Now Available from Roc

SHADOWRUN #5
Aftershock
by Jean Rabe and John Helfers

The troll known as Hood and his fellow
Shadowrunners steal some biological agriculture
from the Plantech Corporation—only to find
themselves framed for murder and tied to an
even greater conspiracy.

0-451-46101-0

THE ULTIMATE IN
SCIENCE FICTION AND FANTASY!

From magical tales of distant worlds to stories of
technological advances beyond the grasp of man, Penguin has
everything you need to stretch your imagination to its limits.

penguin.com

ACE
Get the latest information on favorites like
William Gibson, T.A. Barron, Brian Jacques,
Ursula Le Guin, Sharon Shinn, and Charlaine Harris,
as well as updates on the best new authors.

ROC
Escape with Harry Turtledove, Anne Bishop,
S.M. Stirling, Simon Green, Chris Bunch, Jim Butcher, E.E.
Knight, and many others—plus news on the
latest and hottest in science fiction and fantasy.

DAW
Mercedes Lackey, Kristen Britain, Tanya Huff,
Tad Williams, C.J. Cherryh, and many more—
DAW has something to satisfy the cravings of any
science fiction and fantasy lover.
Also visit dawbooks.com.

*Get the best of science fiction and fantasy
at your fingertips!*